YOU ARE CORDIALLY INVITED

AN AUCKLAND MED WEDDING

JAY HOGAN

SOUTHERN LIGHTS PUBLISHING

Published by Southern Lights Publishing

Copyright © 2021 by Jay Hogan

To request permission and all other enquiries contact the author through the website

https://www.jayhoganauthor.com

Trade Paperback ISBN:978-0-9951326-2-7

Digital ISBN: 978-0-9951326-1-0

Digital Edition Published June 2021

Trade Paperback Published June 2021

First Edition

Editing by Boho Edits

Cover Art Design Copyright © 2021 Reese Dante

Photography for cover Copyright © 2020 Brian Brigantti

https://www.brianbrigantti.com

Proofread by Lissa Given Proofing and L. Parks

Printed in the United States of America and Australia

ACKNOWLEDGMENTS

As always, I thank my husband for his patience and for keeping the dog walked and out of my hair when I needed to work, and my daughter for her incredible support.

Getting a book finessed for release is a huge challenge that includes the help of beta readers, editing, proofing, cover artists and a tireless PA . It's a team effort, and includes all those author support networks and reader fans who rally around when you're ready to pull your hair out and throw away every first draft. Thanks to all of you.

For my family who read everything I write and keep on saying they love it all, blushes included.

And to Cam and Reuben who were the reason I started this fantastic author journey in the first place. They weren't the main characters in my debut book because I wanted to make sure I got them right. They will always be dear to my heart and out of all my characters, I wanted to give these two a wedding to close out the Auckland Med series.

There are also a couple of little 'easter eggs' in the book that I hope you enjoy.

CHAPTER ONE

Cam

"KINKY TRICKS, SIXTY-SIX." CARMEN BENDOVER'S SULTRY VOICE filled the crowded function room of Downtown G to a cacophony of hoots and hollers. Carmen's gay bingo events were legendary.

Dressed in a red sequinned evening gown that was pretty much painted on her curvaceous figure; fuck-me black stiletto heels; an impressive cleavage that defied explanation; and a tiara that sparkled almost as much as the mischief in her eyes, the notorious drag queen had captivated the room from the minute she'd sashayed in and wafted her black feather boa seductively under the current, and very straight, All Blacks' captain's nose. To his credit, Andrew Simons had run with the challenge and got to his feet to waltz the notoriously sassy drag queen up to the front stage, and Carmen had appeared . . . charmed.

"Come on, you sexy young things." She arched a brow at the crowd sipping on cocktails with enough alcohol to fuel the next landing probe to Mars. "Someone must at least have a line. If I have to come down there and check people's cards, I'll be paddling a bottom or two and leaving a mark. And don't think I didn't see the excitement in your eyes at the prospect, Roland James."

The handsome Blues' halfback blushed a deep red and everyone laughed. The room was loaded with enough glitter and rugby muscle to make any young gay boy weep, and quite a few of the older ones as well.

"Hey, Carmen." I got to my feet a little unsteadily and waved my bingo, or rather my bin*gay* card. "I haven't won *anything*, and it's *my* damn bachelor—"

"*Our* damn bachelor party." Reuben's hand glided over my arse.

"*Our* bachelor party," I corrected with a bow to my fiancé, which was greeted with much banging on tables since everyone knew I was a bossy bitch, and yet somehow, Reuben had my sappy heart wrapped up in enough knots to make a Shibari convention ecstatic.

"Mm-hmm." Carmen eyeballed me without an ounce of sympathy. "And exactly how many calls have you missed already?"

Most of them. My chin jutted. "Pfft. One or two at the most."

A blatant lie, which earned me another round of mocking applause. Reuben and I were, in fact, sharing a bingay card—mostly because I'd given up being able to identify any individual numbers a few cocktails back or even hear the calls, apparently.

We were also sharing some increasingly indiscreet gropes, well, at least on my part. Reuben slapping my hand away probably didn't count.

Carmen smiled like the shark she was. "I rest my case, sugar. Besides, I think you've hooked a big enough prize already." She waggled her impeccably coiffed brows and nodded Reuben's way, and yeah, it was hard to argue with that. "So sit that pert arse of yours back down on those impressive All Black thighs and let the rest of us drool in peace."

I did as I was told, which, to be honest, was the least painful way to deal with Carmen. She returned to calling the numbers, and I turned and cuddled up to my fiancé and—fuck, I missed the next number as well.

I grabbed my card and eyeballed Sandy across the table. "Come on, Sandy, you have to be nice to me. It's my party—"

"*Our* party." Reuben bit my ear.

"*Our* party. Exactly what I was going to say, baby." I turned and kissed him soundly on the forehead.

"I'm not telling you a thing." Sandy side-eyed me and laughed. "If it's another manicure coupon, I *need* that prize. Have you forgotten I work in a damn morgue?"

"A pitiful excuse." I glared at him, which only made his eyes roll. I was clearly losing my edge. "And here I thought you were a friend."

"Hey, you." Reuben pulled me back against him in a transparent attempt to sabotage my epic board game skills. "How's it hanging?" His hot breath brushed my ear, and my dick pinged to attention as best it could in its slightly inebriated state. Having said that, the persistent appendage was nothing if not determined, and Carmen and her bingay went up in a puff of inconsequential smoke.

His arm tightened around my waist, and I turned to place a reasonably well-aimed but sloppy kiss on his lips this time. Yeah, I might have had one or six more than I should have, but it was *our* damn bachelor party and Rube had my back.

With the rugby season still in process, albeit winding down to the end of year All Blacks' tour to Europe, Reuben was nauseatingly sober, whereas I . . . wasn't. And I also wasn't about to miss any opportunity to get handsy with my own personal All Black booty, especially since all that glorious six foot three inches of rippling power was currently stuffed into a size-too-small—so sue me—black Henley and a pair of silk mix black slacks that fitted those drool-worthy thighs like a fucking glove.

Ninety kilos of eager-to-please hard muscle, and all mine for the taking.

Read 'em and weep, suckers.

"It's not fucking hanging at all," I answered with a grumble. I'd made the fatal mistake of donning a pair of my favourite black leatherette condoms I laughingly called jeans, especially for the occasion. They hugged my arse in stupendous fashion, but I'd failed to factor in the necessity of getting Reuben's hands down them at some point in the proceedings, and my cock was turning bluer by the minute.

I wriggled awkwardly, trying to loosen the fuckers, and Reuben gave a strangled groan. *Mmm.* I leaned back against his chest, tilted my head up, and gave him an upside-down smirk. "What was that, my precious?"

"You did that deliberately," he complained, nuzzling my ear. "If my cock gets any harder, it's gonna slice straight through my trousers *and* yours and impale you where you sit in front of all our friends and half of New Zealand's rugby royalty. Just saying."

I aimed for my best ogle, which likely missed the mark seeing as I was still upside down. "Oh yeah? Well, don't hold back on my behalf, gorgeous. It might be your best chance to top in the near future, 'cause I'm jonesing for your arse something fierce these days. Must be in the air."

"Is that right?" He lowered his lips to the curve of my neck, pulled my neon-orange net singlet aside, and lightly sank his teeth just below my favourite silver chain choker.

And oh man, those fucking jeans were crippling me.

I squirmed, and Reuben groaned and grabbed my hips. "You really, really need to sit still."

"Yeah, I'll get right on that." I tilted my head to give him more room as he trailed kisses up my throat. "Jesus, Rube, you're killing me here. I think my cock just origamied itself into a swan."

"Flirty whore, thirty-four," Carmen's voice blared through the room and I jerked up on Reuben's lap, eyeballing him accusingly.

"You're deliberately distracting me from winning." I grabbed my bingay card and waved it in his beautiful face, caught for a moment by the light bouncing off the darker specks in his silver eyes.

He leaned forward and rubbed noses with me, a thing he loved to do as often as he could.

"For fuck's sake, would you two cut it out?" Mathew griped from the other side of the table. "Show some respect to those of us who have to watch you with a belly full of whatever the fuck Michael put in these lethal drinks. I figure I'll be making their reacquaintance long before breakfast at this rate. I'm gonna crash and die at training this week, God help me."

"Which reminds me." I waved the bingay card at Mathew instead, and the sucker flew out of my hand.

Reuben snatched it from mid-air like the star number fifteen he was and put it safely on the table.

"Nice hands." I smirked, which made Reuben snort and brought those cute-as-fuck dimples to the fore.

Then I returned my glare to my brother. "I knew it was a mistake to leave organising the bachelor party unsupervised to your *committee*." I cranked my fingers around the offending word. "Whose idea was it to put our good doctor in charge of the damn bar? You're my brother and best man, Mathew, for fuck's sake. Did you lose your collective minds?"

"Okay, so yes, that was my idea," Mathew admitted. "I mean, Michael doesn't drink, right? I figured it made sense to have someone sober in charge of the alcohol. Josh and Georgie had no problem with it."

We turned as one to where Michael was shaking his booty behind the bar and exchanging cocktail shakers through the air with the official club bartender, cheered on by Georgie and Josh's sister, Katie.

"Yeah, okay." Mathew chuckled. "So that might've been a mistake."

"Ya think?" I crashed back against Reuben and elbowed him in the ribs. "I hope someone warned the ER. And that's your best woman up there in the middle of that mayhem, by the way."

Reuben grinned, watching Georgie shamelessly egg Michael on. "I know. Great, right? You can't blame me for that. Katie is Georgie's friend as well. And Georgie makes a mean mojito. That girl has some serious bartending skills herself."

She did. And I loved her to bits. She'd been pretty much the only friend in Reuben's life keeping his head above water before I came along. I owed her a life debt for that one thing alone.

Reuben chuckled in my ear. "Come on, admit it. It's a good party."

I took in all the happy faces of our friends and family and smiled. It was. "Yeah, okay, you guys did a pretty good job, considering."

"Jesus, how did that feel coming out?" Mathew's lips curved up into that gorgeous smile that kept most of Auckland's female rugby supporters in need of fresh underwear and a few of the men as well.

"Like camel turd," I admitted. "And no, you can't ask me how I know that."

He snorted. "Well, it was lucky we had Josh. Those are two of his police mates on paparazzi and social media duty—collecting all the cell phones."

I glanced to the two buff off-duty cops on the door. "Yeah, that was inspired. And I'll admit the double party bus pick-up with an open bar and night tour was an awesome kick-off." I narrowed my gaze. "But the pass-the-cock-under-the-chin dildo exchange around the room was definitely a bridge too far."

He laughed me off because we both knew it had been hilarious. And when the All Blacks' prop Tom MacDonald had dropped it on his lap and the Blues' winger had to retrieve it without using his hands, there wasn't a dry eye in the house.

"I'm also reserving judgement on the bingay," I told him. "Carmen's in wonderful and disreputable form tonight. She's taking no prisoners, and I'm not sure the All Blacks in the crowd are sufficiently equipped."

"Getting plenty, number twenty." Carmen fanned her face, her bright red talons flashing.

I rolled my eyes. "I rest my case."

"And let me assure you, my hunky boys, *plenty* is putting it mildly." She gave a predatory grin. "But I *always* have room for more." Her gaze hovered over the dozen or so beefy professional rugby players whose schedules had allowed them to come. Nearly all seemed to be having the time of their lives, although a few had spent the first thirty minutes of the party looking as if they were single-handedly facing down an entire South African front row.

Carmen could do that to you.

"Particularly you, sugar." Carmen winked at Gary Knowles, the All Blacks' coach—a surprise guest whose appearance had Reuben beaming all night.

The room erupted with whoops and more banging on tables, and Gary flushed a bright red—a colour rarely seen on the serious man. He'd garnered a fair bit of attention from Carmen over the evening—she had a well-known taste for silver foxes—but it was all in good fun. Carmen's own husband, Pete, was in the front row, wearing his usual indulgent smile while knowing he had zero to worry about. The flamboyant queen and the short, stocky, suburban, slightly balding, middle-aged guy were a legend in the gay community for their rock-solid if somewhat unexpected pairing.

Watching Gary splutter, I wondered if Carmen might have pushed things just a bit too far, but then to everyone's delight, he blew Carmen a kiss and exposed his ankle seductively.

The crowd went wild, and Carmen looked momentarily lost for words. But she recovered quickly. "Well now—" She licked her lips. "—aren't you just the saucy tart then?"

Gary flushed a deeper shade of scarlet, if that were even possible.

I glanced over to make sure the official party photographer had captured the moment, and he had. Awesome. Gary's wife was gonna owe me big time. On occasion, she and I had bonded over shopping and noon-o'clock wines while our men did their endless training thing.

Having the wife of the All Black coach on speed dial was no mean thing in the macho world of rugby, especially for a sass-fuelled, card-carrying member of the fabulous-fem-so-fucking-get-over-it gay varietal. *Yeah.* I might've caused a few ripples in rugby's testosterone-filled lake since Reuben had come out and arrived with me on his arm.

A lot of it was great—the fans, the letters from young gay kids, the chance to shatter some walls and watch a few jaws hit the floor. But the media attention and the crap from the bigoted homophobic bullshit brigade, not so much. Still, it went with the territory.

"On your knees, thirty-three. Open wide, boys."

"Oh my god," I choked out, scanning the room. She really was the worst.

"Line!" Ed shouted from behind, so loudly I nearly fell off my chair. I'd almost forgotten he was there. The man was one of the biggest introverts I'd ever met.

When Mark mentioned that he and Josh were going to be a little late to the party due to some burglary case they were working, I'd planted Ed at our table where he could observe all the fun and disappear into the wood panelling if he needed to.

"Look at you." I high fived him. "But watch out for Carmen's prizes. The last line winner got a blow-up dildo."

"Awesome." Ed's eyes swam just a little. "You can never be too prepared." He winked, and I almost choked on my Suck Bang and Blow cocktail.

"Who the hell are you and what are you drinking?" I nodded at his glass.

He grinned like a loon. "Sex on my Face."

I snorted. *Holy shit.* Mark was going to have his work cut out for him when he finally got to the party. I'd only seen Ed drunk once before, but man, it had been epic.

I turned back around and almost tumbled off Reuben's knee, grabbing his hand to steady myself. "I think I'd have less chance of falling if you held me . . . here." I placed his palm over my zippered dick. It had enough alcohol roaming its veins to make sure any chance I had of wrecking Reuben's arse when we got home sat somewhere between zero and zip, but hey, it still felt good.

"I think maybe you're right." He slid it between my thighs and—mmm. There was no way he'd get his fingers past that cock blocking waistband, but a fingernail under the balls? Oh boy, yep, that worked a treat.

I dropped my head back on his shoulder and blew one of his long blond waves off my face. "You have excellent ball-handling skills, Mr All Black." I ran my tongue over my lower lip, which probably didn't look as sexy as I thought it did upside down.

"You're looking very contented there, Mr Charge Nurse."

"The operative word being in *charge,* sweetheart." I fired him a wink.

"Of course it is."

"Sixty-nine, breakfast of champions," Carmen called out.

"What are you wearing under these?" Reuben dropped his lips to my ear. "I missed watching you dress tonight."

"Less talk, more nails," I answered, widening my thighs to give him better access. "And to answer your question, I'm wearing that cute pink jockstrap you bought me last month. The one with the fringe around the top."

He swallowed hard and bit my ear. "Fuck, I love that thing. How do you feel about a short interlude away from the crowd? Do you think anyone would notice?"

"Yes! They would," Mathew barked from across the table.

I laughed and poked my tongue out at my brother, then whispered to Reuben, "I think that's a hard yes to that question, babe, and can you, argh . . . just a little to the right . . . to the . . . mmm . . . damn, that feels good."

Reuben chuckled. "You're a wicked man, Cameron Wano."

"That's why you love me, but hey, it's only two weeks till the wedding." I turned so I could see those magnetic silver eyes. "Not too late to run, you know."

He gave me an odd look and then smiled and kissed me firmly while that fingernail kept tracing sharp lines over my cock and balls. "It was too late to run from the very first time I saw you outside that hall, remember?"

I nodded and chased his lips for more. "I still have the bruises from where you shoved me into the wall, you sexy bastard."

"Mmm. Sorry, not sorry. You were a cheeky fucker, and I was so deep in the closet you couldn't see me for dust." He nuzzled my neck and my sozzled dick briefly contemplated a comeback before throwing in the towel. "If only I'd known how much better my life was going to get." He pulled back to look at me.

"The perfect answer." I lost myself in the warmth of his eyes. I still couldn't believe that he was mine, that I got to be a parent to Cory, and that I had this amazing life. "Come on. I'm sure we can slip away for five minutes—"

"Don't you dare." Mathew glared and threw a balled-up serviette at me. "You live with the guy, for fuck's sake, and this is *your* damn party. Which means you're gonna sit right there and enjoy it if I have to handcuff you both to the chair."

I swallowed a smile and Reuben chuckled against my shoulder.

"You seem a little grouchy there, darling brother." I grabbed Mathew's glass, took a sniff, and screwed up my nose. "What on earth are you drinking?"

He flushed. "It's called an Anus Burner."

I choked on a laugh.

"Fucking Michael Oliver." He rolled his eyes. "He did that deliberately. Even yelled it from the bar for me to collect."

Priceless. "So, I take it you're not being all sober and responsible like Reuben then?"

"On all fours, forty-four," Carmen's voice rang out, and my gaze shot to the front.

"Only missionary for you, gorgeous," someone shouted from the back.

Carmen preened. "Make sure you leave me your number, sugar."

Mathew gave the room a stealthy once over before answering my question. "Our North Harbour coach left about fifteen minutes ago, or at least I hope he did, and this damn plantar injury will see me benched for next weekend's game as well. The weekend after that, we have a bye week, as you well know since you're getting *married*. So I figured, what the hell."

"Yes indeedy, we are getting married." I jiggled in place and Reuben grabbed my hips again. "And we are *not* postponing it this time. There will be no torn hamstrings or changes in the All Blacks' touring dates. *Nothing*. We might have to wait for the honeymoon proper, but we are definitely getting married."

"Hell, yeah." Mathew clinked glasses with me. "You're getting fucking married, bro. Jesus, I'm so happy for you both."

I glanced at Reuben. "I can't wait. Mister and Mister, right, baby?"

Reuben looked at me in that way he had that said I was just too fucking adorable for words and it stole my breath as it always did.

"Well, you both deserve it." Mathew took a swallow of his drink and winced. "Jesus, that shit needs a warning label." He shuddered, then eyeballed both of us. "But as for tonight? If the two of you disappear and I have to come looking for you, so help me God, I will cut off your dicks and you'll spend your wedding night sucking arse 'cause that's all you'll have to work with. Got it?"

I snorted my cocktail through my nose and all over the back of my cousin's clean white shirt at the table in front.

Jake spun, took one look at me, laughed, and flicked my forehead with his finger. "Jesus, Cam, I'll never get that pink out."

"Oops. Sorry?"

Jake rolled his eyes and went back to his bingay card.

Reuben hooked my jaw with his finger and turned my face to his. "You take my breath away." He pressed his lips to my cheek, and I grabbed a lock of his hair to hold him in place and make sure I got a bit of mouth and tongue action as well.

"Mmm." I smacked my lips and narrowed my eyes. "You've been using my watermelon gloss, mister. Come back here."

"Twenty-seven, chocolate heaven."

"Bingay!" Miller yelled and waved his card in the air, and I turned so fast I clocked Reuben on the nose with the back of my head.

"Ow, fuck."

I would've apologised, but I was too busy watching Sandy hitch up his red leather skirt to expose a deliciously naughty pair of lacey black suspenders he'd failed to mention on any of our lingerie shopping expeditions. Sneaky little shit. He straddled Miller's wheelchair and planted a huge kiss on his man's lips, raising a few rugby eyebrows in the process. Reuben's gaze dipped to Sandy's suspenders and I made a mental note to have a chat with the other nurse about sourcing some of the same.

I popped a finger under my fiancé's jaw and lifted it shut. "Eyes up, sweetheart."

"Huh?" Reuben's gaze darted to mine. "Pfft. I was just thinking how much better they'd look on you, baby."

Oh, he's good. "Sure you were. But an excellent save, nonetheless."

Carmen stood and lobbed a terrifying pink cock cage Ed's way. "For the line winner, darling."

He caught the lethal-looking cage and turned it over in his hands, grinning from ear to ear. "Best prize of the night."

My jaw dropped. "Oh. My. God. I don't even want to know. There's not enough bleach in the entire world to erase those images." I covered my eyes and pleaded with Reuben, "Rube, lamb chop, honeybee, I need a whole lot more alcohol to cope with this. How long have we been here?"

"Two hours." Reuben waved a hand to Michael at the bar who nodded and set about making who the hell knew what. To be honest, it was better to remain in the dark. "The night's still young."

Dear God. I wasn't sure I'd survive.

Carmen cocked a hip and waved Miller over. "Get yourself over here to claim your prize, Mister Paralympian. This outshines any silly old gold medal, right?"

Miller hooted and wheeled himself Carmen's way in a decidedly *not* straight line and almost ran over a black stiletto in the process.

Sandy pissed himself with laughter.

Carmen bent low and kissed him soundly, leaving a bright red slash across his lips. "It's your lucky day, honey." She held out her sack of prizes. "Pick one."

He stuck in his hand and eyed her suspiciously. "There *is* only one, you wicked woman."

"I knoooowwww." She crooned and waggled her eyebrows. "Exciting, isn't it?"

The look on Miller's face made it clear he wasn't quite so sure about that. He set the wrapped gift in his lap and stared at it like it might bite him.

There was a better than even chance that it would.

"Open it. Open it. Open it." Sandy led a chant that quickly gained momentum. He flicked a wink my way.

Huh. What's all that about?

"Oh, for fuck's sake." Miller ripped the paper off the prize and . . . frowned.

I leaned forward for a better look. A toy police light? *What the hell?*

Miller's gaze shot to Carmen and she whispered into the mic. "Turn it on, cutie."

Miller flicked a switch on the side of the light and a siren blared through the room. The eighties throwback music ceased, the lights went out in the body of the room, leaving only the stage lit, and the doors to the function room blew open.

Four men surged inside, their flashlights slicing through the crowd.

"Police. Freeze."

What the fuck? I spun to Reuben who was clearly as much in the dark about what was happening as I was, although I had my suspicions—suspicions which were confirmed when I turned to find Carmen's twinkling eyes locked on mine.

Motherfucker.

"Stay here." Reuben pushed me onto my feet before I could warn him.

"Stop right there." One of the officers held his hand up. "Everyone back against the wall."

There was an immediate drag of chairs and rumble of nervous voices, especially from the rugby players who probably saw the headlines already. *All Blacks Caught in Police Raid on Gay Nightclub.*

They had nothing to worry about. I could smell a stitch-up a mile off.

The middle of the room cleared in seconds as everyone lined up against the wall, even the bartenders, although they looked remarkably relaxed for a police raid.

Fuckers.

Reuben pulled me to his side. "Where the hell is Ben?" he hissed in my ear. The club owner was working the downstairs bar to free a bartender to cater our party.

Oh, to be so naïve.

"Sweetheart, I really don't think—"

The siren blared once again, grabbing everyone's attention. Two of the 'officers' dragged a couple of chairs centre stage at the exact same time that a spotlight landed on Reuben and me, and the light finally dawned in Reuben's eyes.

"Oh," he groaned.

"Yep," I said, glaring at a particularly smug Mathew and wondering exactly how many friends we were going to have left after I dealt with those responsible for whatever mortifying calamity was about to happen.

The single instruction I'd hammered into the committee had been clear.

No. Embarrassing. Pranks.

And by that, I meant embarrassing *to us.* Everyone else was fair game.

I was taking names.

I glanced at Reuben to find him surprisingly mellow regarding whatever excruciatingly humiliating torture we were about to endure.

"Stop them, now," I hissed in his ear.

"Hell no." He wore a huge grin. "This is awesome. You only get married once, baby. Relax and enjoy."

Which earned him an immediate place on my shit list for the next eleventy-billion years. It wasn't that I was opposed to a good dose of friend mortification, but only when I was the one doing the mortifying.

"Just think of the stories we can tell Cory and our other children." The fucker even laughed.

"There won't *be* any other children," I snapped back. "Because as soon as this is done, I'm gonna cut off your balls and nail them to your All Blacks' locker. Good luck scoring a try after that, hotshot."

"Aw, you're so cute when you get all threatening." Reuben leaned down and kissed me . . . with tongue.

And a quick grope of my arse.

Ugh.

So maybe he'd get to keep *one* ball.

The siren cut and my gaze landed on Miller's shit-eating grin as he held up the light.

I fired him my best you-are-in-so-much-fucking-trouble look, which he ignored with a casual wink.

Another set of balls was added to the list.

"Would the happy couple come centre stage?" One of the exceedingly buff not-cops waved Reuben and me toward the chairs.

Oh, hell no.

"Come on." Reuben nudged me from behind. "How bad can it be?"

I cut him a sideways glance. "You have got to be shitting me. These are our *friends* you're talking about. Or at least they were," I said loudly enough to send a ripple of laughter through the room.

A slow clap started.

"Oh, fuck me."

Reuben chuckled. "Later, baby."

I turned and glared at those not remotely beautiful eyes. "Don't you 'baby' me. How much did you know about this?"

He threw up his hands. "Absolutely nothing. I promise. Come on, where's that fuck-the-world attitude I love so much?"

"Getting ready to fuck the world of some of our so-called friends later," I grumbled, which earned me another ripple of laughter.

Reuben bent down and kissed me softly, then stared into my eyes. "Come on."

And I melted, goddammit. "All right, all right. But don't say I didn't warn you." I steeled my shoulders, squared my jaw, and narrowed my violet-lined eyes till they were sharp enough to slice through bullshit and badly behaving friends at twenty paces.

I gathered my dignity and sauntered over to one of the chairs, with Reuben close behind. Out the corner of my eye, I caught Gary Knowles making a fast exit. I didn't blame him.

"The rats are leaving the ship," I whispered to Reuben, nodding to where the All Blacks' coach was almost out the doors.

He laughed.

We'd no sooner taken our seats than two of the officers sauntered in front and wiggled their shapely butts at Reuben and me. *Good lord.* The crowd gathered around with way too much enthusiasm as Usher's 'Yeah' began to stream through the speakers.

Fuck me. Strippers.

I groaned and dropped my chin to my chest. *Kill me now.*

The officers spun around, and I lifted my gaze to find—Oh. My. Fucking. God—Mark and Josh—grins as big as the hole that was gonna be left when I removed my foot from their arses.

Their hips rolled effortlessly to the sexy beat, and yeah, okay, they looked damn good. Not that I was gonna tell them that.

I pulled on my best scowl. "If either of you get close to my lap, you're dead meat," I snarled. "And if you think for one minute I'm putting a tip in any jockstrap you might have hidden under there, you've got another thing coming." I ran my gaze between the two smiling men, caught Reuben's chuckle, and slapped his thigh. "You're enjoying this altogether too much."

"I am. Come on, they're bloody good dancers."

And they were, dammit. Almost as good as Sandy and me, although Mark's charisma and playful flirting had as much to do with his riveting performance as any actual dance moves. I stole a quick glance to Ed, whose gaze was locked on his sultry boyfriend, and smiled. They were ridiculously cute together. Apples and oranges.

Josh was a lot less skilled on the dancefloor, but since he looked like he belonged on the cover of vogue, he didn't really have to impress too much with his moves. Our two friends remained in front, while the two professionals focused on us. They were equally gorgeous, ripped and gifted on their feet, and no doubt in other places as well. I doubted either would leave alone tonight if the growing lake of drool on the spectator floor was anything to go by. Even the straight contingent seemed impressed.

Okay, so, maybe it wasn't that bad. I started to relax.

Hands trailed over our chests and backs.

Fingers slid through our hair and glided up our thighs.

Hips checked our shoulders.

A bit of reverse straddling of our laps invited a few butt slaps, which I was more than happy to deliver. The crowd approved and the strippers came back for more.

And yeah, it was fucking sexy. They knew exactly what they were doing and were damn good at it. Meanwhile, Mark and Josh worked the crowd, paying particular attention to the rugby guys and getting a few not-so-subtle, heated looks in return from men I'd never have thought it of.

Fuck me. If there weren't more than one or two confused men heading home tonight, I'd eat my damn choker.

It was all good, if downright raunchy fun, with lots of encouragement from the crowd. I was enjoying the shit out of it when the music suddenly switched to the raspy vocals of Joe Cocker's 'You Can Leave Your Hat On,' and all four men started peeling off their clothes . . . slowly . . . seductively . . . to the beat . . . one item at a time.

Jackets.

Braces.

Trousers.

Socks.

Shoes.

Shirts.

Right fucking down to their skin-tight black booty shorts for Josh and Mark . . . and leather jockstraps for the professionals.

And all with Reuben's All Blacks' jersey number 15 pinned on the back.

Holy fucking crap.

I shot a glance to Michael and Ed to check their reaction to their partners stripping in front of a crowd, but they seemed suspiciously okay with it and were clapping along with everyone else.

I wasn't sure I would've been so accommodating.

But Mark and Josh rocked awesome bodies. The shorts might've been the less risqué choice, but they didn't hide much. They were having a ball, and I couldn't help but smile. Dancing under the spotlight like that . . . man, they took my breath away.

And not just mine.

Michael was front row, staring at his husband like he was two seconds away from licking him like a goddamn ice cream, while Ed sat riveted in his seat, eyes alight, gripping that cock cage with white knuckles.

And then at the line, 'You can take your dress off,' Sandy leapt to his feet and sashayed in front of Miller's chair. You couldn't hear the music for the crowd as he shimmied out of that red skirt to expose tiny matching number 15 shorts, a black fishnet top, and that damn lace suspender belt.

Miller's eyes bugged out of his head and I snorted. Sandy was a master at strutting his stuff.

But when the professionals returned to straddle our laps with a lot more intent this time, I made a quick decision. I let them do their thing for a few teasing, dick-brushing sweeps so the audience got their jollies, and then pulled on the arm of the one jiggling over my lap. "Take it to the guests, sweetheart. This guy here's mine. And be mindful who you choose. No baiting. No drama. Got it?"

The dancer gave me a wink, tapped his mate, and the two of them peeled off into the crowd to wield their magic on what I was sure would be more than a few willing participants.

As soon as they were gone, I pushed to my feet and with only a few swaying missteps, planted myself in front of Reuben instead. No one danced for my guy like that, except me.

The crowd roared, and someone called for a fire extinguisher.

Reuben's gaze locked on mine and he sucked in a breath.

Damn right, baby.

He knew what was coming. This wasn't our first rodeo.

"Play it again," Georgie called from the back and someone flipped Mr Cocker on repeat.

Hell yeah.

I was a good dancer, tipsy or not, no point pretending otherwise. I had Reuben's full attention, and by the sound of all the clapping and cheering, most of the crowd's as well. A third chair hit the floor and Mark swung Ed into it, while Michael took my empty one, and Sandy pushed Miller's chair back to form a line.

The four of us with our men.

This was on.

I had some catching up to do in the undressing department, so I let the other three work their men to the music while I took my time.

Loafers.

Socks.

Zipper down . . .

Aaaaaand that was as far as it got since those jeans weren't going anywhere without a crowbar, and no one got to see Reuben's favourite jockstrap except the man himself. Instead, I reverse straddled his lap, shook my booty in his face, and let him peel down the waistband for a dramatic peek to the cheers of our friends.

The resulting bite mark on my arse might take some time to fade, but the roar of appreciation from the crowd would stay in my brain forever.

Next, my neon-orange top hit the floor, leaving me in just the skinny jeans and the sexy-as-shit silver choker.

A choker which had seen more action in our bedroom on *Reuben* than it ever had on me, a fact most in that room wouldn't credit, and which was the very reason I'd worn it.

Reuben blushed every damn time he saw it.

Which left all four of us non-professionals in little more than skin and a whisper of fabric as the song drew to a climax and the room filled with enough steam and sexual tension to power the Auckland grid for a month.

With a few bars to go, Mark caught all of our attention with a hand signal, and the finale was on. We straddled our men face to face, circled our hips, and at the final note, we sat.

The lights went out and the room fell deathly quiet for all of two seconds before the room erupted and the walls shook with applause and howls and shouts for more.

I dropped my lips to Reuben's ear. "I love you, baby."

The lights came up and his hands clamped around my arse. "I love you too. And I can't wait to marry you."

He took my mouth in a fierce kiss. "I'm the luckiest fucking guy on the planet. Now get those damn clothes back on."

CHAPTER TWO

Reuben

Cam's arm flailed in the air and landed on my chest as he groaned his way over onto his back. "God in heaven, would someone pleeeease remove my brain from my skull." An eyelid peeled open, then slammed shut again. "Who turned the fucking sun on?"

"Good morning, sweetheart." I leaned over and kissed his brow, mourning the loss of the spectacular view I'd had just seconds before of the traditional tattoo on his arse—all swirling lines and pert muscle.

"Oh my god, I've died and gone to hell." He shoved me away. "Look at you all bright-eyed and smelling like a damn daisy. This has to be against the Geneva Convention as cruel and unusual punishment. I blame *you* for letting me drink so much. Oh my god, my head."

I laughed and brushed a lock of hair from the broad eyeliner smudge on his cheek. Yeah, my baby had seen better days. It didn't stop my heart from landing in my throat like it did every time I woke to find him pressed up against me. How had I gotten so lucky? I didn't deserve him, but I'd keep doing my damnedest to try.

"Pretty sure I had zero chance of stopping a single one of those drinks," I told him.

He pried an eye open with two fingers and stared at me. "A likely story. Your arse is mine tonight." He tried to lift his head, groaned, and fell back on the pillow. "Or maybe tomorrow."

I snorted and patted his hip. "Yeah, good luck with that. I'm feeling my chances to top improving by the second. And to be honest, I think it was the shot relay Mark challenged you and Josh with at the end that nailed your coffin shut."

His eyes widened. "That fucker. I'm gonna—ow, ow, ow, goddammit!" He rolled to face me and curled up like a hedgehog. I patted his prickly back. "How many knives have I got sticking out of my head, and who the hell threw them?"

"Aw baby, come here." I wriggled his knees down and pulled him into my arms. "Let me kiss it better." I peppered his cheeks and nose with kisses. "If it makes you feel any better, I think Mark will be hurting worse than you. And seeing as how he's currently comatose on our lounge room floor, you'll get your chance to enact revenge, if you're quick."

"What the hell is he doing in our lounge?" Cam muttered, his face pressed into my armpit.

"You may well ask. We shared an Uber back, and when I turned around after we'd been dropped off, Mark and Ed were standing in our driveway thinking the party was still on. I soon put them right, but it seemed easier *and* safer to keep them both here for the night." I kept kissing. "So don't go in the spare room naked, looking for clean laundry."

"Noted. Mmm. You missed a spot." Cam touched his lips. "Although, fair warning, I suspect I'll taste like the dancefloor of Downtown G after a pride party. I think my pores have shut up shop cos even they can't stand to smell me."

I chuckled. "Maybe so, but you'll always taste sweet to me." I covered his mouth and went in for a quick taste before wrinkling my nose. "Yeah, nah. I definitely underestimated that. Toothpaste is absolutely called for."

A pillow landed on my face and I threw it aside.

He rolled on top of me and smooshed my cheeks together, his face inches from mine, his breath . . . yeah, about that. *Whoa.*

"For better or worse, remember?" He stared down at me with those huge, tawny, panda-ringed eyes. "It's not too late to run. When I'm old and falling apart and carrying round my catheter bag, I'll smell a whole lot worse."

I snorted. "Thanks for the imagery. And yes, for better or worse. Don't forget I'll be right there with you. I doubt Cory will want to visit either of us, but we can hold hands in the nursing home and scandalise the other residents when I cage you against the wall with my walking frame and have my slow but wicked way with you."

The corners of his mouth turned up and he waggled his brows. "Oooh, kinky. I like it. Do they make adult diapers in lace—"

I covered his mouth with my hand. "Oh. My. God. Enough. We are not going there."

He licked my palm until I freed him. "I reckon there's an untapped market right there," he said. "I should talk to Sandy."

"You do that." I kissed him on the nose. "Just as long as I don't have to hear about it." I tucked a few strands of silky black hair behind his ear, which was still sporting a small rainbow gauge from the night before, and lost myself in those eyes. "But I've noticed you keep reminding me it's not too late to run. Are *you* having second thoughts?"

His brows drew together. "No, of course not. I'm all in, rain or shine, whatever fuck traps life throws at us. I just . . ." His gaze slid sideways, then back, but a little less certain. "I just don't want you to regret anything. I don't want you to feel this is a done deal, that you have no choice. I want you to live your dreams, *all* your dreams—"

I kissed him to shut him up and rolled us both to our sides, not letting go until he melted against me. Only then did I lift my lips and tip his head back so we were eye to eye. His worried expression had me falling head over heels for him all over again.

This soft sweetness was the Cam no one saw except me. The vulnerable, unsure, truth minus sass, snark and barbs—all prickles flat, not a wall in sight. I got to have this side of him, and it made me the luckiest man alive. I'd treasure this gift and the man who gave it to my dying day.

I cradled his face and skimmed my lips across his. "This love we have, baby, this is the real deal. Forever. So, no more thinking *for* me, okay? No worrying that I've got any questions, cos I don't. I am one hundred percent in this, with you, for as long as I'm lucky enough to have you. And if you don't know that by now, then it's my fault for not making it crystal clear. We went through hell to make this happen, and nothing, nothing is going to take you away from me. You're it as far as I'm concerned. You and Cory, and those other kids we have planned down the road when I retire from rugby. I want *you.* I want it all."

He stared and I knew he was weighing the truth in my words. It might've hurt if I wasn't already kicking myself for not seeing this coming. I should've guessed. Cam had been left as second-best before, when he'd discovered a long-term boyfriend had actually been married with a family. It had almost crushed him at the time. He'd fought all his life to be true to himself, and I knew he still sometimes struggled with the whole macho rugby thing; the looks he occasionally got; the occasional aggressive arseholery from fans and other players; the innuendo; the snide comments; the media attention both good and bad.

And some of it had been really bad: social media trolls; anonymous 'presents' in our letterbox—once even literal shit wrapped in gift paper; threats to Cory, to me, and a lot to Cam; churches publicly praying for us; even some professional rugby players in other countries calling us faggots and sinners, evil and sodomites; people calling for Cory to be removed from our care; picketers outside Cam's ER, calling for his removal.

Cam put on a great show, rolling with the punches, giving as good as he got, brushing it off with a slice of wit or a killer look, but I knew he worried about me, about whether he was negatively affecting my career, holding me back, even hindering Cory, who had enough going on just learning to live life on the spectrum without adding a media spotlight. We both understood that. But I was exactly where I wanted to be, Cory and I both were, and I should've told Cam that more often.

Rugby wasn't my dream, not anymore. Cam and Cory were my dream. It might've taken me too long to figure it out the first time around, but when I did, there was no going back. Rugby was amazing, fulfilling, and exciting, but it would never top having those two men in my life.

Cam never voiced any of his concerns openly, of course, but I'd always known on some level—a look he sent my way or when he read something less than flattering about us, or him. I did try to raise it in conversation once or twice, but he just waved it aside as a non-issue. He was coping, and the rest of the world could go to hell. And I'd wanted to believe him. It was easier that way.

But as I stared into those soft welling eyes, I knew I'd let him down. My baby hurt and I needed to step the fuck up.

If he wasn't going to ask, I needed to tell him.

"This stops now," I whispered against his trembling lips. "The only thing in this world that I would *ever* regret is letting you slip away from me. Now, maybe someday, you'll have had enough of *my* sorry arse and decide to leave *me*, but I really, really hope not, because it would kill me, baby, and I don't know how I'd ever recover. But it will never, ever be me who leaves, understand? I choose this life. I choose you. I choose Cory. We're in this together. You're stuck with me."

His eyelids fluttered shut and he sighed and snuggled against my chest. "I'm sorry. It's ridiculous, I know."

"It's not ridiculous." I nuzzled his hair. "Fighting the world gets tough sometimes. But you're not the only one who gets worried."

He raised a furrowed brow.

I smoothed it with a finger. "Do you think I don't worry about all the shit the game and the celebrity puts you through? That maybe you'd be better off without me. That you'll come to your senses and see that you could live a quieter life, an easier life, without me, without having to consider the eyes of the world all the time—"

He shut me up with a fierce kiss. "I never feel that way," he said against my lips. "I never want anything other than what we have. I don't want easier or quieter; I just want you. You and Cory."

"And I want you." I cupped his cheek and he turned into the touch, kissing my palm. "But maybe I'll always worry a little," I said softly. "Just like you worry about me. So let's pinky swear to stop hiding all that batshit stuff from now on. As long as I'm in this game and maybe even for a good while after I leave, the pressure is gonna be there. We need to keep talking about it. This fucked-up circus that surrounds us isn't going to pull us apart, but not talking about it might. Agreed?" I held my little finger in the air and he wrapped his around it.

"Agreed. I fucking love you, Reuben Taylor."

"I love you too, Cameron Wano. Now, I really think you need to get in that shower because, phew wee, there's more alcohol in the fumes coming off your body than in Michael's cocktail menu last night, and Craig is dropping Cory back in an hour. Oh, and Miller texted to say Sandy is looking a lot like you, I think."

Cam rolled his eyes, then froze. "Oh, god, it's all coming back to me. Sandy's suspender belt. The striptease. Son of a bitch, I gave you a lap dance, didn't I?" He blanched. "In front of everyone. Fuck." He covered his face with his hands.

I snorted and pulled them aside. "You sure did."

He winced. "Was I any good?"

"The best."

He straightened and narrowed his gaze. "Damn right I was." He wriggled to a sit and his face turned a little green at the edges. "Oh shit, I'm gonna throw up." He fled to the ensuite, slammed the door shut, and I rolled onto my back and listened to the dulcet tones of him regretting the night before, several times.

It was hard to keep the smile off my face, so I didn't.

"You do realise I have a final fitting tomorrow?" he croaked through the closed door, and the water turned on. "My face looks like the freaking surface of the moon, and I'm carrying a million extra kilos of fluid on my hips and waist. It's never gonna clear in time. And how the hell did I get eyeliner down my neck? Jesus Christ, did I mention this is all your damn fault—oh fuck—"

The toilet lid slammed back up and my smile grew.

"Cory, my man, I love you to bits, but you gotta stop driving that truck up my legs." Mark was stretched out on the deep green sofa with an arm slung over his forehead, his expression pained. Kneeling on the floor beside him, Cory rolled his favourite red truck up Mark's left leg, across his groin, and down the other side. Mark had managed to lay a magazine over his dick and balls, offering some protection from the onslaught, but he still squirmed with every pass.

"Reuben?" Mark groaned even louder. "You have to save me, man. I promise I'll send you a copy of the vid I had Georgie make of Cam's lap dance."

"She took a video?" I leaned my head over the granite breakfast bar next to where I was making pancakes on the cooktop. "What the hell, Mark? I thought the photographer had been told to exclude that in case it got out. Plus, I thought all phones were banned?"

He lifted his arm and looked at me sheepishly. "Yeah, well. Rules are for sissies, right? Plus, it was Georgie. And she was one of the organising committee, not to mention your best friend, right?"

"Exactly," I pointed out. "Jesus, you couldn't have chosen someone worse. She might not feed it to the media, but I'll never hear the bloody end of it for the rest of my life, and Cam's gonna fucking kill me."

"So let me get this right. You're saying you *don't* want a private peep show of Cam's sexy-as-fuck pert little arse all up in your face? All those rugby games away from home, the overseas tours . . ." He circled a finger in the air.

Fuck. I scrubbed a hand down my face to hide my expression because, hell yeah, I wanted that. "Fine. Tell her to send it to me, but then I want it deleted. And no copies."

Mark huffed. "She won't be happy about that. She saw endless teasing opportunities in her future."

"Tell her unless she does, I'll sick Cam onto the both of you."

I didn't think it was possible for Mark to look any more sickly than he did, but that was the miracle of Cameron Wano. "That's dirty play, right there." He held his stomach with one hand and jabbed a finger at me. "He's still mad about the whole condom helium balloon bouquet I had sent to the ER on your engagement."

I said nothing and his head fell back on the cushion. "All right, all right. I'll make her delete it after she sends you a copy."

"Excellent choice." I fist-pumped the air.

He rolled his eyes, then winced. "Goddammit, even my eyeballs hurt. Why do you need all this damn colour? What's wrong with black?"

I snorted. "Because we like it." We'd been in our new house about six months, and the only neutral colour space was Cory's bedroom, which remained a calm oasis for sleep and de-escalation. The rest, although painted a bland cream on the walls, was chock full of bright accessories. We'd amassed a wonderful selection of eclectic geometric prints from my rugby tours, which combined amazingly well with a few originals by particular Samoan artists that Cam loved. There were cheerful rugs and cushions, a colourful glass and rock collection that Cory added to regularly, and a lounge corner full of Cory's favourite things all neatly housed in colourful shelving.

Our backyard was full of flowering trees and perennials, and Cam had recently completed a raised vegetable garden where Cory had a section all to himself. Not much got a chance to grow at the rate

Cory pulled stuff out and changed his mind, but he was happy as long as he wore his gloves and could sit on a blanket and not get his legs dirty. Some things didn't change.

"You don't like the colour, you can go home," I pointed out.

"All right. All right. Now can you please . . ." Mark waggled his finger above Cory who was busy running his truck over and around Mark's feet while singing a favourite Disney song just under his breath.

At almost seven, Cory was barely recognisable from the withdrawn little boy he'd been two years ago when he was still with Craig, before I'd come out and before he'd come to live with Cam and me when Craig's life had imploded. He attended a specialist school and was doing remarkably well, noticeably calmer and interacting more. And we were seeing fewer and fewer meltdowns.

He remained quiet and probably always would, and he still needed a lot of time to adapt to new people and environments. But life was a whole lot easier than it had been, and as long as we were careful to consider his needs, our family functioned similarly to other families. We just needed to keep paying attention and plan things ahead of time, things that other parents often never had to consider.

He had his unique set of issues like all kids on the spectrum did, but he was beginning to trust more and more. He was happy to be left with Cam's parents, and Geo and Sandy had been brought into that circle of trust as well, along with the school and a few of the other parents in our support group. It meant we had a good range of people who could look after him if we wanted to go out, or if Cam needed help when I was away, or any number of reasons. Life was pretty good.

My formal adoption of Cory had gone through with minimal fuss, and Craig continued to be in his life on a regular basis. When we were married, I intended to get Cam's name added to those adoption papers quickly. We'd initially filed the application in just my name to keep the process as smooth and fast as possible—anything to keep my arsehole homophobic father quiet. But that was going to change.

"Hey, Cory?" I knocked on the countertop and he looked up. "Do you wanna watch *Up*?"

He beamed. "Yes, please."

Per Cory's current behavioural plan, we were working on trying to substitute other distractions in place of movies, and so being offered the chance to watch one out of the blue was a real treat. His eyes danced with excitement.

"*Up. Up. Up.* Yes. Please. With Mark?" He bounced up and down.

I laughed, and Mark groaned and shuffled his feet off the side of the sofa and onto the floor while keeping his body where it was. He looked damned uncomfortable. Cory climbed carefully into the vacant space, made himself at home, and started up with the truck again.

"Nuh-uh, sweetheart." I walked across with my hand outstretched. "If you want a movie, then you put the truck on the coffee table for later, okay?"

Cory looked at the truck and thought about it. The outcome was never a foregone conclusion as he took his time to weigh up his options. I bit my tongue and waited. Cam had patience in abundance, more than me, as it turned out, which was a surprise to all concerned.

I loved Cory deeply, but Cam was definitely the better peacemaker. Ninety percent of the time, he intuitively knew what Cory needed if he got frustrated. Not that it worked all the time, but he was right more often than he was wrong.

As for me? I just muddled through.

"Okay." Cory finally held out the truck. I chalked one up for Pappy as I slipped it on the table and got *Up* queued on the television. Craig had kept the name Dad. I'd been given Pappy, and Cam got, well, Cam.

"Thank Christmas for that," Mark moaned and turned on his side while I headed back into the kitchen and kept an eye on them over the breakfast bar.

Cory scooted into the curve behind Mark's knees and patted his thigh.

"Okay, Mark?" He leaned forward to peek at Mark's face.

Mark returned a somewhat sickly grin. "Wonderful, little man, just wonderful."

I swallowed a laugh.

"That's good." Cory patted Mark's leg once again. "Did you know Pappy and Cam are getting married? I'm carrying the rings with Tink."

I flipped a pancake and tried not to cry. Cory looked so damn proud.

He loved all the dogs in our tight group of friends, interacting with them in ways he never allowed with people, but Mark and Ed's huge Neapolitan Mastiff was his absolute favourite. It had taken us a couple of months of practice to get the ring carrying thing ready to go —first with our family and friends, then with his class at school who loved the visit from Tink and Mark—and just last weekend Cory had let the mastiff lead him around the park while he carried the ring box.

He might pull out at the last minute with everyone there, but that was fine. We'd work around it. And a dog of our own was next on the Wano-Taylor list of family to-do's—after the wedding.

Family.

Mark shoved another cushion under his head and rubbed his bloodshot eyes. "Yes, I do know. Are you excited? Tink is."

"Yep." Cory glanced sideways, then back at the television. "Shh. It's starting."

"Give him his headset," I told Mark. "Then come and eat. You're making me feel sick just looking at you."

"I can't," he whined. "Someone switched my stomach out for a vat of acid." A long, noisy burp underlined his point. "Oh, my god, yuck. I think I'll join you after all."

He lumbered his way to the breakfast bar and slumped in a seat. "Where's the love of my life, by the way?"

I nodded down the hall as I slid another pancake onto the stack and pushed the dish Mark's way along with the butter and maple syrup. "Eat something. Plates are on the shelf beside you and utensils in that drawer. And to answer your question, Ed's in the spare room. Where I thought you'd be, by the way. What happened?"

He blushed. "I vaguely remember coming out for a drink of water, and then for some reason, I had to sit down . . . on the floor, apparently. Seemed like a good idea at the time." He poured syrup on a pancake, stabbed it with his fork, and lifted the whole thing to his mouth to take a bite.

"Well, that explains that." I pointed at the water glass sitting on the floor by the hallway.

"Huh." He chuckled. "How about that? Guess I didn't drink it after all. Is he okay?"

I snorted. "Who, Ed?"

"Mmm." Mark chewed on his mouthful while I flipped another pancake.

"I have no idea," I answered. "He's your problem, not mine. But I have to say, I've never heard him talk as much as he did last night."

Mark swallowed his pancake and gave a huge grin. "Right? Proper little chatterbox with a few drinks in him. Aces in bed like that too. Just lets loose and—ow! What was that for?"

I returned the silicon flipper to my other hand. "Not another word about your sex life. I've got gym training at ten. It's gonna be hard enough keeping my breakfast down with only four hours sleep without adding any images of you and Ed having kinky sex into the mix."

Mark's mouth dropped open. "Gym training. Holy sh—" His gaze shot to Cory. "Shivers. Sucks to be you." He glanced at the clock on the wall. "Damn, I need to call Carla and get her to pop next door and let Tink and Nana out before they bust their bladders."

He took his cell to the window while I finished the pancakes, just in time for Cam to appear from our bedroom looking like . . . last week's fish. *Holy moly*. I'd have grabbed a photo if I didn't value my balls.

"Feeling better, my sweet?" I bit back a smile.

"I saw that look," he grumbled, sliding his arms around me, his warm body pressed against mine. "And no, not really."

"Well, at least you smell a lot better." I turned to snag those pouty lips in a kiss, slipping a little tongue inside. "Mmm. Taste a lot better too. Now, get some food in you."

"Oh, god, I couldn't." His hand went to his mouth and his olive complexion took on a distinctly khaki tinge.

"You'll feel better for it."

He scowled at me. "Says you. I think I'll take my chances. Besides . . ." His arms dropped from my waist and I turned to watch him creep up on Mark who was still talking on the phone. He waited until Mark disconnected and then grabbed him around the waist.

"BOO!"

The poor guy nearly fell into the giant ficus.

"What the fu-fudge, Cam? What was that for? You nearly gave me a heart attack."

"Shh." Cory scolded them from the couch.

Cam tiptoed over and planted a soft kiss on Cory's cheek. "Sorry, little man. Want some pancakes?"

"Yes, please, Cam."

Cam returned and fisted Mark's shirt before hauling him into the kitchen. "*That* was for exposing me to the terrifying sight of you in those obscenely tiny booty shorts last night." He kept his voice low. "Whichever one of you lot came up with that idea needs their head read. I'm never gonna be able to look at Lycra again without remembering your scrawny arse, amongst other unmentionables. As it is, I may never find my dick again; it's still recovering from the shock of discovering that yes, cocks really do come in extra small." Cam smirked.

"Fuck off," Mark whispered and hauled Cam in for a sloppy kiss on the cheek. "We're talking XXL at the minimum."

"In your dreams. And only if XXL stands for extra, extra Lilliputian." Cam wiped his cheek with his sleeve and loaded a plate with pancakes for Cory, while Mark eased slowly onto his barstool.

"And there's nothing scrawny about this arse." Mark slid his phone onto the counter. "Carla's heading over to feed Tink and Nana and let them out. The little shits probably slept on our damn bed."

Cam returned from the lounge and slid onto the barstool alongside Mark.

"So." Mark turned sideways to Cam. "Honest answer. It was a good night, right?"

Cam gave one of those wide grins that melted my heart every damn time. "Yeah, it was. Surprisingly."

Mark snorted. "You only say surprisingly because you didn't get to micromanage every damn second of it like you usually do."

I chuckled because it was true, and Cam stabbed the back of my hand lightly with his fork. "Yeah, yeah. You're all being very brave at the moment. I can see I've let things slide. Time to tighten those reins."

I leaned around the breakfast bar and pressed my lips to his. "I can't fucking wait."

"Oh my god, I am not sitting here for this." Mark slid off his barstool. "My stomach's barely coping with the pancake. If you want me, I'll be reacquainting myself with my boyfriend in the spare room. It may take a while. Talk amongst yourselves." He took the remainder of his pancake in his hand and headed down the hall.

I walked around the breakfast bar and spun Cam's stool until he was in my arms and his legs wrapped around my waist. "Now, where were we?" I dipped my lips to his just as his phone went off in his pocket with a familiar ring.

His mum.

We broke apart with a simultaneous sigh.

"Hold that thought," he said with apology in his eyes and walked off to take the call.

I let him go and grabbed myself some breakfast, taking just a single pancake alongside a bowl of fruit and cereal. The AB's worked on a 90:10 nutritional plan. Eat the good stuff ninety percent of the time, with ten percent treats. I was tired and the gym work wasn't gonna be a picnic, but with a few weeks off for a hamstring earlier in the season, I needed the strength work.

I tried to listen to Cam's side of the conversation as I ate, but he was unusually quiet. Margaret Wano was a force of nature, just like her son. A fierce Polynesian woman with both Samoan and Fijian heritage, and she protected her family like a big-toothed mumma bear. The two strong personalities fed off each other with often hilarious results, but not today. From the little bit I heard of the other end of the conversation, Margaret sounded upset, and that wasn't like her.

I went across and cupped Cam's cheek as he listened, gently turning his face to mine. "Problem?" I mouthed.

He held my gaze, then frowned, shrugged, and walked the phone over to the window, leaving me standing there.

Huh.

Cam rarely, if ever, walked away from me. Not unless he was solidly pissed about something my thick skull had missed in whatever argument we'd been having at the time. But there was tension in his slim shoulders where there'd been none before, and his free arm wrapped around his waist in a protective stance.

Something was wrong, and I didn't like the look of it one little bit.

When he finally hung up, he didn't explain right away as I'd expected him too. Instead, he simply stared out the window. Even Cory glanced his way—always super sensitive to any free-floating emotions.

A curl of worry wound tight in my stomach and I walked across to slide my arms around his waist from behind.

He immediately tensed.

Something was very definitely off.

"Hey. What's up, sweetheart." I rested my chin on his shoulder. "Your mum sounded upset."

He didn't answer straight away, but rather than push, I waited, sensing a wall slip between us that hadn't been there for a long, long time. He was being careful, considering how and maybe what to answer.

"It's, um, just a family thing," he finally said, and that clench in my stomach grew to the size of a fist. "No one you'd know."

He turned around and I took a second to really look at him. He wasn't lying; he just wasn't telling me everything.

"I'll head over and see them at lunchtime," he added. "I'll take Cory and try to be back before you get home."

I rubbed my hands up and down his arms. "You want me to tag along? I can push back my training to this afternoon?"

"No." He patted my chest. "I'll be fine. As I said, you don't know them. Family, what can you do, right?" The smile never reached his eyes, and I wasn't buying it.

"But this is *your* family, Cam, which means they're *my* family too. I love your mum and dad, you know that. They're better parents to me than my own ever were. And if something's upset them enough to make you this worried, I want to help if I can."

"There's no need," he said sharply.

Whoa. I took a step back.

"I'm sorry." He stepped in and slid his arms around my waist, pressing his cheek to my chest. "I didn't mean it to come out like that. I just . . ." He paused and sighed. "I'll tell you everything after I've talked with them, okay? You have to get to training, and don't forget, Jake's coming for dinner. There's some drama going on with him that he wouldn't tell me about last night. Jesus, what is it with my family at the moment?"

"Jake?"

He shrugged. "I think he and Trent might've broken up."

"Damn. I liked that guy."

"Me too. He was good for Jake. Settled him down."

I wrapped my arms around his shoulders and kissed the top of his head. "Okay, I'll wait. But is it something to do with why your parents pulled out from babysitting last night? They never really explained on the phone."

He hummed against my chest. "Yeah. Just as well Craig's been a surprisingly reliable backup lately. Eight months sober. That's his longest run. And he looks different this time, more solid somehow."

Thank God. Two falls off the wagon were enough. "I think you're right. He seemed grateful for a genuine excuse to stay away from the temptation, even though I'd told him he didn't have to come."

Cam kissed my cheek. "You're a good brother. Now, get going or you'll be late." He patted my chest with both hands and pushed me toward the bedroom.

I gathered my gym bag, gave Cory a hug and Cam a thorough mauling, but it still didn't feel right leaving him like this and I chewed on it all the way to the gym.

CHAPTER THREE

Cam

I ARRIVED AT MY PARENTS' HOUSE ABOUT TWELVE THIRTY, BUT rather than go straight inside, I sat in their driveway beside a vehicle I didn't recognise and wondered for the hundredth time if I was doing the right thing.

There was a dreariness to the weather after the bright spring start to the day—clouds swallowing the sunshine and not looking at spitting it out anytime soon. It fitted only too well with my sinking mood, as every fibre in my body screamed that Reuben should be with me.

It didn't sit right. But I'd still fobbed him off.

And on some level he knew. He'd looked if not exactly hurt, then wary, and I hated that I was the reason for it. But my mother had caught me off guard, and there was way too much going on for Reuben, with the wedding in two weeks in addition to all of his rugby commitments and the upcoming European tour, to add this complication to the mix. Not until I knew more.

But then I thought of our promise that morning.

Pinky swear?

Fuck.

Just a few hours later and I was already screwing up.

No, I hadn't been upfront about my concerns that Reuben might feel trapped or that he might feel his rugby wings were clipped by having me in his life. I wanted the best for him, and I never wanted to be the reason he didn't reach his potential. But I also knew he loved me and that he wanted me in his life. I *knew* that at a bone-deep level.

I should've just talked to him. I don't know why I didn't. The damn wedding was messing with my head. We shouldn't have tried to squeeze it into a rugby bye weekend, for fuck's sake.

Ya think, queen?

But nailing *any* date that worked with Reuben's rugby commitments was damn near impossible. Rugby ran from February to November. First, the Super Rugby competition until mid-year, then the provincial Mitre 10 Cup which followed. And that wasn't even including the All Blacks' fixtures, training, and tours in-between. We'd already postponed the wedding once; it wasn't happening again. If we didn't do it now, it could be well after Christmas and another six months would've passed. Not. Happening.

And since Reuben was still early in his career, there would be no let-up. Little wonder lots of players chose to wait until they were retired. But Reuben didn't want that and neither did I. It wasn't that we *needed* marriage; we wanted it, always had, although I'd been the one to ask—quaking in my boots—but that's another story. Plus there was Cory to think of. It definitely helped to ensure his future with both of us.

"Cam?" Cory leaned between the seats and poked at my damp eyes. "Are we going to see Granna and John?"

Somehow only my mum had got the grandparent moniker, although my dad secretly thought the first name option was pretty damn cute.

Dammit. I blew out a sigh and pulled up my shirt to wipe my eyes. *Get your shit together, Cameron.* "Yes, little man, let's go and see Granna. Take your trucks and headset."

Cory had barely hit the front path when my father barrelled out the front door to meet him. He slowed just in time before Cory scuttled behind my back. It had taken a bit of practice and a few 'incidents' for my dad to calm his generally boisterous approach to life when it came to Cory, but he'd finally got it and the two were best of mates, in as much as Cory ever was with anyone outside Reuben and me.

My dad stopped a short distance from Cory and held out his hand. "I'm working in the vegetable garden, Cory. There's a rug and your favourite road track set up under the lemon tree if you want to come with me. I've got an apple juice and a cheese sandwich for you, crusts removed."

Cory stared at the ground for a bit, then lifted his gaze for just a second to take Dad's hand. "Okay, John."

"Take as long as you need." Dad shot me a wink, then led Cory down the side path to the backyard, chattering about all the spring flowers as they passed while Cory nodded and hummed, happy enough to be led along.

I stared at the front entrance for another few seconds while I herded my mental ducks into a dubious row and then headed up the path—excited or terrified, take your pick.

I'd almost reached the door when a familiar horn spun me in place.

Reuben.

My heart kicked up and my eyes immediately filled as he pulled in behind my car and climbed out. Then those strong legs ate up the distance between us in seconds, and I was in his arms. I wrapped my legs around his waist and he cupped my arse in his hands to hold me up as I buried my face in his neck, into that familiar reassuring scent that never failed to steady my world.

"Pinky swear. We're in this together, right?" His warm breath brushed my ear and I nodded like a bobblehead. "There's no multiple choice here, Cam. If you're upset, I need to know why. And I want to be there for you. That's what we do. That's what this means. You. Me. Us. Don't shut me out, baby, please. I'm a big boy. I don't need your protection, remember?"

But you do. The need swelled in my chest but remained unspoken. "You better set me down before I throw up," I warned, sliding down his hard body to my feet.

He let me straighten my shirt and then cupped my jaw. "I said, do you understand?"

I avoided the question, mumbling something I hoped he'd take as a yes. Because I loved him, and I protected everyone I loved. "But what about training? You needed to be there."

"No," he said, brushing a thumb over my lips. "I need to be *here*. I was so worried about you, I almost dropped a ten-kilo weight on Mac's foot. Andrew sent me away to get my head on right, and here I am. So, do I need to know anything before we go in? Because your mum's staring at us through the window like we've lost our minds."

"No." I slid my lips over his, drinking in the taste of the man I loved more than anything. "You'll pick it up soon enough. Just remember to breathe, and don't say I didn't warn you." I grabbed his hand and pulled him inside, wondering if anything was ever going to be the same.

Twenty minutes, two gulped cups of coffee, and a piece of sponge cake later, and I was feeling a little more alive and a lot more nervous as Reuben grew increasingly still on the couch beside me.

I was too afraid to even look at his expression, keeping my eyes fixed on the two women sitting on the couch opposite—my mother and her much older sister, Colleen.

"And your daughter, sorry, Stella is seventeen?" Reuben asked softly, his hand sneaking into mine. I pulled it onto my lap and held on for all I was worth.

Colleen's gaze followed the movement with a smile. "Yes, that's right. Two months back. Martin and I married late in life." She winced, her cheeks flushing red, and I felt for her. This couldn't be easy.

My mum rested her hand on her sister's arm. "She's a great girl, Colly."

Colleen smiled and put her hand over top. "She is, thank you."

"It's a lot to think about," Reuben commented.

I tried to wring every nuance of meaning out of his words and tone of voice but got nowhere. Also, talk about understatement of the fucking year.

"We realise that," Colleen answered. "Which is why we didn't bring her today, even though this was her idea." She sighed with the combined weight of generations of parents faced with similar circumstances. "It's the first time we've seen Stella smile in a week, and I didn't want to get her hopes up or for you to feel pressured."

Good luck with that. I squeezed Reuben's hand and got a white-knuckled one in response. *What did that mean? Was he thinking yes? No?* I stole a glance to find his expression thoughtful, his brow lightly furrowed, and his eyes carefully . . . neutral. *Fuck it.* He could be deciding on damn curtains for all the information that gave me.

"And you said she's fifteen weeks?" Those furrows sank just a bit deeper, and I wanted to iron them flat with my hand.

I didn't.

"Yes, that's right." Colleen glanced at her sister. "She, ah, she had no idea she was pregnant. Her cycle is irregular, and it wasn't until she missed her third period that she did a home test and our GP confirmed it last week. It was Stella's decision to have the baby and then have someone within the family adopt if possible, in case you're wondering."

"You don't want to look after her baby yourselves?" I asked the obvious question that I knew would be top in Reuben's mind as well.

Colleen's eyes shone with tears. "We will if we have to, of course. But Martin is seventy and I'm sixty-five. We're not really up to coping with a newborn again, and Stella has years of education ahead of her if she wants to fulfil her dream of being a vet.

There are a few others we can approach, and we're almost positive one of those couples will be keen, so please don't feel pressured, but Stella wanted to ask you first. She loves you, Cam, and admires you, Reuben." She took a breath as if steeling herself. "She also came out as bi to us this year—" She hesitated, and my brow arched.

This was news to me. I shot a glance to Mum who appeared unusually flustered.

"Stella was planning to talk to you before . . . well, before this happened. I'm ashamed to say it took us a minute, but we fully support her. However, you know how close-minded some of our church people can be, Cam, even family."

Did I ever. More than a few 'family' had disappeared from our lives after I'd come out, and only later did I learn that my mother was responsible. You didn't look sideways at any of Margaret Wano's children and expect an invitation to her house ever again. Did I mention how much I loved my mother?

"It's changing, but it's slow," Colleen continued. "But Stella doesn't want to take a chance if she can avoid it."

The room fell silent. So no pressure then.

"It would need to be a completely open adoption," Colleen stated firmly. "The baby would have to know Stella as their birth mother, us as their grandparents, and their place in the wider family; *everyone* would need to know. That's how these things go in our culture." She spoke those words directly to Reuben. "And Stella would want to keep contact and be in the baby's life in some way, once you were all settled. May as well be upfront about all that before we start."

So, not complicated at all, then. My eyes fired around my skull like a pinball machine.

"What about the father?" Reuben asked.

Colleen exchanged looks with my mother who nodded. "He's twenty-three and engaged to someone else. Stella didn't know that at the time. Anyway, he's been very clear that he's not interested in being more than a paper dad and is happy to sign whatever is needed and fulfil any legal or financial obligation. Of course, that might change, but it's all we have to work with now."

"Has he told his fiancé?" I asked, hoping she dropped him like a stone for the arsehole that he was.

She shrugged. "Who knows? That's up to him, I guess."

The room fell quiet once again, and I wanted nothing more than to drag Reuben outside to find what was bubbling under that infuriating neutral expression he still wore.

This was *exactly* why I'd wanted to wait. You can't prepare for this. *No one* expects this kind of opportunity, especially not when you're a gay couple two weeks shy of getting married, parents to a high-needs child already, and under an eye-watering media spotlight for the next ten years, give or take.

Hardly ideal, and I could practically see Reuben's mental synapses flashing like Sydney Harbour at midnight on New Year's Eve.

Yes, we wanted more children. But we'd always said we'd wait until Reuben retired from professional sport and Cory was older. But we might also never get this opportunity again. It wasn't like surrogacy was straightforward in New Zealand, especially for a gay couple. We couldn't offer any financial recompense, and the adoption process after the birth, was still convoluted.

But this type of intra-family adoption wasn't easy either. A newborn within a family? Lots of nosy people, lots of well-meaning interference, lots of gossip, and potentially lots of pressure. Plus, a very close relationship with the birth mother. It invited complicated family dynamics, to say the least, Reuben's adoption of Cory being a shining example.

And Colleen was right. LGBTQ tolerance wasn't always high in a strongly church-centred community. If Reuben and I adopted Stella's baby, there'd be more than a few unhappy family members, and Stella would catch some flack too. And that was on top of all the rugby shit we had to deal with already.

Fuck. My. Life.

"We're gonna need some time," I said, reaching again for Reuben's hand. He was starting to look a bit shell shocked, and I didn't blame him. "When do you need an answer? You realise we have our wedding in two weeks."

"We do." Colleen wrung her hands. "And I'm so sorry to add to your stress. Plus, I know you have Cory to consider. But Stella doesn't want to leave it too long to talk to the other two couples if you say no, so she's hoping you might make a decision by Sunday night if that's not too rushed. She's had her first scan in order to date her more accurately, but she said to tell you that if you decide you do want to be parents to her baby, then there's another scan around twenty weeks that you could attend."

She leaned forward and rested a hand atop Reuben's free one. "We've only met once or twice at family get togethers, Reuben, but can I just say that from what I've seen and heard, I think you two have a lovely relationship, and I would be more than happy to put my grandchild in your hands. That said, you need to do what's best for the both of you and for Cory, so I'm going to let you think about it and head home." She stood and brushed off her skirt.

"How about you leave Cory with us tonight?" my mother offered. "I'll run him by your place tomorrow for his bag and get him to school. It'll give you guys a chance to talk. I've got plenty of clothes and he's got all his favourites here."

I glanced at Reuben who looked decidedly pale and serious. *Oh, baby.* I kissed his cheek and his lips turned up. Much better.

He nodded to my mother. "Thanks, Margaret."

Colleen hugged us both, and then the two sisters walked out to Colleen's car with their arms around each other, while Reuben and I watched through the window.

I leaned into Reuben and he threw an arm around my shoulders. "The gym would definitely have been the safer option."

I snorted. "Come on, let's go see Cory and then head home. I'll call Jake and tell him that dinner's off for tonight. Maybe I can get something out of him on the phone instead." I slapped Reuben's arse.

"And I vote for a bit of action before any more talk. I don't know about you, but I've got some serious stress to relieve. You got a problem with that?"

Reuben's smile reached right into his eyes for the first time since he'd arrived at my parent's house. "Not a single one."

Reuben

Oomph. Cam slammed me back against the wall inside the front door, set his teeth to my throat, and proceeded to maul his way across to my shoulder tip. Then he lifted his head and cupped his ear.

"Can you hear that?"

Silence reigned.

"That's the sound of an epic fuck waiting to happen." He stared at me; our faces so close I could make out every single one of those epically long eyelashes that framed his beautiful golden eyes. "Are you ready, baby?"

Hell yeah, I was. Anything to fend off the emotional maelstrom that had taken root in my chest the minute we'd left his parents' house.

Grabbing the hem of my jersey and T-shirt, Cam tugged both over my head and threw them aside. Then he spun me around and smooshed my cheek against the paintwork.

Fucking ninja Taekwondo skills.

"I'm not the one with the hangover, sweetheart," I reminded him. "You sure *you're* ready for this?"

He leaned in close, his breath hot on the back of my shoulders. "Pffft. Are you questioning the readiness of my cock, Mr Taylor?" He held me in place with a hand in the centre of my back as he shoved my sweats and briefs around my ankles. "My Aunt Colleen's sponge cake is known for its restorative powers." He dropped to a crouch and bit my arse. "It's a goddamn miracle."

"For the love of God, please don't *ever* mention your Aunt Colleen and your cock in the same sentence, ever again."

"Lift your feet."

I did, and he threw my sweats and briefs to the side.

"Stay where you are."

I did. I wasn't stupid. Those words only ever meant good things whenever my body was in Cam's sights.

He ran his hands up the outside of my legs as he got to his feet and then fished in the table by the front door for the lube we kept stashed there.

So yes, we might've been in this position once or twenty times before.

The buckle of his jeans hit the floor and a shirt landed at my feet, quickly followed by the snip of the lube cap. He slicked up and pressed a very demanding cock through the top of my thighs to press against my balls and my already interested dick sat bolt upright.

Welcome home.

"Fuck, I love that you're just that much taller than me." He nudged into me until I moaned. "It's the perfect fucking difference."

"Yeah, stop talking and . . . mmm, right there." I shoved my butt back to get the head of his naked cock exactly where I wanted so it slid along my taint before hitting my balls. I reached behind to feel his arse and answer the question that always presented itself whenever Cam was intent on fucking me.

And yessss!

Satin and lace.

Which meant he'd pulled it aside to slick up and thigh fuck me. The visual alone sent a buzzing to the base of my spine.

Damn.

Sex with Cam was never predictable; never exactly the same two times in a row. Every time I thought I knew what he was going to do, he surprised me. The how, the when, the where, the position, toys or not, lingerie or naked. I still couldn't believe how lucky I was.

"You like?" He leaned against me, thrusting in and out between my thighs.

"Red or yellow?" I knew the feel of all his lingerie.

"I was in a red mood today, baby. Do you remember?"

Did I ever. The last time he'd worn those particular omens of deliciousness, he'd fucked me raw in a Sydney hotel after I'd scored three tries in a game against the Wallabies and taken out man of the match. Just as well the team flew back to New Zealand in business class, because I couldn't sit down for two days. It had been a block-buster night.

"I need to train tomorrow," I reminded him. "So maybe go a little easier on me this time."

He withdrew his dick and spun me around, slamming me back against the wall. "I'll think about it." He dropped to his knees and swallowed me to the back of his throat.

Or not. "Holy . . . mphf." The back of my head hit the wall and I made a mental note to call the plasterer. The entrance was looking decidedly pitted of late, and all at head level—mine.

Cam grunted and I looked down to see him working himself—his swollen dick jutting out the side of those bright red satin briefs I knew so well, pre-come dripping to the floor by his toes.

I sucked in a sharp breath, captivated by the sight of him, as always. He was so effortlessly sexy. The man oozed sex appeal in scrubs and a pair of damn sneakers. But like this, on his knees for me? He was incendiary.

He worked my dick like he'd been starving for it, and maybe he was. I liked to think so. I'd pretty much poured him into bed the night before—all wandering hands and zero coordination—cute as a button. He'd been out in a matter of minutes, his hand still holding my cock, a thin line of drool out the side of his mouth as he quietly snored. Fucking adorable.

Between Cory's commitments and training and games and travel and Cam's work, we didn't always get as much alone time as we'd have liked, but that was life. We just made damn sure to make the time we did get count. And if anyone could make it count, Cam could. He never let a second go to waste if he could get his hands on me, or any opportunity to show he loved me. He was a toppy, bossy, sexy, demanding machine in bed—nothing had changed in the two years we'd been together—and I loved every spine-tingling, arse-aching second of it.

I channelled my fingers through all that silky black hair as Cam went to town on my dick. I even attempted a few thrusts into his mouth—poking the bear just for the hell of it.

He glanced up, caught my eye, and immediately went still.

Permission granted.

I wrapped my hands around the side of his head and his throat opened to me like the hot, wet, sucking black hole that it was. Cam had always deep-throated like a champ, whereas my own attempts had initially come with a warning that sounded remarkably like Gandalf when things got serious—'You shall not pass.' But I'd had two years of practice and I was catching up fast.

He stroked himself, struggling for breath as I fucked that glorious mouth. His tawny eyes streamed but remained locked on mine, daring me to hold back.

Never gonna happen. I knew he loved it.

And in less than a couple of minutes, I was teetering on the edge, balls drawn up, spine tingling.

Then just like that, his mouth was gone and my cock bobbed free.

"Bed." He grabbed my hand and tugged me down the hall and into our enormous bedroom—Cam's number one requirement when we'd gone real estate shopping for a larger home in the city. That, and a private, safe backyard for Cory and for us to be a family and entertain without making it easy for the media to intrude.

I eagerly followed, my eyes locked on the bunch and stretch of his firm arse and the tattoo that peeked through a fine layer of red lace. At the foot of our bed, I stretched to cup it in my hands, and he froze.

My palm slid over the delicate material and the silky-smooth skin of his arse. Heat bloomed in his flesh at my touch, and he moved his hips in a slow circle. Then he looked at me over his shoulder and licked his lips. "You wanna taste, baby?"

Desire licked deep in my belly. "You know I do."

He blew me a kiss and crawled onto the mattress on all fours, keeping his knees close to the edge. Then he dropped his head to his hands and wriggled his shapely arse, that red scrap of lace just begging for attention.

"Have at it, sweetheart."

My hands were on him in a second, enjoying the contrast of all that firm muscle wrapped in a pretty lace package. I slipped those siren-red briefs down just enough to give me room to work and then pulled apart his cheeks so I could run my tongue up the length of his taint and over that sweet, sexy hole.

A shiver ran the length of my spine at the first taste—so fucking turned on I wasn't sure I'd last to get him inside me.

He growled into the mattress as my heart pounded in my throat. This gift, this vulnerable place Cam had so rarely given to others— always needing control, always cautious—was mine for the taking. He opened himself up in every way he could for me, as hard as it was— heart, head, and body—and I'd never take it for granted.

I slipped a hand between his legs and over those lace-covered balls and stroked his needy cock. I licked and sucked and probed at his hole, adjusting my approach to the way his body demanded—a fresh angle; deeper; shallower; a zing of pain, if you please. He squirmed and moaned, shifting his hips and growling in frustration when I ignored him. He both hated and loved being edged, and I was the undisputed master of driving him crazy.

I pulled back and slid a finger in to replace my tongue, mesmerised as he fucked himself on it with unrestrained abandon, filthy noises falling from his mouth.

He shunted back and forward, and I added a second finger, keeping them in place as I shuffled around to his side and claimed an awkward sideways kiss. He snagged my lips between his teeth as he kept fucking himself, eyes closed, grunting with the effort. And then he was gone, rolling off to the side and gasping for breath.

"Jesus fuck, I almost lost it." He held his dick at the base. "On the bed," he ordered, scrambling to his feet to get the lube from the bedside drawer.

I fell onto the mattress as he made his sinuous way to the foot of the bed, like a well-fucked cat wanting more. From there he stared at me, eyes burning into my heart as he slicked up his cock and decided exactly what to do with me.

I never knew, never even bothered to presume. The anticipation was one of the hottest things about sex with Cam. I knew I could ask if I was in the mood for something particular, and he'd indulge me without blinking an eye, but mostly I just fucking loved the surprise. In my tightly controlled physical life, Cam was the ultimate release valve.

He threw the lube on the bed and crawled up my body until we were eye to eye, and I lifted my legs over his shoulders with a contented sigh. I was so very, very in the mood for this.

I glanced over his shoulder to the huge mirror on the ceiling above our bed. There were others on each wall, but for tonight, this was the best seat in the house.

Kitchy? Not on your fucking life. When your fierce baby wore lingerie to fuck your brain cells to kingdom come, you wanted to see that shit from every angle God made.

Cam reached down and shoved a lubed finger into my hole, and then two, and I arched up. His cock banged and then nestled against mine, and I was ready.

I didn't need much prep. If Cam knocked, I was ready. That's just how it was.

He guided the head of his dick to my hole and nudged ever so slightly. Then he cradled my face and covered my mouth in a deep, lazy kiss that set my toes tingling as he slowly pressed in. His tongue fucked my mouth slowly as his dick filled me up, and we were home.

We generally went straight at it, but this time Cam shuddered and closed his eyes, his body stilling inside me.

"Baby?" I asked softly, my brow wrinkling.

His eyes flicked open, and a rush of love poured like a waterfall into mine. I couldn't move, couldn't speak.

"You are *everything* to me, Ruby." He kissed the damp from my eyes. "Us—you and me and Cory—you're my world, and nothing will change that. This will always be enough; *we* will always be enough. I couldn't love you any more than I do. You're it for me. We can change our life however we want, or not change it, but nothing will take that away from us, understand?" Emotion ran thick in his words, and I lifted my lips to his.

I did understand, and my heart settled in my chest for the first time since we'd left his parents. "I do understand, baby, and I love you too. We've got this. Either way, we've got this." I kissed his eyelids one at a time. "Now, how about you fuck me like you promised?"

His expression morphed almost instantly from concern into that cheeky, sexy, confident man I knew so well.

Damn. I fisted the sheets. *Here we go.*

With his eyes on mine, he pulled back slowly and then slammed back into me, rocking me up the mattress, handholds be damned. He did it again, and again, until finally settling into a slow, pounding rhythm that echoed through my body and sent me rocketing toward home plate.

"Jesus, Cam," I gasped, the back of my head buried in the pillow. "Right. Fucking. There!"

A flash of red grabbed my attention and I stared up at the mirror, riveted to the punch and thrust of his tight muscled arse as he worked my hole, that damn tattoo teasing as he grunted and rammed home his absolute pleasure at being inside me.

"Whenever you want, baby," he rumbled from above, sounding grimly desperate. "Fuck, you're tight. I can't . . ."

I might've been embarrassed at how little time it took to get there, but Cam so often did that to me: a look as foreplay, a few touches to juice me up, a dirty word, a command, and a few thrusts and that was it. Hang my dick up to dry and go to sleep.

And there I was again. My dick squeezed between our bodies, the friction guaranteed with every thrust, and then I was there.

Still thrusting, he sat back a bit so he could watch me come apart in his hands, and I idly wondered why he bothered. I came apart in my heart every damn day I saw him.

"Yeah. Just like that." He held my gaze as I arched and shot between us, shuddering with the aftershocks. Then he leaned forward and held my gaze as he shuttled in and out a few more times before I felt his cock swell in my arse and explode with a hot gush.

He grunted through the waves of pleasure before collapsing on top of me, his arms falling at his sides as my legs slid to the sheets.

"Holy crap." He breathed against my chest in short, sharp gasps. "That was fucking amazing." He lifted his head and kissed his way across my chest. "I may need an ibuprofen or six, though. My headache just pulled back into town with a few of its mates. But damn, baby, that was worth it."

He rolled to the side, his softening cock sliding free as his hand reached between my legs so he could gently stuff a finger in my hole as his spill ran out. He was such a sap.

"Come here." I slid an arm under his neck and pulled him tight against me, boneless and sated. "I fucking love you, Cameron Wano."

He nuzzled his nose into my armpit and licked it as his finger continued to gently slide in and out of my hole. "Just as well, Reuben Taylor."

We lay quiet for a long time and I guessed that Cam was exactly where I was—enjoying the peaceful interlude while avoiding the inevitable re-entry into the ongoing circus that seemed to be our life together.

It was me who gave in first.

"So." I wiped the drying come from our bellies and shuffled onto my side so I could see his face. He tensed, appearing wary and unsure. It was a look I hadn't seen for a long time, and it took me a few seconds to get my head around it. "A baby, huh? When exactly were you going to tell me?"

He sighed with the weight of a thousand suns. "I deserve all of that. I'm sorry I didn't say anything, but I didn't want you to feel pressured, and I didn't know the whole story, and we'd already talked about leaving expanding our family until later when you were retired, and you know how Mum is about family stuff, and—"

"Shh." I pressed a finger to his lips. "I understand all of that, but we do things together, right?"

He nodded. "I know, I know. I fucked up. I'm glad you ignored me and came anyway."

"Hey." I tipped his chin up. "I meant everything I said just before, and I'm hoping you did too. Our little family is good just as it is, right? We're good as we are, too. So we've got this either way. There's nothing to lose here. Yes, I know your mum would love this to happen, but it's our decision, not hers. And we have Cory to think about. That's why we're not going to rush this."

Cam rolled onto his back and stared at the ceiling. "That's the hardest thing about all of this. Cory is so much more flexible and social than he was; the change has been amazing. But he still needs us and his routines to get through the day, the month, his life. I don't want to jeopardise his progress by adding a baby. Could we still give him what he needs if we did that?"

Right. That told me a lot.

I took a second to digest what he'd said and hadn't said and to make sure how I felt. Then I cupped his jaw and turned his face to mine.

"Question for you."

He frowned and kissed me on the lips. "Shoot."

"If it weren't for Cory—"

"But we can't—"

"Shush, hear me out."

He mock-zipped his lips.

"If it weren't for Cory, what would your thoughts be about this baby?"

"Still a bit worried," he admitted, and I loved him just that much more for his honesty.

"Okay then, list them off," I said.

He sucked in a breath and blew it out slowly as he thought. "Your rugby career takes up a heap of time and you're away a lot. It would be a shame for you to miss out on all the fun things as the baby grew. And I wouldn't want them to miss out on their amazing Pappy, either." He fired me a loving look that crashed around in my chest like a tender explosion.

Oh, my heart.

"And then there's the media circus." He donned a pained expression. "It's bad enough about the two of us. Imagine adding a baby to that. Holy fuck, they'd go off their tree to get photos of the baby or all of us together. Not to mention the whole complexity of it being a family adoption. And when, not if, they found out about Stella, she'd be in line for that invasion of privacy as well. The whole family would become media fodder. We don't have to look further than Craig and your dad to see that. Even your mother's death wasn't off-limits."

The reality of what he said hit me like a train to the chest, and a bolt of fear rocketed through me. I hadn't thought that far ahead and I should've.

"And I'd have to give up work, at least for a bit. With you away so much, I'd *want* to be a constant in their life for at least the first year. I know in plenty of families both parents work, but my job's pretty intense at the best of times, and our lives aren't exactly our own. There's a lot of pressure. So, yeah, I'd be looking to reduce that pressure, and for me that would include staying home at the start. My job would have to go on hold."

I really didn't deserve this man. I pressed a kiss to his forehead, and he snuggled closer.

"And then there's my family." He tapped his head against my

chest a few times as though he was banging it against the wall. "I love them to bits, obviously, but if you thought they were all up in our business now, you have no idea what you'd be in for. And I'm not sure how I feel about sharing a baby of ours in that way. It would be very different from adopting outside the family where I'd feel like we had more ability to draw those lines in the sand—create boundaries for us to live as a family separate from the wider one."

He tilted his head back to look at me, an almost resigned sadness to his gaze that I didn't like.

He continued, "But a family adoption changes a lot of that. It would take some careful negotiation to make sure we established the boundaries we needed, at least in the early days, but making sure to respect Stella and her parents' needs as well. It feels like a spider's web of disasters waiting to happen. Fuck, it's doing my head in."

He shuddered and dramatically shook his hands. "What about you? What do you think?"

That I love you more than I did five minutes ago. "Everything you've already said. I'd feel guilty about leaving you carrying the bulk of the family load so often. And I would hate to miss out on being there to watch the baby growing every day, just like I do with Cory. I'd feel that tug between rugby and my family even stronger. Issues with the family boundaries? Yes, I'd be lying to say that wasn't a concern. And yes, I'm concerned about not setting Cory back as well."

"Yes," Cam gasped. "Oh my god, all of that was without even adding Cory's needs to the mix. I know Cory is so much easier now, but maybe it's still too much, Rube. Maybe the best thing would be to say no. Let Stella ask the others. It's not like she doesn't have options. With the wedding and everything else on our plate, I can't get a single thought in my head to line up with any clarity. We should just say no."

I studied him for a moment, this kind, generous, fiercely loyal man with a heart of gold and the bite of a rattler. "You don't mean that."

"I absolutely do." He stared right back, tawny eyes flashing.

But I'd heard the lie and waited him out.

"Ah, fuck it." He dropped his head. "I don't know what I want."

I tipped his chin up and kissed those full lips. "Oh, I think you do. I think you want this baby, Cameron Wano." I held his gaze. "But I think it all seems too complicated to make happen, and that's why you didn't want me to come today. Your heart wants to say yes, but you're worried that's the wrong decision. And if I wasn't there, it would make it easier to convince me to turn her down."

"Damn, you're good at this." Tears welled in his eyes. "I think it's time to stop those therapy sessions of yours."

I grinned. "Nah. I've got years of daddy issues to solve. Two years of therapy has barely scratched the surface."

Cam forced a smile, but it quickly disappeared. "I guess I also keep thinking, what if we don't get another chance? What if when you retire, we can't get a surrogate or the laws change or whatever? What if it doesn't work out how we've planned?"

I crushed him against my chest and tunnelled my fingers through his hair. "None of that matters, sweetheart. We can't say yes or no based on 'what ifs.' We need to decide if *this* baby at *this* time is the *right* decision for us as a family, *all* of us. We've got till the end of next weekend. So, let's think and talk and not close any doors too soon."

He looked up and I bopped his nose. "And if we even start thinking we might be interested, then we need to talk to Stella and Cory's teachers, as well, and maybe the ASD support group. I know you've got wedding stuff going on, so how about I do those things and then fill you in."

"Then, you really mean it?" He stared at me wide-eyed. "You really think we should seriously consider this?"

And there it was. "I do." It was the easiest decision I'd made in a long time. "Regardless of what we decide, if we don't at least think it through thoroughly, we might always regret it."

He nodded enthusiastically, and I knew that for all of my questions, I'd done the right thing.

"But honestly, you don't have to do the school thing, Rube. I can talk to—"

"No," I said a little sharply and he startled. "Sorry, but I *want* to do this, please?"

Cam hesitated. "Okay. But tell me if you need me to step in." He pulled me into his arms this time, and I sank into his strength. "Holy shit, Reuben."

"Yeah." I sucked in a breath. "Holy shit."

CHAPTER FOUR

Cam

MY LEG JIGGLED AGAINST THE CHARTING DESK. I STARED AT THE pathology report in my hands and tried to pretend I was actually reading a single fucking thing. By the concerned looks my nurses were sending me, I wasn't doing a very good job.

"Here, give me that." Stacey ripped the report from my hands and waltzed back to the nurses station. "I'm pretty sure the patient would like to get discharged sometime before Christmas."

"You're lucky I don't fire you," I called out with zero heat.

"You're lucky I don't kick your arse," she fired back, and everyone laughed. "Go make yourself useful and get everyone a coffee. If this is what the rest of the week is going to be before you go on leave, I'm not sure we'll survive."

She wasn't wrong. But then she had no idea my tightly bound Pandora's box of stress factors had just exploded in my face, leaving the telling scent of baby powder in the air.

Alison, my best staff nurse, breezed past me with our weekly treat box from the bakery opposite Auckland Med's main gates. She sent me a cheeky wink. "Come on, grumpy face."

My stomach might've growled.

"There better be at least two salted caramel donuts in that box with my name on them," I warned. "That's if you want a snowball's chance in hell of getting even half those roster requests you put in for next month. I'm down a nurse already that week, and I'm open for bribes."

She looked over her shoulder and grinned. "I'm surprised you even have to ask. Check out your office desk. They're sitting next to a tube of that new lime lip gloss you admired last week . . . and another request." She wiggled her full hips and shimmied her way into a warm welcome from the other nurses who jumped on the treat box like a pack of rabid hyenas.

I laughed. "Damn, girl, you make me proud. But be sure to put a warning on that box for those medical staff who haven't contributed to the slush fund. I caught our esteemed haematologist stealing a lamington last week, and the last time Jim Foley opened his wallet, bats flew out. And I'd check on Michael as well."

"And good morning to you too, Charge Nurse Cameron Wano." A voice slid over my shoulder and the nurses station erupted in laughter.

Fuck.

"How are you this bright and wonderful Monday? Cheerful and generous as usual, I see."

I spun to find myself face to face with the man I'd been looking for all morning. He appeared fresh, well-rested, and bright as a button, and I hated him on sight. "*Dr* Oliver, how delightful of you to turn up to work, *finally*."

His gaze narrowed. "Did you miss the memo, Charge Nurse Wano? I switched with Alan to start at eleven. It's not like you to be behind in your paperwork." He smirked. "A little worse for wear from a certain party, are we?"

Son of a bitch. I'd missed the damn switch. Checking the rosters was usually the first thing I did when I clocked on, but my head had been cotton wool all morning.

"*Everyone* was worse for wear from the party." I regarded him suspiciously. "And who the hell taught you to mix a cocktail? Those things blew the head off anyone silly enough to order one, and most of the people who didn't, since you only had to be in the general vicinity to risk alcohol poisoning through osmosis."

"I notice it didn't seem to stop *you*." He laughed and picked a bit of lint off my scrub top and flicked it away.

"Stop that." I slapped his hand away. "And I only had too much because Reuben kept calling the waiter over. I blame him."

"I just bet you do."

"Mark fell asleep on our lounge floor—don't ask why they were at our place because no one really knows. And I just passed Ed in the cafeteria. He was headed to court looking for all the world like some old bone Tink had dug out of their garden a week before. Green, of questionable heritage, and definitely not to be consumed."

Michael laughed. "Well, they both had to look better than Josh who was still in our bed at dinner time yesterday threatening Sasha with a ten-year grounding if she didn't turn her music down. Even Paris had enough sense to steer clear."

I snorted. "I was surprised you two hung around after the lap dance, to be honest. You looked ready to eat your husband alive."

Michael pouted. "If I'd had my way, we'd have left the minute it finished. But since he missed the first half of the party, Josh was eager to catch up with everyone first. Enough to say he has a taste for my cocktails. Cooked my own damn goose there. He couldn't have got it up with a hoist by the time we got home."

I snorted. "Serves you right."

"It was a great party."

I shot him a grin. "Yes. Much as it pains me to say, it was. So, thank you." I glanced at the clock. "But you're still ten minutes late."

He rolled his eyes. "I got talking to the neurologist out front about that sailing accident last week. And I don't believe for a second that you actually knew I'd switched with Alan. Which isn't like you, by the way, so what's up?"

"Nothing," I lied. Reuben and I had agreed not to mention the baby to anyone until we'd made a decision. "Just a bit tired with all the palaver for the wedding."

Michael shot me a look. "Also not believed. You've loved every minute of that *palaver* as you call it."

I avoided his gaze, concentrating on the nurses station instead. Auckland Med's resident wannabe playboy cardiologist was busy chatting up one of my nurses who was doing her best to brush him off.

"But whatever," Michael continued. "Keep your damn secrets. But I'll do you a favour and take the ambulance headed our way from that motor vehicle accident in Westhaven. Multiple fractures and a head injury."

"That's . . . good of you," I admitted. "I'll put Alison in with you."

"Excellent. And you could always bring me a coffee, if you're not busy." He waggled his eyebrows.

"In your dreams, hotshot. It took me an hour to get my don't-fuck-with-me eyeliner straight this morning, and I'm not wasting it running around after you." I nodded toward the nurses desk. "I have a cardiologist to skin."

He followed my gaze and chuckled. "Ah, the charming Dr Long. Go get 'em, tiger."

I stabbed a finger at his chest. "Be in my office at one for a wedding war party. Sandy, Miller, and Georgie are coming. Don't be late."

"But the accident won't be done—"

I fired him a glare.

He scowled and studied me for a long second. "All right. I'll make it happen, somehow."

"Do that." I turned a steely eye on the nurses desk. "Dr Long." I made my way over, Michael's chuckle at my back. "Unless you want billing for half of Sarah's daily wage, I suggest you let her get on with her work. I doubt she has any idea what those cheesy seventies pick-up lines mean."

Dr Long rolled his eyes and flipped me off but turned and headed out of the department, nonetheless.

Sarah gave a full-body shudder before sending me a grateful look. Long was a great cardiologist but an even greater sleaze, and I kept a close eye on him whenever he was in my ER.

No one fucked with my nurses.

Two hours and half a billion cups of coffee later, I'd just finished the next month's roster when Sandy breezed into my office in a dapper green tartan skirt, black tights, black ankle boots, and a tightly fitted royal blue button-down. And with his blond locks slicked back, peaches and cream complexion, killer cheekbones, green eyeliner, and pink lips, he looked fucking fabulous.

"Hey, gorgeous." I pushed up from my seat and leaned across the desk to exchange cheek kisses. "Mmm. You smell good today. I'm not sure how you made it out of the house unmolested in that get-up."

He winked. "Who says I did? And hey there yourself. It's Sandal-wood. Miller should be here any min—oh, here he is." Sandy held open the door for Miller to wheel his chair inside and the two exchanged a lingering kiss.

"Ah, young love," I teased. "How long has it been?"

"Nearly four months." Sandy took Miller's hand and eyed me up and down. "Are we still on for the final fitting this afternoon?"

I nodded. "See you at four. But the, um . . ." I glanced at Miller who simply smiled smugly. "The thingy hasn't arrived yet."

Sandy frowned. "The thingy?"

"You know, the *thingy*."

Sandy's eyes widened. "Oh right. The *thingy*."

Miller chuckled and got an elbow from Sandy.

"Don't worry, it'll get here," Sandy soothed, but I wasn't so sure. "You ordered it months ago."

"I know, but there's only twelve days left and it's still not here." I chewed at my nails. "And now I'm second-guessing the whole outfit. Maybe it's a sign. Maybe it's too much. Maybe I should change it."

Sandy's eyes popped and veins bulged in his neck. "Oh, fuck no. Don't do that. It'll be fine—no, great. I mean it'll be great. It's an amazing outfit. Just pleeeease don't change your mind. It's too late."

Miller laughed, which earned him another elbow from Sandy who said, "I'm not sure that assistant will ever let us back in the shop."

I frowned. "Oh, come on, she loves me. I gave her two freebie tickets to the last Bledisloe Cup game. She was practically worshipping at my feet."

Sandy glanced at Miller. "I think that might be overstating it."

He was right. Her delight had, in fact, grown in direct proportion to the realisation that I'd finally made a decision and she wouldn't have to see me again, bar the final try-on."

"Don't start without us." Michael swooped into the room and swept his arm for Georgie to follow, then shut the door. "I've got twenty minutes while this guy has his CT scan, but I might be paged sooner, so make it quick."

Georgie grabbed the last chair and said a round of hellos. As best woman to Reuben, I really hadn't expected any extra of her on the day, but she'd offered, sweetheart that she was.

"Okay." I rapped a pen on my desk. "This meeting is called to attention. Sound off. Waiheke Vineyard."

"Contacted and ready to go," Michael answered with a salute. "Menu checked, place settings checked. Everything checked, checked, checked."

I regarded him dubiously. "Cake?"

"To be delivered to our home the day before the wedding," Michael replied. "And I vow, on pain of death, I will get it safely to Waiheke Island on the ferry."

I checked that off the list. "Honeymoon night?"

Sandy's hand shot in the air. "Please, miss, that one's mine." He smirked and ducked when I fired my pen at him. "Booked and checked, *sir*."

"Music?"

"Done." Miller raised a brow. "Although considering I'm new to this group, I'd like to lodge a pre-emptive complaint about the unfairness of landing me with such an important—"

"Next." I blew him a kiss. "Cars?"

"Ed assures me they're booked and checked," Sandy answered. "And he also told me to tell you to stop leaving him messages or he'll downgrade you from a Mercedes to a Kia, if you're lucky."

"He wouldn't dare."

Sandy merely raised a brow, and I hesitated. Of all our friends, quiet, reserved Ed was the most immune to my charms, dammit. "Okay, okay tell him I'm—"

"Sorry?" Sandy proposed.

"Watching," I corrected, and everyone laughed.

I fell back in my chair and glared at the four of them. "I'm glad you're all having so much fun with this."

"Oh, believe me, we're not," Michael commented drily. "This is entirely self-preservation in the fervent hope that if we can only get this done and dusted, you will never *ever* get married again, and we can all live a blissful and contented life. As it currently stands, I wake up on a nightly basis in a cold sweat and with the dulcet tone of your voice in my ear screaming to know where the third tier of the cake is."

I narrowed my gaze. "There are *four* tiers."

He threw up his hands. "I rest my case."

I stared a moment longer, but he was giving me nothing. *Bastard.* "Okay, Sandy, you had Cory, right?"

Sandy smiled. "Geo and your mother are booked for the night."

My mother. Stella. The baby. Fuck. "C-celebrant?" I croaked, then looked to Georgie who gave a small frown at my stumble.

Michael looked at me sideways.

"Whatever you're gonna say, keep it to yourself." I flashed him a warning glance.

He snorted and sat back in his chair.

Georgie answered, "I sent her and her husband an invite to the reception like you asked and emailed everything else *in triplicate.*" She winked. "She says she'll ring you next Wednesday to check in unless she sees you at the game on Sunday."

"Great, thank you." Discovering that the wife of the coach of North Harbour Rugby—Reuben's Mitre 10 Cup team—also happened to be a celebrant was a huge win. She understood only too well the importance of remaining tight-lipped in the face of the circling media. Which reminded me.

"Security?"

"Josh has it all in hand, including a drone no-fly zone," Michael answered. "There'll be security at the gate and around the vineyard perimeter. He's talked with Reuben and the Blues and All Blacks' media guys. Every guest will be checked as they enter."

"Good." It was, but what a freaking nightmare to go through just to get married. I was pretty sure half the country would think we were being too precious about our privacy, but I didn't care. I wasn't having our wedding ruined by fucking media, and I refused to let it get to me.

I ticked another box on my checklist. "And I've confirmed with the photographer, and the million and one other things that needed seeing to. I think that's it."

"What about the spa?" Georgie asked softly.

"Oh shit." I slapped a hand to my forehead. "Who had that?"

"Mark," Michael reminded me. "And he says it's all in hand."

My heart skipped a beat. "Oh, fuck. Will someone check up on him?"

"I will," Georgie offered. "But as far as I know, the wedding party and the few extras you asked will meet there at two on Saturday. You boys will go one way, while Jasmine, Katie and I go the other. Thanks for that, by the way. It would've sucked to be on my own while all you guys got to have fun together. And if I remember correctly, that's you, Mathew, Michael, Sandy, Jake, Reuben, Tom MacDonald from the AB's, and Mark, since Reuben's brother turned it down, right?"

"Right." I swallowed hard. "I think that's it. I just hope I haven't forgot—"

"You haven't," Michael reassured me. "You've done him proud, you prickly pear. He's a lucky guy. Even if you haven't let him get anywhere near the planning."

Shit. My brows crunched. "Has he said something? I didn't cut him out. I just didn't want him to have to worry about anything other than his training and games. I can do what needs to be done."

Michael's expression remained neutral. "Maybe he wanted to help?"

I snorted but couldn't ignore the small knot of worry in my belly. "Have you met my fiancé? Reuben said more than once that he couldn't care less about how or where we held the wedding. I was to have what I wanted."

Michael held my gaze. "I guess you'd know that better than me." He got to his feet and wrapped me in his arms. "Anyway, I can't wait to see you married, you hellhound."

"Arrogant arsehole."

"Drama queen."

I let myself be held for a couple of seconds longer than I'd normally allow because, well, because this was Michael. And if I whispered something sappy about being grateful for his friendship, I made sure to keep that just between me and the man's scrubs.

"You're welcome," he said softly.

Fuck.

CHAPTER FIVE

Cam

"OH. MY. GOD." SANDY SPRANG FROM HIS CHAIR OUTSIDE THE
fitting room and ran to take my hands. He held them out to the sides
and ran those sharp brown eyes over me from head to toe. "You
look . . . bloody spectacular. Turn around." He stood back while I did
a couple of spins. His hand covered his mouth and his eyes filled.
"Damn, you look so beautiful." He sniffed.

"You do, indeed." Gayle, our long-suffering retail assistant walked
across to pin the fit a little tighter around my hips. "There, now it's
perfect." She took my shoulders and gave me a cheeky wink. "He's
gonna love it."

"Do you really think so?" I turned to look at myself in the full-
length mirror, dismayed at the shake in my voice. I was a single gushy
tear away from having to hand in my slash and sass membership card.

Carmen would be appalled.

Or maybe not. I thought of the sappy looks I'd caught her sending
her husband during our bachelor party.

Sandy and Gayle took a spot either side of me, the assistant primping the multi-layered tulle skirt, while Sandy lifted my vest and tightened the thin leather harness strap just a little at the back.

Reuben would rock the simple but elegant black tuxedo we'd chosen for him—he looked hot as hades in it. But I'd wept blood trying to decide on my own outfit.

It had taken a stern talking to by both Sandy and Gayle, two glasses of complimentary bridal shop bubbly, and an entire box of Kleenex—which neither of them were ever to mention again—to talk me out of the near-fatal mistake of letting media pressure and worry about what the rugby powers would think influence that decision.

I had to choose something for *me*.

For me and for Reuben.

They were right, of course. Reuben wanted me to be me, the me he knew, the me he loved, and not to worry about what others might think. In particular, not to worry about his career or the vicious media, because for sure my choice would be eviscerated by some, if not most of them. I could count on a few being on my side, but the rest, who knew?

I should've known not to question Reuben's courage. He'd proved it time and time again. Plus, Sandy and Gayle had also been fiercely adamant, and they were right. That morning of bubbly and tears had changed everything. I threw the conservative options out the fucking window, and we started again.

Gone was the black and white idea, with all the fem and frillies safely hidden underneath where no one could see them. In its place, an ocean of pale pink tulle fell from a skirt with a tightly fitted waist and hip. At the back, the tulle ended in a short sweep of train, while at the front, it curved up and was slit to the thigh, revealing cream stockings tucked into white button-down, high-heeled ankle boots, with just the glimpse of a black lace and satin garter when my leg slipped through the opening, just so. A soft pink-and-cream satin fitted waistcoat completed the outfit, its run of thirty tiny pearl buttons catching the light, with nothing underneath bar a thin black leather harness peeking out. The *thingy* had arrived in time.

And I loved it.

Fuck the haters.

I stared at my reflection in the mirror and—

"Dammit." I held out a hand for Sandy to slap a few Kleenex into. "I promised myself I wasn't going to fucking cry, again."

He slipped an arm around my waist as I wiped my eyes, trying not to smudge my eyeliner, something else that was becoming a habit.

"And why the hell not?" he said, clutching me close. "You're getting married, babe. This is big, right? And you don't have to hide yourself from me, you know that."

I turned and cupped his face. "I do know, and thank God for that." I looked to Gayle and smiled. "You too. Thank you."

I ran my hands down the vest and stood a little straighter. Yeah. It was fierce. "The media are gonna wet their fucking pants." I fired Sandy a wicked grin.

He laughed. "Hell yeah, they are. You look awesome. It's exactly who you are. It's pretty, and sexy, and tough, and daring but not sleazy, and totally appropriate. With the eyeliner and makeup, the outer layer says sweet, willing, and fuck me please, while the harness says I'm male to the bone and don't presume anything."

He rested his head on my shoulder. "Every person in that room is gonna see you as the breathtaking force of nature that you are. And I'd bet even the straight ones are gonna wonder what it would be like to be the centre of your attention for a night. It couldn't be more perfect, and Reuben will get it straight away. Everyone will."

I turned at the snort to find Gayle's eyes sparkling. "What he said." She fanned her face. "This has been an . . . education." She beamed. "And I wouldn't have swapped it for the world. Please, please tell everyone where you got it made."

"It's already on the thank you cards," I assured her, and she blushed brightly.

"Oh yeah." I turned back to the mirror. "This is a done deal."

We headed for the closest bar for a celebratory drink after slamming my credit card with a bill equivalent to the gross national debt of a small country. But I had not a single regret. I couldn't wait to wear it.

Sandy slid his flute of prosecco to the side, leaned back in his chair, and crossed his ankles. "So now that the outfit is done and dusted—" He arched a brow my way. "—you can tell me what particular hornet's nest is rammed up your arse today. You're way more spikey than usual."

His perceptiveness was bang on, as usual, dammit.

I rolled my eyes and gazed out the window, ignoring yet another text from my mother. "I'm fine," I said, dodging his question. The Viaduct Basin, jam-packed with restaurants and bars that fed off its America's Cup heritage, was hardly enthralling on a quiet Monday evening. But if I stared at the burnt-orange sky reflected on the flat surface of the water as long as possible, it kept Sandy from reading the lie in my eyes.

My phone buzzed again, and my mother's face lit up the screen. I switched it to silent, glanced up at Sandy, and saw his brows draw together. Damn. I loved my mother to bits, and he knew it. Ignoring her wasn't something I normally did, but I had no answers to give her, and she wasn't the right person to ask any questions of either.

"The wedding is close, that's all." I brushed his concern aside. "There's a lot of balls in the air." I took a slug of champagne and set the glass back on the table.

He reached across and tapped my nose. "Liar."

Told you.

"I've survived wedding shopping with you for six months. I should get a damn Nobel Peace Prize for that effort alone."

He had a legitimate point.

He continued, "So don't you dare fuck with me, Cameron Delaney Wano. What's eating you? And don't tell me you're having second thoughts because I've never seen two guys more determinedly in love than you two. You're disgustingly happy and you're my damn role models."

I snorted. "You really need to get out more. Because if you only knew how close we've come on occasion—ow—Jesus fuck!"

Sandy withdrew his foot from my shin. "Don't you dare joke it off. Of course you've had arguments. You guys are hugely different in lots of ways, just like Miller and me. Not to mention you've been squeezed by the media and public opinion till your eyes popped. And yet, you're still here, stupidly in love and making it work. We all come close. Life isn't a fucking romance novel. But it's exactly *because* it hasn't been easy that it matters, right? If you don't want to tell me, fine. But don't lie to me."

The back of my head hit the booth and I closed my eyes. In truth, I was desperate to talk with *someone*—my head a mess of conflicted emotions, bile churning in my stomach. Also true—there was probably no better choice than Sandy.

Oh god. I swallowed hard and opened my eyes, hoping I was doing the right thing. "Okay, okay." I leaned forward on the table. "I'll tell you, but you have to swear to say nothing, and only because you mentioned that you and Miller were thinking of starting your own family."

Sandy's brow creased.

"At your brother's fortieth a couple of months back," I reminded him.

"Oh, right." He smiled. "So is it something to do with Cory?"

"No." I locked eyes and took a deep breath. "We've been given the opportunity to adopt a baby."

"A baby?" His eyes popped and a smile instantly appeared. But he schooled it to something more neutral when my lack of excitement became apparent.

I explained, "An adoption from inside my family. My young cousin's pregnant, fifteen weeks, and she's asked us if we would be interested in being her baby's legal parents."

He fell back against the booth and blew a long, low whistle. "Wow."

"Yeah, wow."

"But that's great, right?" He smiled once again. "I mean, Miller and I have just started looking into surrogacy, but man, that's a complicated path. To have the possibility of an adoption just come out of the blue like that, well, shit, that's amazing, Cam." He noted my frown. "Isn't it?"

I slipped down in my seat and pushed my champagne flute aside. "You'd think so, but it's not that simple."

He studied me for a few seconds. "Okay. Tell me."

And so I did. And by the time I was done, Sandy's expression was as pinched as my own.

"Well, fuck me. You guys sure know how to complicate shit."

I blew out a sigh. "Tell me about it."

He looked thoughtful and I waited. Sandy was one of the few people whose opinion I paid the slightest bit of attention to. He'd been through a lot learning to accept himself, and we kind of got each other in that way, except he was one of life's nice guys, whereas I . . . was a work in progress.

He met my eyes with a soft look. "But regardless of all that shit, I'd have thought the decision is still kinda simple."

"Funny, I must've missed that bit," I deadpanned.

He huffed. "I'm not saying all that other stuff doesn't matter, babe. I'm just saying that it probably boils down to the same question at heart, and sometimes our brain just overcomplicates it. I mean, Stella didn't have a *choice*, right? She's had to face this life-changing event, along with millions of others who fall pregnant at inopportune moments in their lives, or whose families disintegrate for lots of reasons and need someone to take up a parent role they weren't expecting."

I saw where he was going. "So, what you're saying is that actually having a choice might be crowding out the basics?"

"Yeah, I'm just playing with it though, so feel free to ignore me. But I wonder if it would help to clarify things, if you just imagine what you'd feel if this landed on you *without* a choice? What if you'd just found out you were pregnant?"

My brows hit my hairline. "I'd earn a fuckton of money on the talk shows. Also, you worry me sometimes, but okay . . ." I closed my eyes and imagined being hit by that life-changing information.

Panic filled my chest, and all those same worries alarmed in my head. "Terrified," I answered, opening my eyes to find him watching me intently.

He wasn't fooled.

There'd been more than just panic.

"And?" he pressed.

I narrowed my eyes. "You are way too good at this, but okay. *And* excited. *And* . . . full." My hand covered my chest. "In here." I side-eyed him. "Fuck, you're clever."

He smirked and blew me a kiss. "I know. It doesn't mean you should agree to adopt this baby, but—"

"At least I know that I want it, yeah, I got that part. And Reuben saw the same thing in me, so you can wipe that smug look off your face." I blew out a shaky breath. "But it helped to think of it like that, without a choice, I mean, so thanks. And if you asked my mother—she's practically got booties swinging in her eyeballs already. God knows what she'll say if we turn the baby down."

I twirled the stem of the champagne flute slowly in my fingers, around and around and around. Sandy called the waiter over to refill our glasses but otherwise left me to think as a loudly chattering group of patrons were seated at the table beside us, the restaurant filling with the early dinner crowd.

"I worry about Reuben," I finally said. "In case it's a bridge too far for him at the moment. We've both got a lot going on, and to think of adding a baby to that . . ." I sighed.

"What's he said?"

I shrugged and emptied my glass, letting the bubbles rattle up my nose before answering. "He said he has all the same worries and that he's concerned about Cory just like I am. I know he never thought about us having another child until he retired from rugby. With a new baby, I won't be able to just pack a suitcase and join any of those

All Blacks' tours for the odd week or two, either. We'll be apart a lot more."

The waiter arrived with two fresh flutes of champagne and a bowl of nuts. We clinked glasses and I took a handful of nuts and a long swallow of my drink before continuing. "The truth is . . ." I stared out the window again—the sky a little darker now, and there was a small chop on the water that wasn't there before. "Reuben and I haven't really talked since that first conversation. He's asking our support group, and Cory's school, about things we should consider, but it's like the subject is this hot potato we don't want to eat in case we burn ourselves. As if it might affect the wedding."

"Would it?"

I shot him a horrified look. "Of course not." Then I winced. "At least I hope not."

"Mmm." He gave me a pointed look. "I get the feeling that *we're* not really talking about it, actually means *you're* not really talking about it. And maybe because you're worried if you can't agree, then it *would* change things."

I pursed my lips. "You're an irritating fucker, you know that?"

He raised his glass. "At your service."

I rolled my eyes and my gaze landed on the superyachts berthed in the basin. I bet their owners didn't have to put up with this shit from their friends.

"Yes, they do," he said.

Okay, so I said that aloud.

"That's what friends do," he added. "You're just not familiar with the rules because you haven't had any like me before."

I arched a brow. "You're very sure of yourself there, Mr Williams."

He smiled and took another sip of his drink. "I am, actually."

I threw my hands to the side. "Ugh. See, this is *why* I haven't had friends like you before." I flopped my hands on my lap.

"Aha! You just admitted it." He fired me a shit-eating grin.

"Oh for fuck's sake. And also, there are rules?"

"None that you need to worry your pretty little head about. I'll tell you what you need to know as we go along." He smirked.

"Why do I get the sense I'm being had?"

"I have no idea. And don't think you've distracted me from the question. Why haven't you told Reuben what you've told me?"

"It's simple," I said, knowing it was anything but. "I don't want to add to the pressure on him. I don't want him to say yes just to keep me happy and then regret it."

Oh fuck, I was doing it again.

Pinky swear?

Sandy covered my hand with his. "That's a lot of assumption you've got going on in that big brain of yours. How do you know he'd do that for you? He's a big boy. He knows the difficulties as well as you do. Maybe you'll both decide it's too much. Just because you want something doesn't mean it has to happen. But at some point you have to stop juggling the hot potato and eat it, right? Talk about it. Only you two know what your limits are."

"You sound just like him," I grumbled, lifting my glass and firing my drink coaster at him. He ducked it skillfully. "But thanks." I reached for his hand and squeezed it. "You know how much I love talking about my feelings."

He laughed. "I do. But you don't always have to carve through life on your own, you know?"

If only it were that easy.

"Reuben loves you. Let him in."

I bristled. "I *do* let him in." *Like no one else, ever.* "We're partners."

Pinky swear?

Fuck.

"Does he know that?"

"What the hell does that mean?" I glared.

He sighed, glanced at the next table who were busy ordering, and leaned closer. "This is me you're talking to. You and I have had to build some pretty solid walls growing up just to survive. It's taken a lot to believe in ourselves, and we like to control our lives tighter than most so that no one fucks with us or the people we love. But those walls don't just fall down when we meet someone, even *the* one. In fact, I reckon that only makes us worse, because finding someone who accepts and loves us for who we are is such a goddamn surprise that we're terrified of doing anything which might jeopardise that. Giving up control isn't like flipping a switch, you know."

"I do realise that," I said, fidgeting with the serviette and feeling my pulse quicken.

"Maybe you do." He looked a little sheepish. "But you'd be surprised how many times I look around to find I've kept stuff from Miller without even realising it. Either because I think he won't get it or doesn't need to know, or maybe that he might not like what I'm feeling. Now that doesn't matter when it comes to ordering pizza or even buying a car—although the man's taste in colour leaves a lot to be desired—but it sure waves red flags when it's anything about relationship stuff."

"This isn't the same thing."

"Isn't it? Look, I'm not saying that's what you're doing, just that maybe it's something to consider. *You* think you're letting Reuben decide for himself by keeping quiet, but really what you're doing is holding back information he needs to make that decision. It's just another form of control." He sat back and studied me from the other side of the table, nervous, as if I was about to pronounce sentence on him or our friendship.

I wanted to.

I wanted to get up and walk out and leave all those dangerous words of his to get kicked around on the restaurant floor until someone swept them into the bin. Words that sank like a depth charge in my heart. One twitch in the wrong direction and all those glittering sharp edges I'd so carefully crafted over the years might just disappear in a puff of diamond dust.

Take an even closer look and I might actually have to . . . change.

Pinky swear?

It's not too late to run.

Fucking, fuck, fuck.

I slumped in my seat and scowled at him. "Son of a bitch, I hate it when you're right."

"I live but to please." His lips quirked up.

"Well, don't smile too soon," I snipped, hailing the waiter across the room. "Next round's on you. And you can up it to a damn Moët."

CHAPTER SIX

Reuben

GEORGIE WATCHED ME THROUGH HER KITCHEN WINDOW, TIGHT brown curls bouncing around her elfin features and green eyes, a notch of concern dipping between her brows. I'd stopped on the way home from Tuesday training to ask her opinion on the whole baby thing. Only Cam knew me better. Before him, it had just been Georgie and me.

And I needed to talk to *someone*. Cam had made it clear he wasn't ready, saying he wanted to wait until I had all the information we needed first. I fucking hated this awkward dance we were doing around each other, but there weren't that many people I could turn to who weren't too involved as it was, like Cam's mother for example.

And so I'd come to my best friend and had just finished telling her about the baby when Cam's mum interrupted us.

"He's not answering any of my texts or calls." Margaret Wano sounded more than a little pissy on the phone as I walked our conversation to the far corner of Georgie's deck and took a seat out of the cold gusty wind. Potted daffodils danced in the stiff breeze, brightening the space and reminding us it was spring even though the day's temperature hardly reflected it.

"I don't think he wants to be influenced by *anyone* at the moment," I explained. "Be patient with him. Both of us want to be sure how *we* feel first before we talk to anyone else." I glanced at Georgie through the window and hoped Margaret didn't hear the stretch and snap of the truth. "We also need to talk with Stella. I think she—"

"But she'll want an answer from you."

"Then she'll be disappointed," I said flatly. "We won't be pressured, Margaret, and we can't make a decision without knowing what role Stella sees for herself with the baby, in the future. What 'contact' and 'involvement' mean for her. Surely you understand that?"

She went quiet. "Yes, of course I do. I just—"

"Can you text me Stella's mum's number?"

She sighed down the line. "I'll do it as soon as I hang up."

"Thanks." I loved Cam's mum, but she was as much a force of nature as her son. The two of them together were dynamite. "We understand just how much you want this to happen, Margaret. We know you'd love us to adopt Stella's baby, and maybe that's exactly why Cam isn't quite ready to talk to you, yet."

"But . . . I just . . . my sister . . . ugh, okay, yeah. I can't lie. I do want that." She paused. "Too much, maybe."

"There's nothing wrong with that. But you know what our lives are like, Margaret. This wouldn't be easy for us or for Cory, and we have to think of the family we already have first. Make sure a new baby would be a good fit. Please try and understand."

She was silent for a minute before blowing out a long sigh. "Okay. Zip it and step back. I hear you. But I want to say one last thing. If you do decide to take this baby, I promise I will help in any way I can to lighten your load, both of you. John and I have talked about it and he agrees. I don't know if it helps, but the offer's there."

It did, in a way. "Thank you. But we can't make any promises. This will be *our* decision and no one else's. We love all of you, but this can't be done on a wish and a hope. And Stella's mum said there were other people they could consider."

"There are. None as good as you, for what it's worth, but then I may be biased."

I snorted. "You? I don't believe it."

"Cheeky little shit." She laughed. "Okay. I hate it, but I understand. And I promise I won't say anything if you decide not to go ahead."

"I'd really, really appreciate that. Cam won't ever say anything, but I know he'll be worried sick about letting you down."

Margaret drew a shaky breath. "That boy could never let me down. He brings sunshine into my life every day just by being alive. Make sure he knows that, will you?"

"I will. And thank you."

A few seconds after we ended the call, my cell buzzed with the promised phone number, and I called Stella's mum to set up a meeting at their place for Friday after Cam finished work. I explained we wouldn't be giving them an answer that day, but we wanted to meet and find out what relationship Stella and her parents saw happening with the baby in the future.

Just as I was done, Georgie appeared at my side with a cup of tea, and I wrapped both hands around it for warmth.

"So what are you thinking?" she asked, pulling a chair beside mine and stretching her legs out in front. "It's no small thing, another baby on top of everything you've got going on."

I looked her straight in the eye. "I want it."

Her eyes popped. "Wow. Just like that?"

"Yeah, just like that."

"In that case, what do you need to talk to me for?" She toed the pot of daffodils out of the way.

I rolled my eyes at her. "Because Cam *isn't* talking, and I've spent two sleepless nights trying to figure it out." I took a sip of the hot tea and grimaced as it burned its way down my throat.

"And I'm not the one who's gonna be hit with the lion's share of the work; Cam is. I'm pretty sure he wants the baby, but he's not saying anything, and I don't know if that's because he's really concerned about how we'll cope, or because he wants more information like he says, or what. But I don't want to tell him *I* want the baby in case that pressures him to agree. Fuck me." I fell back in my chair. "The point is, we need to have a solid plan in place before we go forward, *if* we go forward, because there's Cory to consider."

She rolled her teacup around in her hand and studied me. "What did the school say?"

"That it was hard to predict how he'd react. Shocker. That lots of kids with a similar level of ability as Cory manage just fine, and a few have setbacks, but overall they didn't have any real concerns. Once we were sure of our decision, then we could start introducing the concept slowly and they would help with preparations before the birth, and then after, to help him understand and cope. They also said it would be good if we planned for as much help as we could afford to make sure Cory gets enough one-on-one time."

Georgie nodded. "Good advice. What did Cam say about that?"

"Not much. I think we both knew that would be their answer. I'm going to talk to the support group tomorrow, but I'm guessing they'll be the same."

"Mmm." Georgie regarded me with a wary look. "Are you sure you're not looking for someone else to make your decision for you?"

I closed my eyes for a long second. "Maybe. It would be a whole lot fucking easier, that's for sure."

She snorted. "No, it wouldn't. And you do realise that lots of loving families have challenges to face, and they cope, right? Yours would simply be another one of those families. I mean, it's not like you're short on love, is it?"

My pulse kicked up as I thought of Cam and Cory, and my eyes sprung a bit of a leak. "Hardly." I blinked the tears away and Georgie squeezed my hand.

"And with Cam by your side, you and Cory, you're not short on courage or determination, either. Don't hate me for asking, but does it worry you that the new baby might come with some challenges as well, like Cory did?"

I couldn't help the wince. "Not worry as such. But I can't say it hasn't crossed my mind."

She smiled softly. "I'd guess that was perfectly normal. And you have to be bluntly honest with yourself."

"But, as you said, other families face that too. And I look at Cam and think there isn't anything we can't do together. He's an amazing father to Cory, and he'll be exactly the same with another child. He'd fight to the death for our family, no questions asked. He's my fucking hero, but even heroes have limits." My voice broke and I wiped at my eyes. "For fuck's sake, look at me. I'm getting married next week to the love of my life and I'm a fucking blubbering disaster."

Georgie wrapped her arms around me. "Welcome to the messy world of families, baby. You should know that tale better than most."

I kissed her cheek. "Yeah, let's try not to use my family as an example for anything other than how not to do shit, yeah?"

She shuddered. "Amen to that. But that doesn't solve the problem that you haven't yet told Cam that you really want the baby?"

I looked away.

She sat back and nudged my foot with hers. "Remember the last time you didn't tell him how you felt?"

Shit.

"You almost lost him."

I closed my eyes and my chin dropped to my chest. "I was coughing up dust balls in the closet. It's hardly the same. I'm not that guy anymore."

"Potatoes, potahtoes. Don't make that same stupid mistake. And so what if he's not talking. Cam doesn't get to call all the shots, Reuben."

I cocked an eyebrow at her, and she kicked me in the ankle.

"Well, don't let him get away with it, then."

I sighed. "He knows I'm thinking seriously about it. And no one can *make* Cam do anything he doesn't want to."

"That's where I think you're wrong," she said softly. "The way he looks at you? He'd give you the world. But sometimes you have to step up and ask. And you've never been good at that, Reuben. That's how you got stuck in the closet for so long. Cam's an Energizer-bunny, take-charge kind of guy, and you love watching him eat up the world. The dynamic clearly works for you both, until it doesn't."

Here we go again. "Wow, don't hold back."

"I won't," she scoffed. "Because you damn well know it's true. You're a nice guy, Reuben, too fucking nice. You're so busy protecting each other, neither of you are really thinking. But you can't do that *and* make a good decision. Tell him *everything, now,* and ask him to tell you."

Damn.

Pinky swear. Guess it went both ways.

"Yeah, I know," I grumbled. "But holy moly, can nothing in our lives ever be easy for a change? I feel like we've been pushing a rock uphill ever since we first met. A bit of luck would be nice."

Georgie patted my thigh and sipped on her tea. "Is he easy to love?"

And everything fell away as a huge smile stole over my face. "So fucking easy."

She smirked. "Then you've got all the luck you need and more than most ever have. So shut up and drink your tea."

"Hand me the lube." Cam dropped my needy cock and pushed his open hand through the jets of steaming water in our huge double shower.

Not tonight. I slapped his hand away and spun him to face the wall.

He looked over his shoulder with a sultry smile and wiggled that sexy butt. "So, it's gonna be like that, is it?"

"It is." I squidged a mountain of lube onto my fingers and slicked both our cocks before running my fingers up his taint and tapping at his hole. "Knock, knock," I whispered in his ear.

"Who's there?"

"Ivana."

"Ivana who?"

"Ivana fuck your brains out."

"Oh. My. Fucking. God." He laughed and walked his feet back, widening his stance and putting his glorious arse on full display. "You did not just say that."

I took a few seconds to drink in the sight of his tight, lithe body and then angled the water away and pushed up against him, bending my knees so my dick nestled nicely into his crease. Then I reached around and stroked him slowly.

"Mmm." He rocked his hips back and forth and turned his head for an awkward kiss. "Damn, that feels good. What's got into you tonight? Not that I'm complaining." He paused. "Ugh. Right there . . . yesssss. Mmmmmm. It's been a while since I've had the pleasure of riding your dick, but I have to say, I'm fucking excited at the prospect."

"Just needed to feel you wrapped around me, sweetheart." I nuzzled his hair and kissed the nape of his neck as I kept stroking his dick, while the fingers of my other hand slid between our bodies to tease his hole.

"Yeah. Right there," he huffed, pushing back.

Two fingers immediately slid up to the first knuckle and he gasped and rocked harder—forwards into my fist and backwards to fuck himself on my fingers. Then he dropped his forehead to the tile wall and wrapped a hand around mine to tighten the grip on his cock.

"Such a bossy fucking top," I snorted in his ear and he laughed.

"You love it."

I so fucking did.

"How do you want me?" He grunted as I pushed deeper.

"Just like this." I removed my fingers and lined up my aching dick.

He pushed his arse back a little more and I bent lower. Thank fuck for a strong core.

"Keep stroking," I told him.

"Now who's bossy?"

"I'm just warning you I won't last. It's been too long."

"I should ask you more—ow!"

I soothed the red hand mark on his tattooed arse. "That's not your job. I'll let you know. That's what we agreed, and this is me letting you know."

"Okay, okay—arrrrrgh."

I breached him and slid up to full hilt in a single long glide.

He panted and bore down. "Jeez Louise, warn a guy next time."

"You love it," I grunted, holding back, trying not to rush him.

"I so fucking do."

"And you've got altogether too much to say for yourself tonight." I rocked a little in his arse, just enough so he could feel the stretch around the base of my dick, and he sucked in a breath.

"Jesus, you feel big back there." Cam panted in and out. "But so fucking good." He pushed back hard to hammer home his point, and then pulled forward, almost unseating me before slamming back again.

Cameron Wano—the very definition of topping from the bottom.

"Nuh-uh. Not this time, baby." I sank my fingers into those lean hips and wrested control back. He growled and tried to wriggle free, but I was having none of it, my gaze locked on those few centimetres where my cock slid in and out of his tight, hot hole as my orgasm rocketed toward me.

"Son of a bitch, you're tight." I dragged my dick in and out of the stranglehold Cam's furnace of an arse had around it, feeling that clench and release action he was so fucking good at. "You better be close because I'm nearly—fuuuuuuck!"

I slammed into him, a wave of pleasure rushing up my spine. Heat flooded my body as my spill flooded his arse, and I just kept thrusting, losing myself inside him, in his heart, in all that fierce, sweet promise that made up this mystifying man I loved so dearly, claiming it over and over again. Sometimes I just needed to grab it like this and bury it safe inside me until I needed to touch the power of it again.

"Keep going," he yelled, and I slammed into him again.

And again.

He pushed back, his hand flying on his cock.

And again.

And again.

He tensed and arched up and I thrust one last time.

"Yesssssss!" He groaned and spurted ropes up the tiles, shuddering against the arm I had wrapped around his waist, the tide rolling through his body as he jerked softly to a final stillness, leaning on the wall, hungry for air.

I pulled out gently, but he winced just the same. Then he slid down the wall and rolled face down onto the tiled floor. I grabbed the showerhead and washed his spill from the tiles before rinsing his back and between his butt cheeks. He rolled over so I could sluice his front as well, and then I sprayed myself before joining him on the floor to sit with my back against the wall.

The warm water fell gently on our spent bodies, and I manhandled him between my legs, pulling him tight to my chest, my arms around his waist. He curled against me like a sleepy child, and just like that my world fell into place.

"I think you put a hole in my arse," he mumbled, feeling around his hole with a hissed intake of breath. "The wind's going to whistle through there like fucking bagpipes. The next good blow from the Antarctic and I'll be playing 'Scotland the Brave.' If you tap my balls, I might even change key."

I turned his face to mine and gently kissed his lips. "Your brain is a scary place and one of the great mysteries of the world."

He snuggled sideways as the water sprayed over our feet in a soft arc, and I counted my lucky stars I could claim this man as my own.

"I don't know how to have this conversation," I said softly, kissing his cheek. "But we need to have it."

He went stiff in my arms, staring earnestly at the wall. "I'm guessing this is about the baby?"

I nodded against his wet shoulder and then kissed it. "Georgie said she thinks we're protecting each other because we're frightened the other one will just agree with whatever we say to make us happy."

Cam snorted. "Yeah, Sandy says we need to eat our hot potato."

What the? I leaned around to stare at him, and he rolled his eyes. "Don't even ask. It made sense at the time."

"I'm sure it did. Anyway, I have an idea," I said. "How about we count to three and then hold our hands out. A fist means we're thinking yes to a baby, and a flat hand means probably not."

Cam's tawny eyes flashed a cautionary warning, although it was hard to take seriously with all that water running down his cute nose.

He glared at me. "Now I know you aren't suggesting we rock, paper, scissors such an important decision about whether to adopt a baby or not, right? Because that would be pushing ridiculous into straight-up outrageous."

"Pffft. Of course not." I tapped the end of that nose and he wrinkled it like a rabbit. "Just a show of where we are in our thinking. No decisions, just cards on the table. How about it?"

He frowned, his fingers drumming on my bare knee. "Okay. I guess it makes a crazy kind of sense."

We both held out a hand and I called it, "One. Two. Three."

We stared in silence at the two fists hanging between us.

My gaze shifted to Cam's face, his expression unreadable as he continued to stare at our hands. I leaned forward to put my lips right by his ear. "I want this baby, sweetheart."

He twisted in my arms, eyes wide, searching for something in my expression; I wasn't sure what. "You do, really? Even though it's earlier than we planned?"

"Yes. If we can get all the groundwork clear with Stella about expectations, talk to a lawyer, and tick a million other boxes that I can't even begin to imagine, then yeah, at heart it's what I want. What about you? You're not worried about how much work it will add for you? Or the extra pressure, or your job?"

He snorted and slipped his arms around my chest, his hot, wet body nestled right where it belonged, with me. "Hell yeah, I'm worried, but mostly about my family's interference. But like you, my heart says yes. I just didn't want you to say yes simply because it was what I wanted."

I kissed his hair and trailed my fingers down his back to cup his hip. "And I didn't want you to say no because you thought I wanted to wait. Or say yes, for my sake, if you were worried about the workload.

"Jesus, we're dorks." He tipped his head back so I could kiss him, and so of course I did, nibbling on his plump lower lip before finally letting go.

I reached above my head to turn the water off and then hooked a towel with my foot and dragged it over to wrap around us both.

"You're right. We are dorks. But this has always been our life, right?" I gently dried his face with a corner of the towel. "As much as we try to plan *anything*, the universe shits on us every time. Look at my All Blacks' selection; my coming out; people finding out about us, about you; Dad's arseholery. And what about setting a wedding date? How many times have we tried to do that?"

"Four," he grumbled. "Although only one got to the planning stage. Damn All Blacks. Why the hell—"

I squeezed his lips together with my fingers. "Four. There you go. And that's in spite of all your efforts, Mr Control Freak. You can't bend the universe to your will."

He scowled. "I can damn well try."

God, I loved him. "I'm just saying that it seems kind of apt that the chance of a baby happens the same way, slap bang in the middle of a whole lot of other stuff going on. We don't always get to choose the timing; we just have to decide if it's what we want."

He turned his head, a cautious hope lighting up his eyes. "And this is what you want?"

I leaned forward and covered his mouth with mine, taking a few seconds to ground myself in the taste of him, the rightness of *us*. "Yes. But I think we should talk to Stella first. And *you* will have the final say—"

"But—"

"No. Listen to me. Of the two of us, you'll be the one carrying the bigger load at home, at least until I retire from rugby. Cory's life is busy, and we'll be adding a baby to that. I have absolute faith that we can do this, but we'll take all the help we can get, including from your family—"

"Oh, god," Cam looked mortified. "She called you, didn't she? I wish she wouldn't—"

"It's okay. She was worried." I nuzzled his still-damp hair and set about scrubbing it with the towel. "I asked her not to push, but she did get me thinking about what we'd need."

"I'm still sorry. I should've answered her calls, but sometimes she just drives me batshit."

"I get that. It's easier for me in some ways. But as much as the potential family over-involvement thing might need watching, it could also be a really important backup for us, for *you*. Especially when I'm away. We're going to need help, Cam, especially with Cory, and your parents love him to bits."

"Yeah, I guess." He blew out a weary sigh as I dried his back and then cocooned him in the towel and pulled him close.

"I'll be there as much as I possibly can," I promised. "But there's no denying that I'll be away a lot, and you're gonna feel it. So, if you have any doubts at all, we can say no and wait. I'll be absolutely fine with that." I drew the towel up over his head until he almost disappeared under it like some feisty monk. "You are so fucking important to me, to our family, and I won't risk what we have for anything."

I wasn't sure whether they were tears on his cheeks or dripping hair as he cupped my jaw and kissed me softly on the lips. "I love you so much bab—"

"Pappy? Cam? What are you doing on the floor?"

We jerked our heads to where Cory stood in the ensuite doorway, watching us. "I thought you locked the door," Cam whispered.

"I thought you did." I chuckled.

"We were waiting for a cuddle from you, Mr Awesomeness." Cam held out his hand and Cory walked over to take it, then lowered himself onto Cam's towel-shrouded lap.

I wrapped my arms around the two most important people in my life and let the idea of adding a third begin to take root.

Cam's head fell back against my shoulder with a purr of contentment.

Yeah, we could do this.

CHAPTER SEVEN

Cam

Stella sat at the far end of her parents' deep-cushioned couch with her legs curled under her hips. She hugged a pillow to her stomach and picked at the sleeve of the bright red sweatshirt that bore her school's logo. A tall, pretty, full-figured girl with kind, smiling eyes and a self-conscious expression that screamed she'd rather be anywhere else in the world than where she was.

My heart broke for her. This was a huge decision for everyone, but mostly for her. She'd been stumbling sweetly over her words for about ten minutes, thanking us for considering being parents to her baby, and attempting to offer embarrassed and unnecessary explanations for how she found herself in the unenviable position of having to even ask. They were explanations we hadn't asked for and ones she didn't have to give.

I finally put up my hand. "Stella, you don't need to do this," I said quietly, and Reuben squeezed my hand in approval.

She turned to me wide-eyed. "I thought you'd want to know."

I aimed for my most reassuring non-judgemental smile. "We

know how the world works, sweetheart. We also know that you're an amazing, talented, and courageous girl who finds herself in a position she never asked for. All you're trying to do is plan the best future for your baby and yourself. We're incredibly honoured that you chose to ask us first, and we don't take the responsibility lightly."

Reuben leant forward, still holding my hand. "You already know that I adopted Cory from my brother, so we're familiar with the process. You probably also know that my family is hardly a model of functionality. Hell, most of New Zealand knows it."

She bit back a smile.

"For that reason, we kept the adoption to my name just to begin with, but I'll be righting that as soon as possible once we're married. I want Cam's name on those adoption papers. And if we agreed to be parents to your baby, we would want to do it under both our names as well, right from the start."

My gaze jerked sideways, my heart hammering in my throat. We'd talked about my adoption of Cory at some stage, but the fact Reuben wanted it so soon filled my heart to bursting. It was all I could do not to scramble onto his lap and kiss him silly. I settled for a whispered, "Thank you."

He returned a warm smile. "You're welcome." Then he looked to Stella. "This is an amazing second opportunity you've given us, but there's a lot to think about and I know your mum warned you we wouldn't be giving an answer today. We did, however, want to talk about what you saw happening after your baby's born, the type of relationship you wanted with them in the future."

Stella glanced at her parents who'd said very little since we arrived, encouraging Stella to take the lead instead, and for that I admired them. Colleen sat at the opposite end of the couch to her daughter, her expression pained but sympathetic. She nodded to Stella to answer.

Martin Waters sat in a chair next to his wife, a small, wiry man with a gentle gaze. Tears welled in his eyes and he appeared a heartbeat away from swooping across to wrap Stella in cotton wool and hide her away from further scrutiny, but eventually he, too, nodded.

"I don't want to be a problem," Stella said softly, still worrying the sleeve of her sweatshirt as her gaze flicked nervously between Reuben and me. "I know that you'll need time to bond with the baby —the counsellor I've been seeing has talked a lot about how important that is. She said that you'd need to establish yourselves as the baby's parents, and I wouldn't want to interfere with that, but I'd still like to see the baby now and then. I plan to keep talking with her, by the way."

Relief coursed through me.

"So you like her?" Reuben asked.

Stella's smile reached her eyes for the first time. "Yeah, she's really nice. And I know the adoption won't go through until after the birth, but you don't have to worry that I'll change my mind," she said seriously.

My heart squeezed. The words were nice to hear, but we all knew there were no guarantees. Not to mention approval would still need to be completed, no different than any other adoption even if the criteria were a little different with me being family. After Cory, we were familiar with the process, and having one approval under our belts should theoretically help, but you just never knew.

Reuben's grip on my hand tightened. I rested the other on his thigh, knowing the wait for that approval and those papers to be signed after the baby's birth would be an incredibly stressful time.

Holy shit, what were we thinking?

My gaze dipped to the cushion hiding Stella's belly and the incredible life it contained. Warmth flooded my chest and all the churning in my gut settled. We were *thinking* we wanted to grow our family, and that made everything worthwhile.

Still . . . "And you're sure you want to go the adoption route and not just a guardianship?" Guardianship would make our decision even harder with the possibility of it being revoked or challenged down the track.

"No," she answered with surprising force. "I want things to be clear for the baby's sake. I don't want *him* changing his mind—"

We all knew who him was.

"—and *I* won't change my mind, no matter what you think." Her gaze dropped to her lap. "I'm too young. I know that. I've got . . . plans. I want to do stuff. And Mum and Dad are too old."

Colleen snorted. "Not so much of the old, if you please," she teased her daughter.

Stella smiled, and the whole room lit up. Then her expression sobered. "I want the baby to know I'm their birth mother and that Mum and Dad are their grandparents as well as your parents, Cam." She slid a nervous look Reuben's way and he shook his head.

"My dad will be completely out of the picture," he reassured her.

Her relief was evident. "I would want to visit the baby, but I'll fit in with whatever works best. Maybe we could agree on a minimum or something before the baby's born and then just take it from there. Mum and Dad too."

"Absolutely," Colleen agreed. "The baby will be *your* baby. We'll work in with you for visits and we'll keep an eye on Stella."

My stomach clenched. No matter how you looked at it, it was a minefield with no easy answer, and that's how it would stay. That was the risk. It could be the best thing in the world or an unmitigated disaster.

Stella said, "I agreed that Mum could tell you I'm bi."

Reuben nodded. "I take it that's one of the reasons you asked *us*?"

A small frown crossed her brow. "Partly. But it was mostly because you guys always seem so in love when I see you at family stuff, and you're wonderful with Cory. Aunt Margaret talks about you all the time."

Oh god, way to make me feel guilty. The whole avoiding my mother issue had blown over with a phone call and some unsightly grovelling on my part, although things still remained a little strained. But I had an inkling I was hardly going to win the prize for hands-off father of the year, myself. Helicopter parent had a nice ring to it.

"Everyone says you're great parents."

They do?

Reuben leaned sideways and kissed my cheek. "It's mostly down to this one," he said, causing me to shoot him a stunned look as he continued. "You understand I have to travel a fair bit, don't you, Stella? That means Cam would be the primary parent, but we make it work as best we can."

I punched his arm. "Quit that. You're an amazing dad." I faced Stella. "He's the best."

She laughed. "See, that's what I was talking about. You're there for each other. And yes, I get that you travel and also that this isn't going to be easy for you with the paparazzi and stuff."

"So you realise the media are likely at some point to get hold of this, and they might not be kind to you?"

She nodded. "Mum and my counsellor warned me, but you guys are still my first choice."

"Makeup and all?" My words sounded light, but my expression was deadly serious because it had to be said. "This is who I am, Stella. I won't be changing that for anyone, not even a baby."

"I don't want you to," she answered, equally serious. "And Mum and Dad are fine with it."

I glanced to Colleen and caught a genuine smile. Rob's cheeks pinked, but he nodded.

Well, all righty then. One more box ticked.

I turned to Reuben and saw every one of my feelings reflected back. Worry. Confusion. Fear. Hope. And so many questions. This was miles away from the circumstances of Cory's adoption, and Reuben looked as overwhelmed as me.

Colleen got to her feet and smoothed her dress. "Right. I think it's time for a hot drink and some of that chocolate brownie Stella made this morning. Then you boys can tell us more about Cory and *your* life. You're not the only ones making decisions today. What do you say?"

I was grateful for her matter-of-fact approach, and she was right. Reuben and I were under the spotlight too.

"I'll help." Reuben sent me a stealthy wink, got to his feet, and followed Colleen and Stella into the kitchen.

That left the extremely quiet Martin and me alone.

I was gonna kill Reuben.

———

"First thoughts?" I shuffled onto my hip so I could face Reuben in the driver's seat, nerves jangling uncomfortably in my belly.

We'd pulled into a car park at Mission Bay just down the road from Stella and her parents. We'd left Cory with Geo, which meant as soon as we entered our front door, he'd want our attention. We needed to talk while things were fresh and we had the time.

Reuben killed the engine and dropped his window. The rush of cool evening air carried a fresh salt tang that always made me think of family holidays at the beach. Daylight thinned at the edge of the darkening sky, and only the soft lap of waves broke the silence.

Reuben stared out the window and I reached for his hand. "Talk to me."

He put his back to the door, those defiant blond waves wafting forward in the breeze to lick at his face. He frowned and tucked them back behind his ears, looking so very . . . young, and my heart burst in my chest.

I'd always loved this soft, vulnerable side of Reuben from the first time we'd met. There was an innocence about him that was surprising, and so at odds with the tough upbringing he'd had. Reuben Taylor was a conundrum: athletic, focused and driven, a leader on the field and in his sport. But with Cory and me, he was this gentle, generous man, big-hearted and honest.

I was all too well aware that he'd give everything else away in a heartbeat for us. It was my job to make sure he didn't need to.

"There's a lot to take on faith." Reuben lifted my knuckles to his lips. "We don't know how Stella or her parents will feel after the baby's actually born. Or maybe she'll have problems with the pregnancy. Maybe they'll change their minds. We could go through all the prep stuff and end up with nothing. And you and I aren't made to keep our hearts on hold, baby. We'll have committed to this little miracle long before, and it's gonna hurt like crazy if it all falls through."

"I know. I know." My head fell back against the passenger window with a thunk. "Does it put you off?"

"Not a bit." He cocked his head. "You?"

I took a second to think. "It probably should cos it's a bit of a mess, but no. I keep thinking that we got Cory safely into our family, even with your dad doing his dick-headed best to stop it, *and* in the middle of the international rugby incident you caused by coming out with a potty mouthed queen on your arm, so I think we'll manage just fine. Shit." I gulped, eyes widening. "Does that mean we're actually going to do this?"

He gripped my chin and pulled me forward into a kiss that left me humming for more. "Yes, it means we're actually going to do this. You with a baby in your arms? Damn, I can't wait to see that. Although I'm not sure the preschools are gonna be ready for you. I can see some fiery parent-teacher interviews in our future."

I batted my lashes at him. "I have absolutely no idea what you're talking about." I rubbed a circle on the back of his hand with my thumb and watched him closely. "You're not worried about Cory?"

He shrugged. "No guarantees, right? But I think Cory will be fine because we'll make sure he's fine, like we always do, and he's come so far already. We'll prepare him as best we can, get help, and deal with the rest. Same with working out the family involvement thing. One step at a time. I think the more we get to know Stella and her parents now, before the baby's born, the better chance we have of developing a good relationship with them later. That's what families do, right? Although what would I know?" He gave me a lopsided grin that I just had to kiss.

"I sometimes think you handle my family better than I do, so I have zero worries on that score," I said, meaning every word. "But I hate having to live with so many balls in the air."

"No." He tweaked my nose. "You *hate* not being in control."

I narrowed my gaze. "Maybe. I still can't believe we're doing this. No, that's wrong. I *mean*, I can't believe the timing. We were probably *always* going to do this, from the minute she asked, right?"

Reuben's eyes glittered. "Yeah. I figured that too. But how about we still give ourselves till Sunday to sit with it. We've got the spa thing tomorrow—and holy shit, I can't imagine what that bag of snakes involves. How the hell you got me to agree to that madness I'll never know."

"I got you in a weak moment with your balls hanging out your arse from an epic blowjob."

His eyes crinkled at the corners. "Ah yes, I believe it's all coming back to me."

"Aw, Boo." I walked my fingers up his arm. "I'll protect you."

He levelled a glare at me. "Yeah right. I have a bad feeling about the whole thing, and your name is written all over it."

I fluttered my lashes at him.

He snorted. "Good luck with that. I'm immune to your winsome wiles, you little harlot."

My mouth turned up in a slow, sexy smile. "Liar."

"Maybe." His eyebrow twitched. "But putting that aside for the moment, how about we head to Stella's after the rugby on Sunday? It's a noon game, and I can get out of the post-match thing. Maybe we could take Cory with us so he can start to get used to seeing them more often."

I couldn't have loved him more in that moment. "I think that's a great idea." I slumped in my seat. "Jesus, Reuben, we don't do things by half, do we? Which reminds me—" I slapped his chest. "You want to start the process of me adopting Cory as soon as we're married? Were you going to tell me about this sometime?"

"The sooner the better as far as I'm concerned," he said with a cheeky grin. "And I love that I can still surprise you. As soon as we're married, we file, if that's all right with you?"

I squeezed my eyes shut in a vain attempt to conceal the well of tears threatening, as if I could hide anything from him. "It is. I want that more than I can say."

He reached over and ran his thumb under both my eyes. "If only your nurses could see you now. You're such a softie, Cameron Delaney Wano."

I glared and shoved his hand away. "Lies, all of it. And you have to promise to keep this to yourself." I palmed my eyes, no doubt smearing my liner. "For fuck's sake, I hardly recognise this sappy chump I've turned into and I hold you totally to blame. You've loved off all my sharp edges."

He slid a hand around the back of my neck, pulled me over, and kissed me soundly, sliding his tongue between my lips until I melted into his touch, and all I knew was the taste of him. It was enough. It would always be enough.

I pushed him back into his seat, crawled over the handbrake, and plonked myself sideways in his lap, no easy feat with the room he took up. He slid the driver's seat back and I snuggled in close, the stiffening breeze raising goosebumps on the back of my neck.

"Oh, I think you still have plenty of sharp edges left." He nuzzled my hair, and god, how I loved that.

"Shows what *you* know," I grumbled. "People are taking advantage. I can see it in their eyes. They smell blood in the water and they're circling. I need a good fight to sharpen the blades again. I'm thinking of calling a few of the surgeons in for a meeting on response times. They're a good bet to rile me up, and what's more, they fight back. Not that it gets them very far, but at least they try, poor bastards."

He laughed. "Have I told you how much I love you?"

"Not nearly enough." I tugged at my ear lobe. "Hit me with it."

He pressed his lips to my ear, and I shivered. "I love you,

Cameron Wano, every sharp-needled, snark-filled, lace-covered, bossy, prickly, glorious centimetre of you. Don't ever change."

I turned and lost myself in those beautiful grey eyes which had snagged my heart in a wet parking lot over three years ago. "I love you too, Reuben Taylor. And if this baby venture all falls through, we'll be fine, because it's us."

His forehead pressed against mine. "Yeah, because it's us."

CHAPTER EIGHT

Cam

"THOSE DID NOT COME FROM THE VENTS." I POINTED AN accusing finger at the stream of bubbles surfacing between Tom MacDonald and me. "I saw you lift a cheek, you arsehole."

"Nature's a bitch," Tom answered with a smirk. "Better out than in, right? Not good for the body to hold back."

A rumble of laughter circled the enormous sunken hot tub.

Michael shoved his palm into the pool, sending an arc of water heading toward the All Blacks' lock. "Damn, Mac, I think something died inside you. Call by the ER and I'll have a colonoscopy with your name on it."

"Fuck off." Mac's pale freckled cheeks lit up.

"You think that's bad?" Reuben's eyes danced. "Our All Blacks' lockers are next to each other. You wanna add some pregame jitters to those unfortunate bodily issues Mac seems to have, and it's lucky I can make the field on time without oxygen support."

"Shut up." Mac threw a balled-up towel Reuben's way. He ducked and it hit Jake in the face before falling into the water.

Mark grabbed the sodden thing, squeezed it out, and three-pointed it into the hamper.

"What the hell did *I* do?" Jake reached behind for another towel.

"You're too damn pretty." Mark roughed up Jake's hair. "I liked you better when you were straight."

Jake laughed and flipped him off. "You just can't handle the competition, old man."

"Yeah, yeah, yeah. Keep dreaming. Where's Trent, by the way?"

Jake's face fell. "He's, um, not in the picture anymore."

Mark glanced to me and I gave a small shake of my head, telling him to drop it. When I'd finally caught up with my cousin after the bachelor party, it was only to discover that Jake's long-term boyfriend had broken up with him and headed off to the States with zero explanation. Jake was devastated.

"Then he didn't deserve you. You'll find a better one," Mark told him.

Jake looked less than convinced and my heart squeezed for him. He'd been very much in love. To be honest, I'd thought they both were. I just didn't get it.

"Maybe," Jake answered. "But I think I'll swear off guys for a bit. You're all way too fucking complicated. None of you can talk worth a damn. It's women for me all the way from here on in."

"See how long that lasts. You'll miss dick," Mark shot back.

"Yeah, yeah. Well, unlike you lot, I have options."

A small-framed man in his twenties with a towel wrapped around his waist popped his head into the room and interrupted the laughter. He took one look at us and froze. "Um, is this a private group?"

We'd tried to do just that, but the day spa didn't offer that possibility for the hot tub. However, they did assure us that phones weren't allowed in the public areas, just the private function rooms, plus we had to wear swim trunks, so we figured, what the hell? We were just a bunch of guys having some fun, and if someone joined us, we'd keep it fit for public consumption or retire to our private lounge that we'd booked with our own supply of catered nibbles.

Not that it had been an issue since up until then we'd had the pool to ourselves. Although it could hold about a dozen guys, all those who'd ventured into the room so far had taken one look at the eight of us sprawled across its seats and rapidly changed their plans. Or maybe it was the eyeliner I wore, who knew? Either way, I counted it as a win.

"Yes," Michael and Mathew answered at the same time.

"Ignore them," I told the slender man. "Feel free to hop in."

He hesitated, giving me a lingering look with a familiar question in his eyes that I might once have considered. No longer. I kept a straight face, and his gaze swept the rest of the group, eyes widening as he obviously recognised a couple of the impressive muscled bodies on display, and I saw the cogs turning in his brain. His gaze lingered on huge, hairy Mac, which brought a smile to my face. And when he'd put the pieces together, he glanced back at me with curiosity and a fair amount of trepidation.

It warmed my heart.

"Um, I think I'll come back later," he said. "Good luck tomorrow." He nodded at Reuben, then gazed longingly at Mac once again before exiting fast.

We watched his pert little arse shimmy out of the room before breaking into laughter.

"You could've been in there." I dropped my voice and elbowed Mac in the ribs as he reached for his water bottle. Mac had come out as bi to Reuben and me and a few of our friends the year before, but nothing official to the All Blacks or his other teammates.

He blushed adorably. "Nah." He glanced back at the door and frowned. "Ya think so?"

I grinned. "Absolutely. The poor guy was practically drooling. You need to come out with us to the G sometime for a dance. Rainbow 101—a masterclass by yours truly."

He almost choked on his mouthful of water and had to wipe his chin. "Hell no. I can only imagine."

"Oh, honey, you have no idea." I ran my gaze over his huge,

muscled chest. Locks were some of the biggest built athletes on the planet. "They're gonna eat you alive, baby. You're gonna need someone to have your back till you get the hang of it."

"But I'm not out," he hissed.

"The perfect excuse to keep the tigers at bay. Come along as a friend and you can watch and learn without being mauled . . . much."

"You make it sound so inviting." His brow creased as he thought about it. "I don't know. Do you really think they'd be interested in someone like me—"

"Yes!" I waggled my brows. "Oh. My. God. You have no idea. I really, *really* do." I shrugged. "But it's up to you."

A spark of interest lit up his expression. "I mean, it's not like I haven't done *anything* with guys, I just—"

"Hey. You do it in your own time. All I'm saying is when you're ready, let me know. We'll ride shotgun on your maiden outing, official or not."

His expression softened. "Thanks. I think maybe I'd like that."

"You're welcome. And by the way." I eyed him speculatively. "You're way too at ease in this fancy-schmancy place for a guy who looks like sasquatch in the very best way."

"There's a good way to look like a hairy giant?"

I bit my lip and eyed him pointedly. "Oh, boo, there is *absolutely* a good way to look like that, and you totally rock it. You're a huge freckled grizzly bear, sweetheart, in the very, very best way."

He snorted. "I'm not sure I believe you, but yes, I might have visited a place like this once or twice. I like the hot oil head massages."

I snorted and stared at him with newfound appreciation. "Look at you. Who'd have guessed a budding metrosexual lay hidden under all that hairy mmmm. We'll make a queen out of you yet."

His eyes bugged.

"Next up." Sandy sauntered into the room in his swimming briefs looking decidedly sleek and shiny after a full-body wax.

"Very nice work," I commented, running an eye over him as he sank into the water with groaning approval. "Bronwyn, I take it?"

He nodded.

"The woman's a magician, albeit with a slightly sadistic bent. Reuben, I believe you're next on the list." I schooled my expression as best I could.

His head spun like a top. "What the hell do you mean, I'm next?" His eyes glittered dangerously, and my cock perked up. Man, I really, really needed to get *that* look on tap.

I waved a hand at him. "Come on. We're all getting it done. You know, all for one and one for all."

"No, I do not fucking know," he spluttered, his gaze sweeping the other men who deserved a fucking gold medal for their collective composure. "Did you know about this?" Reuben eyeballed Mac.

"Of course I did." Mac's mouth turned up in a Cheshire grin. "I've been dying to give it a go on my . . . you know."

Reuben blanched. "Your what?"

Mac pointed down his front. "My balls."

Reuben's gaze dipped to the bubbling water in front of Mac, and he swallowed hard. "Your balls—Jesus." His voice cracked and his frantic gaze landed back on me. "If you think I'm setting one foot in that room, you've lost your damn mind." He crossed his arms over his chest, which looked all kinds of ridiculous considering he was sitting up to his armpits in water.

"Aw, you scared, baby?" I asked, knowing the reaction I'd get, and I wasn't disappointed.

He glowered. "Yes, I fucking am. You know very well I hate pain. And I'll be roasted alive in the locker room if I go in looking like . . ." He waved an arm Sandy's way. "No offence, Sandy."

Sandy beamed. "None taken. Not everyone can handle this much sexy."

Reuben snorted.

"Oh, come on, Reuben," Mac goaded. "Jeremy Dodds has his chest done all the time."

"Jeremy Dodds is an idiot." Reuben glared. "And he plays for the Broncos, enough said."

"His chest is mighty fine," I said wistfully, earning myself an unrelenting scowl.

"Jeremy's chest is a damn forest. It's likely a fire hazard which is why he has it done. And he only started with the waxing after one of the French front row snagged a handful of the black fuzz in a tackle. When he changed his ripped jersey out on the field, it looked like a moth had been at him."

I bit back a laugh. "So, are you saying you're not as brave as Jeremy?"

The warning in his eyes had my dick sitting up and paying attention. "I'm saying I'm not as stupid."

"Well, I don't know so much." Michael leant back on the lip of the tiled floor. "It keeps things nice and slick down there. No . . . snags." He winked.

"Slick isn't everything." Reuben blushed brightly. "Besides, I thought you liked my hair . . . down there." He glanced my way.

Oh baby. "I do. Of course I do. I just thought . . ." I sighed and tried not to cave at Reuben's troubled expression. "It doesn't matter. I'll go next."

Reuben's jaw worked; his worried eyes locked on me as I started to climb out of the spa. "Fuck it. Okay, okay," he said, his eyes rolling in his head. "I'll do it. But only for you, baby. You should've told me you wanted a change."

I blew him a kiss. "You're my hero."

"Yeah, right. You're gonna owe me big time, and I've got a list running already."

"Oooohhhhhhh," everyone chimed in as one.

I flipped them off. "May the force be with you, darling."

"I'll need it. And as for you!" Reuben pointed straight at Mathew. "One word of this to the team tomorrow and I'm gonna fuck you up on the field next time you play, understood? You won't get a single pass from me, and that fancy best-season record you're chasing will be squiddly shit."

Mathew nodded sagely. "Understood. Fuck me up. No passes. No season record. Squiddly shit. Got it." He snorted.

Reuben huffed, "I hate you all." He stood and water coursed off all that hard muscle like every young gay boy's fantasy come to life.

I was hard as nails in an instant.

Still fuming, he made his way out of the room to rapturous applause while I feasted my eyes on that awesome, dripping wet arse, clad in the teeny tiny swimsuit I'd bought for him to wear. The man made a damn fine exit.

Everyone burst into laughter while I crossed my legs and imagined my own waxing in an attempt to wilt my inconvenient erection. Fail. Michael caught my eye and smirked. I should've known he hadn't missed a thing. Canny fucker.

Sandy noted the time, and fifteen minutes later Reuben was back. It had taken longer than I expected, but we clapped him into the room with accompanying howls of laughter. And if there was a deeper red than beetroot, his fiery complexion had that sucker nailed.

"You are all seriously fucked," he growled, the corners of his mouth twitching. "So very, very fucked, you may as well sell your arseholes now because they're toast, do you understand me? Think you're all so damn funny, don't you? The poor woman nearly laughed herself into a coma when I walked into that room—I was shaking so hard."

He slid into the water and scooped an armful of water at Jake and Mark. "There's no way in hell *you* didn't have something to do with that." He glared at Mark who was pissing himself with laughter. Sandy was already sprinting for the bathroom holding his junk and squealing he needed to pee.

"You nailed it, babe. It was *all* Mark's idea." I swallowed a laugh because it was total lies. "You know what he's like."

Mark fired dagger eyes at me, and Reuben's face lit up in a shit-eating grin. "I thought so. Well, as it happens, Mark, you're up in five minutes, and I made sure to tell her to wax those tiny grapes of yours super clean."

"Fuck." Mark blanched and swallowed hard.

Reuben then eyeballed Mac. "And you're not getting bloody waxed at all, are you?"

"Of course not." Mac's mouth fell open in horror. "Are you fucking crazy?"

And then it was my turn.

"And as for you, *babe*, don't think for a second I believe you didn't plan the whole thing—"

"Eep—" I landed on his lap, my cheeks aflame. "Dear God, will someone please erase that from the soundtrack of my life?" I begged and everyone laughed.

Hands spread my butt cheeks and I found myself astride a very eager cock. A *very* eager cock. "Um, I ah . . ." I cleared my throat and glanced at the others, noting the pointed smirks and knowing smiles. I turned back to Reuben who was eyeing me like a delicious treat he was figuring out the best way to eat. I'd normally have been all over that excellent idea if it weren't for the clarity of the water and— "Ah, Reuben, we have an audience, sweetness."

"We do indeed. I'm just giving you fair warning."

My eyeballs blistered with the heat of his look and I might have gulped, but only in a sexy, completely bossy top way, of course. "Message received, baby. I'll make sure to polish the mirrors."

"You do that." Reuben nuzzled my neck.

"Oh. My. God. Please someone make them stop," Jake groaned, then slipped under the water before surfacing with a splutter. "Oh fuck, I'm gonna need antibiotics, aren't I?"

The entire group nodded.

"Besides, you should know I would never make you wax down there." I cradled Reuben's face. "Your hair keeps my dick warm in winter. I can nestle it in alongside yours."

He chuckled. "Whatever am I going to do with you?"

"You can start with that punishment list you were talking abo—

wait." I pushed his wet hair off his forehead and leaned in for a closer look. I gasped. "Reuben Taylor, you've had your eyebrows waxed." My hand flew to my chest.

"What?" The water in the spa rose and fell as everyone surged across for a look.

Reuben waggled his newly manicured brows to emphasise the point and I kissed him on the nose. "Aw, baby, I'm so proud of you. Another gay achievement unlocked."

He smirked up at me. "It's not the only thing I had done."

My gaze narrowed and my heart did a little flutter. Always with the surprises. "Tell me, right now."

He pushed me off his knees, stood, and turned his back. Then very, very slowly, he lowered those skimpy swim trunks just enough to reveal a perfectly waxed number 15 spread over both butt cheeks.

"Oh. My. God." Jake grabbed his sides and dissolved into laughter.

"Holy shit, you are dead meat in those change rooms tomorrow, bro," Mathew wheezed, trying to catch his breath as he collapsed against the side of the spa. "You can threaten me with anything you like, but there is no way I'm keeping quiet about this."

"Damn, I thought I'd seen it all." Michael held his chest like he was in pain, eyes streaming.

Meanwhile, I couldn't shift my gaze where it was glued to Reuben's arse while he watched me over his shoulder. I reached out a finger and traced the number.

"You like?" He wiggled his butt and I finally unglued my eyeballs from the hotness.

"I'm gonna fucking wreck you." I breathed the words just loud enough for him to hear.

"Bring it on," he whispered back and fired me a wink.

I tugged his swim trunks back into place and patted his arse.

He laughed, knowing exactly what was going through my head.

So sue me. I'd had more than enough of sharing my man's assets.

Reuben

Ninety minutes later we were all buffed and oiled and ready to go, bellies bulging with excellent food, high on laughter and friendship. While the others waited, Cam and I paid since it had been our treat, and then we collected our things and headed out.

"Whoooaaa!" Mac came to a sudden stop as we pushed through the reception doors into the lobby, and I nearly ploughed into his back causing a knock-on effect with the guys behind.

"What the hell?" Mark called from the back of the group. "I nearly had a consent issue with poor Jake in front of me."

Jake snorted. "Shut up, arsehole."

"My point entirely." Mark chuckled. "And I'm not entirely sure Ed would've bought the explanation."

I peered over Mac's shoulder and Cam slid to my side. "Fucking hell."

We all stared through the glass doors to the street.

"Jesus Christ." Mathew whistled low. "Who the hell tipped them off?"

At least twenty people stood milling on the pavement outside the day spa, cameras or phones at the ready. It took a couple of seconds for someone to spot us, and then the whole group surged forward.

"Back into reception." I grabbed Cam's hand, and everyone followed me back inside. Mark stood guard to stop people pushing through.

"I'll check if there's another way out." Georgie scuttled to the front desk.

Jasmine pulled her phone out and started scrolling social media. "There don't appear to be any photos, at least. Just a Twitter post from some douchebag about the wedding party getting the full treatment. It's gaining traction, unfortunately."

"Let me see." Sandy leaned over Jasmine's shoulder to check the man's Twitter handle where the fool had a photo of himself. "That's the first guy who came into the pool room, just after we got there. Bastard."

Jasmine's gaze darted to the raised voices in the foyer. "Leave this to me. Any of them put a foot out of line and I'll have their arses in court." She looked to the desk. "This is private property, right? No one in without an appointment? Do I have permission to enforce that?"

The woman on the desk nodded, glancing nervously to the doors. "Please."

"You need me to wave my badge?" Mark checked.

Jasmine shook her head. "Let's avoid any blowback on the police if we can. This is a grey area."

"Thanks, sis." Cam gave Jasmine a quick hug before she blasted across the room looking every inch the pissed-off lawyer that she was.

Georgie called out from the desk. "There's a loading bay out back that Lena here says we can use. It brings us out on the same street but a little further down."

Mac shook his head at me. "Anything's better than that shitshow. How the hell do you and Cam live with this."

I blew out a sigh and glanced at the door. "It's not usually this bad. It's the wedding."

"Well, fuck 'em." Mac straightened to his full height. "Right, team. Roman tortoise formation. Let's fuck up their chances of getting any good pics of our boys."

Cam rolled his eyes. "Good lord, the man thinks he's Spartacus."

"Spartacus was Thracian, not Roman," Michael corrected with a glint in his eye.

"Whatever." Cam fanned his face with his hand. "The man looked hot as hades in that leather skirt, and those thighs . . ."

I smiled and put my lips to his ear. "Should I be jealous?"

He leaned back against me. "How do you feel about breastplates? And oh my god, is it wrong that I'm getting hard?"

I laughed and pulled him tight against me. "Come on, let's get out of here."

We followed Lena from the front desk to the loading bay, and then quietly made our way up the alley and onto the street, flanked on all sides by our friends. It was a half-baked plan at best, and we had to have looked fucking hilarious with all the shushing and idiotic tiptoeing.

So much for a discreet getaway, we may as well have worn fruit bowls on our heads and held hands for a chorus of 'Mamma Mia.' Sure enough, about thirty metres from the alley, shouts and the unmistakable sound of running feet let us know we'd been spotted.

"Run for the hills," Michael yelled, and we all burst into laughter as we sprinted toward our vehicles stashed in a parking lot about a hundred metres away.

I kept Cam's hand locked in mine and turned to find him flushed and smiling, his eyes dancing with undisguised glee. It almost took my breath away. Dodging the paparazzi wasn't a favourite sport of ours, but having a crowd of people to share it with was kind of epic.

Not that the feeling lasted.

Locks popped and we tumbled into the safety of our vehicles, thanking the stars we'd prepaid the parking fee, only to find ourselves immediately surrounded and locked in place.

"Jerks," Sandy muttered.

"Can we back up?" Mac asked, trying to see out the rear window. "There's no one behind us."

"No, there are blocks behind the rear tyres," Mark answered. "I backed in thinking it would make for an easier exit."

"Just start the car and we'll see what they do as we inch forward," Mac directed.

"How are you feeling a week before the wedding?" Kelvin Greene, one of the sports journalists shouted from beside my door. "Are you nervous?"

I ignored the guy. He was one of the worst offenders. *Fuck.* I hated when we got caught like this. Hated putting Cam through it every damn time. Hated that this was a part of our lives we couldn't just walk away from.

It had eased a bit over the last year, but with adopting Cory and then the wedding, interest was almost back to what we'd put up with when I'd first come out. My heart squeezed at what the news of a baby was likely to do. They'd be salivating for sure, and how the hell was Stella going to cope with something like this?

Was it even fair to put her in that position?

Were we really doing the right thing?

Cam sat wedged between Sandy and me in the back seat. He kept his head up, eyes forward, not hiding—that had never been his way. He smoothed his hair and glanced sideways at the cameras and phones shoved up against the windows of Ed's car, his face a picture of serenity.

It was a well-proven approach.

Outside of a game, the media focused way more on Cam than me. The makeup, the clothes, the fabulousness he wore so effortlessly. He was a conundrum they couldn't get enough of—fem and whip-smart but also strongly masculine with a fuckton of leadership and take-charge attitude. Well, join the club.

They couldn't pigeonhole him, and it drove them crazy. They ached for him to slip up and give them something salacious to print: a snarky comment or a drama queen moment to feed to their readers. He never did, but I hurt for him, nonetheless. It was so tempting to let loose on their bad manners and ignorant comments.

"Will it affect your game, Reuben?" Kelvin pressed.

"Who are your best men?" A woman's face leaned close on the other side of the glass and it was all I could do not to turn and give her the furious footage she so craved. "Cam, are you wearing a dress?" she addressed him.

Cam snorted but said nothing.

"What do you think about your father's interview?" someone on Sandy's side of the car shouted. He leaned forward to block the person's view.

Cam and I glanced at each other and his hand tightened around mine, the unspoken question lying large between us. *What bloody interview?*

"Is he right?" the same woman pushed. "Are you stopping Cory from seeing his grandfather?"

Oh for fuck's sake. Too bloody right we were. It was called a restraining order. There was no way my scum of the earth father was getting anywhere near Cory, not after trying to give him away to his dead mother's dropkick family in the past, just to make his own life easier, and to punish me for being gay. The order didn't extend to us, but at least Cory was safe.

"Is your father invited to the wedding?"

No fucking way.

"They put a scratch on this baby and Edward's gonna skin me alive," Mark grumbled, trying to inch forward through the throng.

"Walk it back, guys," Jasmine's voice broke through the shouts and tangle of questions as she pushed her way through the throng to stand beside Mark's driver's door. "Let them leave, or I'll have you for obstruction."

"Like hell you will. We've a right to be here," some ballsy guy I didn't recognise challenged Jasmine. He clearly hadn't run up against her before.

She walked straight up to the jerk and stood toe to toe. "That won't stop me fucking you up in legal shit for a good long while though, will it? Wanna call my bluff, arsehole?"

The crowd thinned in front of the car as people grumbled and argued but moved to the side, and Mark slowly pressed forward until we'd finally left the crowd behind and were safely on our way.

"Jesus." Mark sighed and his shoulders relaxed. "Is it always like that?"

"Not for a while. The wedding has given everyone a hard-on." I turned and kissed Cam's cheek, noting the way his chest heaved up and down. He didn't usually let this shit affect him. "You okay, baby?"

He nodded but said nothing. I pulled his hand into my lap and he sighed and dropped his head to my shoulder. "I love you."

"I love you too," I whispered, and my head fell against his.

"I hope this isn't an omen for the next week, or we're all fucked," Mark grumbled.

"I'd be prepared, if I were you," I warned him.

"What did that reporter mean about your dad?" Cam pulled his phone from the pocket of his leather jacket and started to scroll.

I'd almost forgotten. I watched as he scrolled, then hit a link. I didn't need more than the heading. "Fuck."

"Holy crap. That bastard." Cam's jaw set in fury as he read, and I didn't blame him.

Mark indicated and took the onramp for the motorway south. Then he caught my eye in the rear-vision mirror. "What's the jerk done now?"

"I'll give you the highlights," I muttered, then read as Cam slowly scrolled from the top. "Dragging rugby into disrepute; morally corrupt and degrading role models for our youth; this is what happens when you bow to political correctness; mocking the institution of marriage; Rugby New Zealand should know better; a sham wedding; a disgrace to New Zealand child services for allowing adoption by a perverse couple; illegal obstruction of his right to visit his grandchild; and so on and fucking so forth."

"Fucker." Cam dropped the phone on his lap and fell against me with a grunt. "I'm surprised the jerk even knew some of those words."

So was I. "Why the hell would anyone give him *any* airtime? That's what gets me."

"You know why." Cam spoke against my shoulder, his body warm against the chill of my father's words. "Most of the arseholes who subscribe to that particular sport talkback agree with him." He finally turned so I could see his face and cupped my cheek. "He's a fuckup and everyone knows he is. This is exactly what he wants, to ruin our wedding day and set the vultures on us. I vote we don't give it to him.

You, me, Cory, and our friends and family? *They're* who matter. He doesn't even rate. And we're okay, right?"

We were. I just wished we didn't have to fight all these fires. My heart pounded in my throat.

"Right?" A frown creased his forehead as he waited for an answer.

I found a smile for him. "Of course we're okay." I pressed my lips to his. "Because it's us."

The corners of his mouth curved up in a lazy smile. "Yeah, baby, because it's us."

CHAPTER NINE

Reuben

"WATCH FOR CHAPPY KEENAN OUT THERE TODAY. HE'S BEEN IN fucking good form." Mathew stretched his legs beside me in the change room. He was one of the designated water boys, his plantar injury keeping him off the field and on the bench. "Waikato is starting him today."

We looked up, both wearing a smile as the crowd roared and clapped to something happening outside. The sound never got old, sending shivers down my spine exactly the same way it had the first time I'd run onto the paddock for the Chiefs all those years ago—pre-Cam, pre-everything.

"Sell-out crowd, best of the provincial season so far," he said, handing me the strapping tape for my hamstring. "The gap's too wide." He pointed to my leg and set to righting it. "How they expect us to play from February to October without fucking our bodies is beyond me. It's hard enough getting through the Super Rugby competition injury-free without having to go on and play the provincial Mitre 10 Cup afterward. And then there's all the All

Blacks' stuff on top, for guys like you. Our bodies weren't made for it, man." He elbowed me. "You're gonna miss me out there today."

We would. "Oh, I don't know about that," I teased. "Rawiri's been damn fast this week and I'm feeling the love."

"Aw, don't be like that." He shoved me playfully as I finished with the extra strapping. "You know I'm the man." Mathew's boyish grin had got him out of more trouble on the field than the rest of the Waikato players put together, but it had stopped working on me a while back. I'd seen it too often at his parents' dinner table, and I'd learned from the best, his mother. Still, he had a way of getting under your skin, just like his damn brother.

"Okay men, time." Our coach clapped and threw the change room doors open. "Line up."

"Come on." Mathew tugged me to my feet, and we slotted into our spots in the line before running onto the field to the elation of the capacity crowd.

Once on the field, I carefully re-stretched my newly recovered hamstring and glanced up into the stand to find Cam exactly where I expected him—slap bang in the middle of the other SAPs—the centre of fucking attention, as always. No longer the WAGs since Cam had appeared on the scene, the North Harbour partners had renamed themselves the spouses and partners, or SAPs, a name that was catching on with the Blues' and All Blacks' partners as well.

Cam wasn't exactly enamoured with the new label, but he wasn't about to rock the boat either, not with the majority of the women proving incredibly supportive. To that end, I made a point of calling him my SAP as often as possible just to light the pissy fire in his eyes.

'Slice of Heaven' blared through the speakers as I shot Cam a wave, and the crowd roared again, adrenaline surging through my veins, kicking up my heart. Nothing beat a home crowd. This was the first game in Auckland for three weeks, and the last before our bye the next weekend when Cam and I were getting married.

Married.

I couldn't fucking wait. If someone had told me three years ago when I first met Cam and was deep in the closet that I'd be out as an All Black *and* getting married to that same man who I loved more than anything, I'd have told them they'd lost their damn mind. And as I jogged across the field, it still took my breath away—all the rainbow flags, the volume of supporter jerseys with the rainbow number 15, and even the occasional drag queen cheering in the crowd in full dress. I had to pinch myself.

A couple of kids from Cam's LGBTQ drop-in centre had even started a queer youth rugby supporters' club, and the membership numbers were rocketing. Visibility mattered. Representation mattered. I just couldn't believe those words actually meant me.

It was a universe away from my experience as a young rugby player—talented but too damn terrified to come out. But as I looked at the crowd, it hit me that *we'd* done this, Cam and me. Credit to New Zealand Rugby for sure, and all the hard work that had gone on behind the scenes, but someone had needed to come out for it to matter, not that I'd had a choice at the time. But maybe for the first time, I was really, really glad it had been me; media be damned.

With only a couple of minutes to go until the start whistle, my attention shot to a teenager seated in the stadium front row, not twenty metres away. He was jumping up and down, waving to attract my attention—pink hair bouncing, full makeup, his number fifteen supporter jersey in place, and a rainbow flag in his hand. The other hand was wrapped around that of the boy next to him who was a lot more subdued but looking at pink hair like he hung the moon. An older man stood on the other side of pink hair, chatting on and off and smiling, a lot. Was he father to one of them?

What if I'd had that?

Shit. I wiped at my traitorous eyes and ran over. It wasn't something we were encouraged to do pre-game, but it felt important. The teens' eyes bugged as I pulled up and asked if they had a pen. The older man immediately rummaged in his jacket and held out a marker, which I used to quickly sign their jerseys.

The crowd hollered and clapped, and I glanced up at the big

screen to find it all being streamed live. I might get my hand slapped by the coaches, but PR and management would be kissing my damn arse. I shook the boys' hands and ran back into my position ready for the whistle. I chanced one last look at Cam who blew me a double-handed kiss of approval.

Because it's us, baby.

Damn right.

My heart roared in my chest and every muscle readied.

The whistle blew.

We surged forward.

And everything fell apart.

By the end of the first half, I was almost puking bile. We'd played like we'd never heard the word rugby. My kicking game was off, and I dropped two catches on the go in the first fifteen minutes. I wasn't sure I'd ever done that, and by the whistle for half-time, we were twelve points down to Waikato, who were without a doubt the weaker team.

But Mathew had been right. Chappy Keenan on the wing for Waikato was firing on all cylinders and had been hard to contain. But it was no excuse for my horrendous form. Maybe the naysayers had been right. Maybe the whole wedding thing really was fucking with my head.

The coach chewed everyone out, but a lot of the responsibility for the score rested squarely on my shoulders, and the team knew it, even if they were nice enough to keep it to themselves. It was my job to read the game and the ball, to nail the high catches, and to keep a cool head. Fifteen was a high-pressure position, and I was playing like a jelly-legged scatterbrain.

My father would be having a fucking field day watching from home. He'd switched allegiance from the Blues and North Harbour after I came out. Now he supported whatever team we happened to be playing against on the day. As long as it wasn't me, he didn't care. He'd die if he knew that nearly every Super Rugby team had a rainbow player on its list—he was so sure I was the exception. Most of those had made themselves known to me on the quiet, but yeah, I couldn't wait for the day I didn't stand alone, and my father could choke on his opinions.

Coach pulled me aside as I rehydrated to check where my head was at. Everyone knew what had happened at the spa, and most had read my father's interview.

"Don't let them win. Don't let *him* win." His words drilled into me. "Turn it around and use that bloody energy to hammer home how wrong they all are. This isn't you, Reuben. Show them who you really are."

It was exactly what I needed to hear.

And whether it was the stinging words of my coach, the thought of my arsehole father, the text from Cam telling me to fuck them up in the second half and that my butt looked cute out there today, or the two teenage boys watching eagerly from the stand, I took the field in the second half a different player with a fire lit deep in my belly.

I was going to finish my last game before getting married like the fucking All Blacks number fifteen that I was.

My team deserved it.

I deserved it.

And every one of our die-hard supporters deserved it.

In the first ten minutes, we scored twice across the line, once when Rawiri caught an awesome blind pass I fired his way, and the second time I managed to fly through their forward pack myself, grounding the ball right under the posts. We converted both, and just like that, we were ahead 17–15 and hope ran like a river through the team.

We had this.

Then the game stalled for the next twenty minutes, neither team able to capitalise on their plays until finally Waikato came back with a try. But they couldn't convert it, leaving them ahead by only three points, 20–17.

But the game was ours, I could feel it in my bones. And a couple of minutes later, we scored a three-point penalty, evening the score.

Yes!

But we needed to keep the pressure on, and with only three minutes on the clock, our brilliant number ten booted the ball damn near fifty metres down the field to give us a ten-metre scrum.

The crowd surged to its feet.

The scrum packed down and our line spread out, waiting for the halfback to pick the ball clear. He'd indicated a throw to the short side, but by the time he had the ball in hand, two Waikato players were blocking his pass.

He threw to the other side instead, and the ball made its way across the field and slowly forward toward the try line. On the far wing, Rawiri got into position for a run down the sideline, but there were two opposition watching him like hawks. And then just like that, a gap formed almost in front of me. A miscommunication sent two Waikato players on a collision course and the run was there for the taking.

I called for the ball and it flew high in the air, bypassing my team-mate and straight toward me. The opposition scrambled to switch focus and block my run, but they were too late. Hands grabbed and slid off my hips as I caught the ball on the fly and flew between the only two opposition players who had a chance of stopping me. With my heart hammering and my lungs on fire, I hoofed it toward the try line, sensing imminent victory.

Then from nowhere, a massive shape appeared in my peripheral vision, offside and powering toward me, the ground shuddering under the force of his feet.

Five metres to go.

I punched down through my hips and thighs, and the studs in my boots caught the ground and kicked my legs up a gear as I pushed toward that oh-so-fucking-close white line on the grass.

A few more steps. Almost ther—

The Waikato prop slammed into me at full speed, all 135 kilos of him.

The crowd gasped and the ball flew from my hands as I was

propelled into the air, past two teammates to land metres away with the force of a sack of concrete.

A sickening crack ricocheted through my brain as I hit the turf with my shoulder, and molten lightning seared the length of my arm. Somewhere in the distance the crowd roared, and for a second or two my heart rocketed with joy that we'd won.

Yes!

But the shout in my mind never left my lips, the words jammed in my brain, a crowd of syllables tripping against some closed door, my body sparking random sensations . . .

> fire flash down my neck
> jangling buzz in my fingers
> arm jerk
> slicing pain
>
> have . . . to . . . get . . . up . . .
> can't . . .

"Reuben! Reuben!"

> need . . . to . . . get up
> voices . . .
> . . . help
> . . . please

Cam

"Will you just stop for a minute and listen to me, Cam. I don't think it's a good idea for you—"

"Don't." I stabbed my finger at my best staff nurse and her mouth snapped shut.

Fuck.

She didn't deserve my anger, she was doing exactly what I would've done in her place, but I had no time for hurt feelings. "Tell me what room he's in, Alison, before I completely lose my shit here."

She stared at me for a couple of seconds, then threw up her hands. "Jesus, Cam, you're impossible. Trauma two. I'm so sorr—"

"Who caught it?" I interrupted.

"Will, but Michael's riding shotgun. He got here just before the ambulance; saw it happen on TV and rang to check we were expecting the admission." Her eyes pleaded with me. "But you need to let them do their j—"

"Thanks." And I was gone, heading for trauma two, every nervous eye in the place locked on my exit. Ancillary staff scattered like pins in a bowling alley as I ran down the hall, my nurses quick with sympathetic nods and more than a little wary concern.

I didn't blame them. Hell, in their place, I'd have stopped them at the front door, not taking no for an answer, and redirected them to my office, platitudes falling from my slick nurse's tongue like a silky balm: give them time; let them work; you can't help yet; you'll just be in the way.

Well, fuck that. No one was about to stop me from getting in that room and laying eyes on Reuben. *No. One.*

And certainly not in my own damn ER.

I was well past ropeable and steaming unchecked toward ferociously pissed off, having spent thirty minutes being held at bay by the fucking security at Eden Park. When I'd seen Reuben go down on that angle, I knew it was bad and immediately raced to try and get into the restricted team zone, nearly breaking my leg on the stairs in the process, and with Sandy hot on my heels trying to calm me down.

Good fucking luck with that.

The security people recognised me and were sympathetic, but they still wouldn't let me into the change room area, let alone anywhere near Reuben, and I'd had to watch from a screen just outside the player's entrance until I had no nails left on either hand. I understood the reasoning, but I was beyond desperate, and for thirty minutes Sandy stood with his arm around me as the paramedics fixed a collar around Reuben's neck, got him carefully onto a spinal board, and then stretchered him off the field on the back of a quad.

We'd run around to catch the waiting ambulance, but that too was sealed off, and all I'd seen was a flash of Reuben's ashen face as he'd passed by a few metres away. I called out to one of the paramedics who I recognised, and he spared me a few seconds after they got Reuben safely inside. Just long enough to tell me they were headed for Auckland Med and that Reuben was breathing but in and out of consciousness and not moving.

Mathew had followed the stretcher out and had needed to forcibly pin me in place so I didn't flay someone alive just to get in that ambulance with Reuben. I'd shoved him off with a few choice words as soon as the ambulance took off and run for my car. Sandy had got there before me—the man had some legs on him—and fought my keys out of my hand.

"Just think about it," he'd snapped, eyeballing me until I loosened my grip. "Jesus, Cam, get in, for fuck's sake. Let's at least get there alive and without killing anyone."

I'd flung myself in the passenger seat for the fifteen-minute motorway slog to the hospital, the ambulance miles ahead of us, my heart thumping in my chest. To his credit, Sandy ignored every furious curse and threat I'd thrown at him to drive faster, instructing me to call my mum instead and make sure Cory was taken care of. It was a good distraction and Mum answered from her car. She'd seen Reuben fall and was already on her way to relieve Geo, our babysitter.

I couldn't have loved her more.

Finally at the hospital, there hadn't been a damn parking spot anywhere near the ER—of course there wasn't—and so I'd flung the passenger door open and simply taken off while the car was still crawling, almost getting my foot run over in the process. I headed for the ambulance bay with Sandy's curses ringing loud in my ears, bypassing the front door since I guessed they'd be warned to head me off.

Good luck with that.

And now, two seconds away from finally laying eyes on Reuben, I was itching to go toe to toe with the next person who even tried to get in my fucking way.

Outside trauma two I hesitated at the closed curtains and didn't even know why. Fear, hope, taking a second to not completely lose my fucking mind, a silent prayer before the chaos hit?

All of it and none of it, and a million pounds pressing on my chest.

The eyes of all my staff at the nurses station burned into my back, and a hand landed on my shoulder.

"Take a breath," Alison said softly.

I did, letting her hand rest there for a moment as I gathered myself. Then I brushed the curtains apart and strode inside.

The room fell quiet as every head turned my way.

Will looked up from where he was threading a central venous line and rolled his eyes. He hissed just loud enough for me to hear, "Jesus fucking Christ, just what we need."

"I heard that." I glared at him as the voices picked up in the room, but I couldn't see Reuben's face for one of my nurses standing in front.

"You were meant to," he spat back, taping the line in place and connecting the bag of fluid. "Just stay out of my way, and no questions until I'm ready, okay?"

"Okay," I grumbled.

"Someone get those bloods on their way, and Sarah, will you please put a hornet's nest up X-ray's arse. We need that spine imaging stat."

Spine imaging.

Sarah moved and I got my first decent look at Reuben, the breath jamming in my chest and threatening to explode through my ribs. He lay still, his eyes closed, an airway shoved between his lips, electrodes slammed on his chest, and lines going every-fucking-where. Sandbags either side of his head kept his spine straight, and all those blond waves, stiff and crusty with dried sweat, lay plastered haphazardly on his forehead. They annoyed me and I wanted to smooth them to the side. I wanted . . . I wanted him to move.

Shaky breaths stumbled in and out of my mouth, going who the hell knew where, since my lungs had clearly left the building.

I reached for the wall to steady myself and tore my eyes from the stark reality of Reuben's body to the familiarity of the monitors instead. This I knew, this I could do—gathering information, calculating, assessing, triaging.

Heart rate good; blood pressure a little low; oxygen saturation okay; catheter bag filling and no blood—kidneys still working. On and on. I pushed off the wall and prowled around them, too fucking terrified to look at the man attached to all of it in case my heart evaporated from sheer panic.

Equilibrium returned. As long as I didn't fucking look at him.

He's okay.

He'll be okay.

We'll be okay.

"Where the hell is X-ray?" Will asked, snapping his ripped gloves off and exchanging them for a new pair.

"I'll get that, Sarah," I barked at one of my nurses and reached for the phone on the wall. Seconds later I was threatening to shove someone's balls in a cage if I didn't see X-ray in the ER in two minutes flat. And yes, I might've been yelling. And yes, a half dozen pointed looks flew my way as my team evaluated my current mental state and found it sorely lacking.

And no, I didn't give a single flying fuck.

But I did keep out of their way, even if I couldn't help interfering.

"Alison, call the lab and see what's holding the bloodwork up," I ordered.

She rolled her eyes at me. "It's only been ten minutes. Give them time."

"Just do it," I said, then winced at the tone in my voice. "Please."
She sighed and left the room.

"Patricia, what the hell are you wearing?" I pointed to the pair of slip-on shoes one of the junior house surgeons was sporting on her feet. "You'll collect a damn cord in those and end up on your arse, or worse."

"Don't yell at her," Will snapped back. "She had heel spur surgery two weeks ago. Jesus, Cam. Can someone not get him out of here?"

"Don't look at me," Will's smart-arse registrar answered. "In fact, I'd pay good money to see someone try."

"Sorry." I sent Patricia an apologetic grimace.

She waved it aside.

A groan from the table suddenly drew all my attention. Reuben.

I crossed the room in seconds and reached for his hand, my gaze locking on the ghostly pale of his skin and slack features. No smiles, no cheeky smirk, no bedroom eyes, no outpour of love like a waterfall from his heart every time he looked at me.

Oh god. I couldn't breathe. I couldn't think.

Will loosened my hand from Reuben's and I almost punched him.

"No," he said firmly, brooking no argument. "Step back, Cam. If you think I'll let you be involved in *any* way, you've got another thing coming. He's *my* patient, and I won't have anyone cock it up, not even you."

I dragged my gaze up and drilled Will with a glare. "As if I—"

"*No one.* Do you understand me? You're taking up room. We need to work. You know I'm good at my job. I'll take care of him. Now step back, or I'll remove you myself and put security on the door."

Determination set my jaw. "You wouldn't da—"

"Don't push me, Cam," he snapped, then his expression and voice softened. "Come on, sweetheart. Just let me do my job."

My knees almost buckled at the endearment from someone affectionately known as the iceman. "Okay. Okay." I nodded and stepped back. Because Will *was* good. He was one of the best.

"He's too still," I said, watching them work. "That can't just be a simple concussion."

Will sighed, then answered as he worked, "He woke on the field, and then in the ambulance, and a few times since, but he's stayed drowsy, in and out. And no, it's not the usual, but we won't know more until the imaging."

Fuck. Fuck. Fuck.

"Cam." Michael's voice fell softly in my ear and a hand guided me back. "Take this." He handed me Reuben's ring, the one I'd given him six months after we'd moved in together as a family. "It's safer with you."

I stared at it, tears welling as my hand started to shake. I swallowed them down as Michael closed my fingers over the cool metal. There'd be time for falling apart later. "Thanks." I slipped it on my hand and Michael pulled me against him.

I drew on his strength for a minute as my heart threatened to break apart. Then I forced my lungs to accept a few deep breaths and watched Reuben's chest rise and fall. Monitors beeped, alarms sounded on and off, and in the middle of it all, the man who'd carved a place in the centre of my universe and around which everything else moved.

Nothing worked without him and no one was taking him from me without a fucking fight.

I took a couple more breaths until I felt the blood begin to sing in my veins, and the nurse in me kicked back in.

There were things I couldn't do, I'd give Will that, but there was a whole fucking lot I could. I wriggled free and shot Michael a look just as the X-ray technician wheeled in the portable machine, finally.

"Tell me everything," I demanded.

He squeezed his eyes shut for a moment, then sighed and opened them again. "We won't know anything until the X-rays are done—"

"Don't screw with me, Michael," I spat the words. "I'm not some naïve relative. *Tell* me, honestly."

He fell back against the wall. "I'll always be honest with you." He looked almost upset. "But the truth is, we simply don't know. From the video replay, we can see he landed awkwardly on his head and shoulder, his neck hyper-extending, but because of the concussion, he hasn't really been able to talk to us fully about what happened or what he's feeling. He's come around but he keeps drifting. All we can do is be cautious and assume a spinal injury until proved otherwise—"

I drew a sharp breath.

"*Assume*, Cam, nothing proven. Breathe."

I gulped in a breath.

"Good." He patted my arm. "Now, what I *can* say is that when he roused a little in the ambulance, he was trying to move his head and he jerked as they tried to put an intravenous in his arm, so he felt *something*." His gaze drilled into me.

"What about reflexes and pulses?" I asked.

"All intact except for some deep tendon ones, and he still seems sensitive to pain although not everywhere. His shoulders and biceps are better than his hands, and his legs are patchy."

"So." I blew out a slow breath. "X-ray, MRI, ultrasound, CT scan, right?"

Michael nodded. "The mobile set of X-rays are simply to check for any obvious or critical instability before we take him upstairs for more extensive imaging. It's gonna be hours until we know anything, and if they find a problem, it could even mean surgery tonight, and more waiting."

I turned to face him. "You're looking for a spinal fracture, right?"

He nodded. "But also herniated disc or subluxation. They're all things we need to rule out before we can go any further. If there's anything that needs stabilising to reduce the risk of further damage, they'll want to get in there straight away. I've just been on the phone with Leyton Robertson, the neurosurgical spine specialist. He's coming to take a look."

Thank God. The air whooshed from my lungs and my knees wobbled just a little as the potential severity of what we were facing hit me. "Fuck, Michael . . ." I tunnelled my fingers through my hair. "What if . . . Jesus, I can hardly breathe. What if—"

"Come here." He enfolded me in his arms. "One step at a time. It's gonna be a long night."

"No." I pushed him away. "Don't. I . . . I can't afford to lose my shit, not now. I have to be here for *him*." I glanced at Reuben's too still body on the gurney as the technician positioned the X-ray plates.

Michael raised a brow. "You mean you have to triple check everything that's being done."

I narrowed my gaze. "Wouldn't you? I doubt you'd let anyone send *you* to the fucking waiting room if that was Josh on the table."

Michael glanced at Reuben and sighed. "Yeah, no chance. I'd be worse than you. But can you please trust me to do the heavy lifting regarding any medical oversight? Will's a great doctor. I don't need you pissing him off."

I grimaced and caught Will's eye. He looked . . . focused. He nodded sharply and got back to work. "I'll try," I said.

Michael gave a wry smile. "I guess that'll have to do. Now let me go and help Will. I've sent Alison to get you a coffee, and you're to sit on that damn stool and keep quiet, understand? I love you, Cam, but if you cause us any problems, so help me, I'll chain you to that chair in your office without a second thought, got it?"

"I'd like to see you try," I growled. "Fucking bossy boots." But I did as he said and took a seat on the stool, my overwhelming fear for Reuben a burning itch under my skin I couldn't scratch.

Michael kept an eye on me, Alison brought me a coffee, and the universe kept spinning as if my heart wasn't laid out on the gurney in this room and ripped open for the world to see.

I hated it. Hated sitting. Hated waiting. Hated watching people do things I could've done quicker, better, maybe. Hated feeling powerless. Hated that I couldn't function. And hated that everyone was watching it happen, watching me fall apart. Hated that I couldn't throw my weight around and demand they get Reuben fixed right the hell now. Hated that I couldn't hold him. That I couldn't touch him. That I couldn't make it better.

"Cam?"

"What—shit." I fumbled to hold on to the half-empty mug of cold coffee, but it slipped through my fingers and smashed on the floor, spewing its contents across the room.

Alison was there in a second with a towel to throw over it. "I'll see to it when he's gone."

"Gone?" I spun to Michael.

He tipped my chin up. "They're taking Reuben upstairs to get the imaging done, and no, before you ask, you can't go with him."

"But—"

"No." He looked at me kindly. "X-ray made me promise, and I don't blame them. But while he's up there, I want you to head to the private waiting room where they've stashed your family and friends and bring them up to speed."

"But if he's going, then that means the portable X-rays came back." I jumped from the stool. "Are you sure he's safe to move? Why the hell didn't you tell me?" I shoved him hard. "Where are they? I want to see them."

Michael sighed. "To be honest, we didn't tell you because we didn't need you hovering over our shoulders the first time we looked. Have at it."

"You're bloody lucky I like you," I growled as I shoved him aside and stormed out of the room and over to the nurses station to see for myself. He followed at a distance.

My gaze darted over each image and found . . . nothing. I looked again, taking my time, just to be sure. Still, nothing.

"Please tell me there isn't a fracture I'm missing?" I white-knuckled the desk, still staring.

"No," Michael answered softly. "They appear to be clear so far.

It's a good start, but we need the rest of the imaging before we can be sure."

We filled in a few minutes talking about the possibilities while I grabbed a fresh cup of coffee from the break room and kept an eye out for the arrival of the orderlies who'd be taking Reuben to imaging.

Then as we headed back toward trauma two, Alison stuck her head out of its curtains and waved for us to hurry up. "Reuben's awake if you want to say something before they take him."

"Thank Christ." I shoved my coffee into Michael's hand and ran, not stopping until I was at Reuben's shoulder.

"Oh my god, baby." I leaned right over the gurney so Reuben could see me past the neck and head brace that now splinted his spine. His mouth curved up in a shaky smile and my heart burst in my chest at the sheer beauty of it.

I fired Will a killer look. He was perched on a stool and writing up his notes. "How long has he been awake?"

He shrugged, looking completely unapologetic. "Five minutes. I needed to ask him some questions first, Cam, in case he drifted off again."

"You still should've told me!"

"Hey," Reuben whispered. "Don't be mad. Let me see you."

I huffed my displeasure at Will and looked down at Reuben's sweet face.

"You look so good." He smiled a little crooked, his focus wavering. "I love you."

"I love you too." I ran my finger along the cool dry curve of his lips and over the trace of blood from where he'd bitten his tongue when he landed. Bruises from the impact also tugged at his jawline, mud flattened his hair above his ear, and one eye flushed a startling red.

He tried to kiss my finger as it passed, and just like that, I was done pretending everything was okay. Big, fat, ugly tears rolled down my cheeks and I didn't give a damn who saw. A few dropped to his face and he blinked one away from his lashes.

"You're gonna smudge your eyeliner, baby," he croaked, his eyes closing again.

"Baby, shh." I touched his face, touched everywhere I could reach, and then lowered my lips to press kisses to his forehead, brushing back those crusty blond locks and resting my cheek on the dirt-smudged skin that lay beneath.

His eyelids fluttered open and I felt it on my jaw.

"I've been so fucking scared, Ruby." I lifted my head and stared down at those beautiful pale ash-coloured eyes with their flecks of soot. "They're gonna take you for imaging. The bastards won't let me come." I glared at Will who rolled his eyes, again. Oh yeah, I was taking lots and lots of names.

"I wonder why." Reuben tried for another smile, a scrap of life returning to his eyes.

"Don't you start," I warned him, sniffing back a charming run of mucous from my nose. "My list of retribution is lengthy."

His attempt at a smile turned to a wince, and my gaze quickly ran the length of his body. "Are you in pain?"

"No." He flinched again. "Just a mother of a headache, and my vision's a bit off. Will says I was out for a bit."

And the rest. "Do you remember *anything*?"

"A bit about the tackle. I remember hitting the ground, but nothing after. Have you been here the whole time?"

I patted his cheek. "Where the hell else would I be? I'm gonna kill that damn Waikato prop."

He stared at me for a second. "My hero."

I snorted. "He'd snot me, right?"

Reuben's lips twitched. "Probably."

I sighed, then grinned slyly. "But I'd get a few quick punches in first. Dazzle him with my Taekwondo."

He almost laughed and I leaned down to brush my nose against his, the simple gesture taking me back to when we'd first got together. It was one of Reuben's favourite things and had always struck me as such a gentle act for a big, tough rugby guy.

Two orderlies appeared in the doorway and I stepped back to let them work, my hand drifting to Reuben's. "I'll let them take you upstairs and I'll see you after. Everyone's waiting for an update. I've been sending Alison out. I couldn't face anyone until I knew more. Now, at least, I can tell them I talked to you."

"Okay." He tried for a smile, but this one didn't reach his eyes.

The orderlies flicked the brakes off the gurney, and I kept my eyes on Reuben until he was out of sight. Only when he was gone did I realise that he'd never reached for me, never squeezed my hand.

My gaze shot to Will and I jolted at his sombre expression. "You tested him?"

He nodded and put a hand on my shoulder. "Right now, Reuben has a flaccid quadriplegia. He can't move anything from the neck down."

CHAPTER TEN

Cam

"WHAT?" I STARED AT WILL, MY MOUTH OPEN AS HIS WORDS sank in. "But . . . but his X-rays are clear. I saw them myself. There's no obvious fractures or any reason—"

"From what we can see," he corrected gently, "we need a more comprehensive set of images than the portable can give us before we can be sure, plus all the other imaging. There might be a disc herniation we've missed or soft tissue damage or a fracture we simply haven't picked up. Cam, you know as well as I do that cases like this are decided as much on ruling things out until you're left with the only thing it can be, as opposed to having any definitive clinical diagnosis."

"Cases like this," I muttered and ran a worried hand over my mouth, squeezing my eyes shut. "Jesus Christ. Why didn't he say something?" I glanced to where I'd last seen Reuben in the hallway.

Will's expression softened. "You know why. We *need* that imaging, Cam. No one wants to jump to any conclusions, Reuben least of all. And he still had some feeling; his sensation is largely intact, but he can't move."

I slumped against the wall and tried to get my thoughts together. "Okay, okay. So what are the differential diagnoses if it's *not* a fracture? And it just can't be that. I won't fucking allow it."

Will gave me a soft smile. "That oughta do it, champ."

"Fuck off." I gave him the stink eye. "So I'm guessing a stinger slash burner from a brachial nerve or cervical root injury from how he fell?"

Will folded his arms and leaned back on the supply cupboards behind. "That would be the best option and is the most common injury from a fall like that. You see enough of them in here, and he said he felt a sharp burning in his arms, almost like an electrical shock. If that's the case, we should see a return of sensation and movement any time. It's usually only minutes, but a stinger can last up to a day or so, max." He hesitated.

I sharpened my gaze. "But?"

He sighed. "*But* you'd also know that a stinger is usually—"

Shit. "One-sided. I know." I drew a deep breath. "And not the length of his body either."

Will nodded. "Correct. Whereas Reuben felt the burning pain in both arms and has changes in all limbs."

Goddammit. "So that leaves what?"

Will blew out a sigh, and for the first time, I noticed the deep-drawn lines around his mouth and eyes. A well of gratitude tugged at my heart.

"Transient Quadriplegia or TQ."

I frowned. "I've heard of it but haven't ever seen it."

"It's not common, but it happens especially with whiplash-type injuries or sports injuries. It's most common in elite athletes because of the way they play—always on the edge of what's possible."

"But that must mean he'll recover," I pressed. "I mean, *transient*, right?"

Will shrugged. "If that's what it is. In TQ the actual internal spinal cord itself has been roughed up, for want of a better phrase, not just the external nerve root. A TQ would help explain Reuben's symptoms, and yes, in that case we should see an improvement within hours, up to thirty-six but sometimes forty-eight, and an eventual full recovery. He could be home in days."

Please God, let it be that. "So that's good, right?" It was getting blood out of a stone, and I was developing a real sympathy for relatives trying to get answers from medical staff. "Will, talk to me, please."

He studied me. "Yes, it's good, Cam, but the problem with TQ is that we can't say for sure if that's exactly what it is, even with imaging, until we see if it resolves in the time frame. We can't see if the cord is just a bit bruised or irritated because it won't always show up. All we can do is wait for him to recover, and if he doesn't, then we're back where we started, looking for a fracture that maybe we missed."

"Shit." I couldn't hold Will's gaze, my gut-churning, my hamster brain turning somersaults in my head. Jesus fucking Christ. My eyes burned and my skin sucked too tight to my bones. This couldn't be happening.

I closed my eyes for a moment and drew a long breath. "Okay, so we do the tests, and then we wait."

Will loosened my hands from the crash cart I was holding onto for grim death and pulled me in for a hug. It was so out of character for both of us, I almost wept in his arms. "Yes, Cam, then we wait," he murmured against my hair.

A few seconds later, another arm slid around my waist. "Hey, you." Michael pressed against my back.

"Oh, fuck me," I groaned. "If anyone sings 'Kumbaya,' I'm gonna throw up."

Will handed me off to Michael with a low chuckle. "Good god, no fear of that from me. I'm gonna have to go and ignore a fuckton of important people just to recover my rep, as it is. Now if you'll excuse me?" He gathered his notes and headed out.

Michael brushed the hair from my face.

"You know?" I asked him, and he nodded. "I think we should go and tell everyone where things are at and then send people home. I've heard they're about to storm the castle looking for you."

I pulled a face. "What do I tell them? Is it fair to worry everyone when we don't know anything for sure?"

Michael's expression sobered. "I always think the truth is a good place to start. Don't protect them, Cam. They won't thank you for it. They're your closest friends and family. Do you really want to keep them in the dark?"

Yes. No. "You're right. But just for the record, I totally deserve major kudos here for not reminding you exactly how much *you* kept *Josh* in the dark about *your* feelings not that long ago." I sent him a pointed look and he flushed.

"Nobody's perfect." He tilted his head and eyeballed me for a minute. "But before we do anything, you're going to fix your damn makeup. Reuben's gonna need as much fierce as he can handle when he gets back, and when Cameron Wano's eyeliner is smudged, it causes a disruption to the space-time continuum that cannot be righted until it's fixed. I know this to be true."

He smiled, turned me towards my office, and gave me a little push. "Go on. I'll wait. And if you're really, really good, after we get rid of everyone, I'll take you to the medical lounge so you can chew on a few doctors' arses. I heard the orthopods had a big surgery tonight. There should still be one or two junior staff around to provide you with a snack."

The thought raised my spirits just a little. Teasing the orthopaedic surgeons was like tag-and-release hunting in a zoo. The targets were fucked but didn't know it. I cupped Michael's cheek. "You sure know how to show a girl a good time. Promise?"

He waggled his brows. "Cross my heart."

I took a minute to peer unseen through the small window into the private ER waiting room. It was jam-packed with well over a dozen people, including the North Harbour coach, the Blues' PR man, and an assistant All Blacks' coach as well.

Dad and Mathew sat in one corner looking grim, while my mother was presumably still with Cory. Georgie's pale face was turned to the ceiling, her eyes closed. She had an arm looped through Craig's while he glared at his phone looking like he'd been hit by a truck. And Tom MacDonald leaned forward on his knees, his brow furrowed, staring at the floor like it would offer all the answers he sought. Reuben had landed a good new friend in the big All Black lock.

Then there was Jake and Sandy and Miller in quiet conversation; Josh with his arm around Katie; and Ed and Mark leaning into each other. And almost hidden from view in the far corner sat . . . Colleen?

I jolted at seeing her there, my gaze lingering on her pained expression. We should've been with them now, almost to the minute, but there was no answer we could give Stella anymore, not until we knew something. And that could be days, weeks if things turned to shit.

Fucking, fuck, fuck.

"You ready?" Michael's hand landed on my back.

"No." I drew a deep breath, straightened my shoulders, and pushed open the door.

Everyone turned at once and I stared at the expectant faces, my heart clenching. My gaze landed on Miller in his chair and I almost fucking cried while shame hit me at the exact same time.

Stop it.

If that was in any way to be a part of Reuben's future, so what? He was still Reuben. We were still us. It wouldn't change a thing, at least not about what really mattered. The rest we'd deal with one day at a time.

"Cam?" Georgie shot to her feet, but I waved her back down as Sandy set a chair out in front so I could sit and face everyone.

I looked to Michael and he raised a brow that said, 'You want me to do it?'

Yes. I shook my head, took a deep breath, and began with the fact that Reuben had woken, and I'd talked to him. That he was lucid and even joking. Strangely enough, getting that out helped soothe my own fears as well. Traumatic brain injury was a real risk, and that seemed less likely now.

Every held breath in the room gushed out in a single sigh.

"Oh, thank God." Sandy sagged with relief.

The news of possible transient quadriplegia, the uncertainty surrounding it, and how long we might have to wait was received with solemn expressions, a mountain of concern, and a lot of questions. I answered them as well as I could, but in the end, I let Michael take over and caught my breath.

Miller wheeled alongside and silently took my hand. He didn't have to say a word. Of all the people in the room, he understood most about the open-ended nature and stress of waiting for a diagnosis for something like this, not to mention the fear of the word quadriplegia. We sat hand in hand until Michael was done.

"If anyone desperately needs an update, you can text me," Michael finished, and I wanted to hug him. "Leave Cam alone, rugby powers included." He eyeballed the coaches. "Cam will let you know as soon as there's something to tell. Until then, assume there is no news and leave him be. Josh and I are bunking down in the hospital tonight," he said with his arms around Josh who nodded and kissed his cheek.

My gaze jerked to them both. "You don't need—"

"Like hell I don't." Michael smiled. "You didn't really think I was going to leave you here unsupervised, did you? Good Lord. Chances are good I'd come back tomorrow and find the entire hospital reorganised and sparkling clean and you an exhausted bag of bones. Remember what happened when you and Reuben were doing your ridiculous dance around each other before you got some sense? The damn ER sluice room gleamed bright enough to land a plane, and I couldn't find a sterile dressing or suture in the size I needed for weeks."

Everyone snickered and I rolled my eyes because he was right. I stress cleaned, so sue me.

"And Josh is taking paparazzi patrol to ensure no one sneaks into the orthopaedic ward or Reuben's room—the vultures are already circling ER reception and clogging up the car park, and a TV crew just pulled up. We all remember last time they got into Craig's hospital room where you two were holed up. It resulted in the most spectacular outing of a certain up-and-coming rugby star. It won't happen again."

"Thank you." I teared up again but couldn't find a fuck left to give. These people knew us, knew me. I was safe. And Josh taking on the media meant damn near everything. Outrunning those fuckers had become a dismal part of our lives for so long, I barely remembered what life was like before.

My thoughts went again to Stella and the baby, and I cringed. How the hell could we bring that shit down on anyone else?

When Michael was done, the room cleared with much hugging of my body, which felt good, if a little weird. It was getting easier to accept, but I wasn't sure I'd ever be truly comfortable. Dad damn near squeezed my lungs out of my chest and told me to call my mother, like I needed the reminder—I appreciated my balls exactly where they were.

Josh headed off to read the riot act to the gathered media with accompanying threats and much police posturing, while Michael headed back into the ER with a promise to call X-ray and see how Reuben was doing.

When he was gone, I made my way across to where Georgie was still sitting with Reuben's brother.

Craig looked devastated.

I squatted in front of his chair and took his hand. He jolted like I'd hit him, and I silently cursed. Craig was getting better about the 'whole gay thing' as he called it, but it had been a slow process. I removed my hand, but to my surprise he grabbed it back.

"Sorry," he said looking sheepish. "I'm an idiot."

I arched a brow. "This we know."

He snorted. "Fair enough." Then his smile dropped and that haunted look reappeared. "What if he doesn't get better? What if it's *not* temporary?"

Trust Craig to lay out the naked fear everyone had so nicely tucked away. "Then we deal with it," I answered, sounding a fuckton more composed than my jangling nerves and need to wash every wall in the damn ER would tend to indicate.

"Yeah, right. Of course." His chin dropped to his chest. "But Cory—"

"Will be fine either way." I stopped that thought in its track and tipped his chin up, forcing him to look at me. "You understand that, don't you? Nothing is gonna change in that regard."

"But if Reuben can't—"

"No," I said firmly. *What the actual fuck?* "Reuben adopted Cory, Craig. It's done and dusted. Nothing will reverse that. And I'm not going anywhere. What's this about?"

His gaze slid and flicked around the room. "Dad's been texting—"

"Oh for fuck's sake." I pushed to my feet and stalked to the window. It was the last thing I needed.

"Why didn't you say?" Georgie shot Craig a stony look. "And why the hell are you listening to anything that douchebag says?" She glanced at the phone in his hand and her lips flattened. "Now, I know you didn't just text him what Michael said, right?"

He flushed bright red. "He's our dad. He has a right to know."

I was two seconds away from strangling the guy. "Are you fucking kidding me? You told him?"

Craig flustered. "He wanted to know how Reuben was—"

"No," I shouted, then stopped and drew a ragged breath to calm down before I unloaded all my frustration on him—it was too damn tempting. Craig might be a walking disaster, but he was at least trying to change, and he didn't deserve that. "He's not interested in Reuben for any other reason than to fuck things up while Reuben can't fight back. *That's* what he wants, Craig. That's *all* he wants. Did you even read what he said in that interview yesterday?"

Craig frowned. "What interview?"

I threw up my hands. "Look it up later. You realise he'll go straight to the media with this new information and stir up another hornet's nest. We'll have every rugby media outlet in the world breathing down the hospital's neck looking for updates. What on earth were you thinking?" I drilled him with a glare. "And what the hell did he say to you about Cory that's got you so tied up in knots."

Craig fiddled with his phone, refusing to look at me. "He said they wouldn't let Reuben keep Cory if he . . . well, you know."

"Oh. My. God. Stop talking to him, Craig. He's wrong and he's only trying to cause trouble. Reuben's going to recover just fine. *No one* is taking Cory from Reuben. Not your dad, not you, no one." I sent him a pointed look. "Why the hell are we even talking about this? If that son of a bitch texts you again, I don't want him knowing anything other than if he thinks he's gonna turn up here and see Reuben, he'll have to walk over my dead body first. He's banned from whatever ward Reuben ends up in, and I'll make damn sure every single staff member knows that. This is my territory, and he's not stepping one foot in it."

"Okay. Okay. And I'm sorry. Will I be able to see Reuben?" Craig asked in a small voice, and my heart squeezed just a little.

"Of course, but he's tied up in imaging for ages tonight and he'll be exhausted by the time he gets to his room. Come tomorrow when he's had some sleep."

"I'll bring Craig with me," Georgie offered, and I sent her a grateful smile. "And you can tell that fiancé of yours when you see him that I'm gonna kick his arse for scaring me half to death, and if he can't feel it, I'll save it for when he can."

I snorted and pulled her into my arms, appreciating the dark humour more than I could say. "You'll have to get in line, sugar. There's a lot I want to do to that particular arse first."

"Ew." She shoved me away with a horrified look. "Come on, Craig, it's time to go." She tugged Craig to his feet, then paused. "So, the wedding?"

I shrugged. "One step at a time. But yeah, it's not looking good. Maybe it would be best to—"

"Shh." She reached for my hand and squeezed. "One step at a time."

I watched them leave, wondering how long it would be until Brian Taylor tried to see his son. The only upside of that particular shitshow was the fact I was spoiling for a fight, and that arsehole would make an admirable target.

CHAPTER ELEVEN

Cam

Two hours later

THE DOOR TO REUBEN'S ROOM IN THE ORTHOPAEDIC WARD opened and I startled from the mindless social media scrolling I'd used to fill in time while he was tied up in imaging. I leapt up and shoved my La-Z-Boy chair into the corner to make room for his gurney and the pair of orderlies pushing it. Michael, Will, and Leyton Robertson all followed.

It felt like a damn funeral procession.

It had taken every ounce of self-control I possessed—and most of the inside layer of my cheek—not to just head down and storm X-ray for answers about what was taking so damn long. Only Michael's text updates had stayed my hand. The bastard took great pleasure in telling me the senior radiologist had bribed him with a free lunch to keep me off their backs for as long as possible.

That list of names was growing longer by the minute.

I stood impatiently to one side as the orderlies did their thing, crossing and uncrossing my arms, checking that they were handling him safely as they slid Reuben onto the bed while keeping his spine protected. My gaze flitted between a drowsy Reuben and the waiting medical team, trying to read their minds by sheer force of will. Their unwillingness to meet my gaze told me a lot. That and the way Reuben's hand flopped to the side once they'd moved him and stayed there.

Dammit to hell.

As soon as I could, I was at his shoulder, tucking that hand against his side and under the sheet. The way he stared at me told me he hadn't felt a thing. "Hey, baby." I kissed him firmly on the mouth.

He smiled against my lips. "Hey, you." He glanced down at his body. "Just the same. No movement yet, although I can still feel a bit."

I kept my expression neutral. "Early days. Did they tell you what they're looking for?"

He nodded.

I narrowed my gaze. "So, I can kill that prop now, right?"

His smile was broken by a yawn. "Sorry. Pretty tired." His eyelids fluttered shut, then open again. "Damn concussion."

"Don't fight it," I said, holding back the tears, shocked the well wasn't dry. The mud had been mostly cleaned from his face at some point, and I guessed I had Michael or Will to thank for that. I tucked the covers under his chin and kissed his lips. "Go to sleep. We can talk later. It'll be a long night. They'll be waking you for recordings and to test your sensation, so sleep while you can."

As if I'd summoned him by my words, the night nurse, Neville, a particularly waifish, handsome guy that I knew from the hospital queer community, strolled into the room to make a start on those recordings. I gave him a tight smile. "Watch those hands, Nellie." His nickname needed no explanation.

"Good lord." Reuben rolled his eyes.

Nellie snorted at my less than subtle counsel. "As if, Cam. Jesus,

I'm not stupid. I'd prefer to be walking tomorrow, thank you very much. I saved a meal for you, by the way. It's in the kitchen."

Reuben fired me a pointed look.

Okay, so I might've fucked up. "Thanks," I told Nellie as he wrapped a blood pressure cuff around Reuben's slack arm. "I'm sorry for—"

"No, you're not." He laughed. "Now get out of here and see what they have to say." His gaze shot to the hallway where the doctors were waiting for me. "I'll take care of your guy."

I glanced at Reuben who was struggling to stay awake. "Have they talked with you?"

He nodded. "A little. But you'll get more from them."

"Okay, well, I'll go see what they have to say, and you try and get some sleep."

"Promise you'll wake me when you get back."

"Okay." I kissed him gently and his eyelids fluttered closed.

"Don't come back without eating something," Nellie warned me. "I promise I'll stay until you do."

"Thanks." I pulled the door shut behind me and headed for the ward office. A couple of nurses charted in one corner, while at the far end, the three doctors had their heads together in serious conversation. They looked up when I came in and waved me to a seat.

It didn't take long.

"So, basically you found *nothing*?" My gaze flicked between the three of them in disbelief. I didn't know whether to be ecstatic or disappointed. No spinal fracture was a hugely positive sign, but Reuben still couldn't move, and they had nothing to go on.

Leyton shrugged. "Some soft tissue inflammation around a couple of the vertebrae, but no obvious spinal cord contusion— nothing to explain the level of flaccid paralysis, which is also a bit denser on his right side. There's no fracture, stenosis, or herniated disc, and no cerebral bleed from the knock to the head. And remember, these are good signs, Cam. It's about eliminating causes as much as finding one."

"I know, I know." I ran both sets of fingers through my messy hair and laced them at the back of my neck. "And I don't need the lecture." I glared. "But they're only *good* signs *if* he gets some movement back in the next day or so, right? If he doesn't, then they are *bad* signs that we might've missed something."

Leyton opened his hands. "It's the best we've got. I know it's frustrating, but TQ is still the most likely option, which is a good thing. Stay focused on that. The concussion is fucking with a diagnosis as well. Numbness, weakness, and tingling can happen with head injuries too, although not usually to this degree. We have no choice but to wait it out."

I blew out a long heartfelt sigh. "We're supposed to be getting married next weekend." I wanted to scream. *How fucking hard can it be to get married?*

"I know. And it sucks," Michael said with a sympathetic look. "But honestly, Cam, we've done all we can."

He was right, and I knew that. But it didn't make it any easier to stomach.

"What do you think you'll do about the wedding?" he asked softly.

My heart plunged in my chest. "I have no fucking idea. It's such a damn mess. Even if it is a TQ and he recovers—" I paused and swallowed hard, fighting back the seemingly endless press of tears. "Who knows if he'll be ready for Saturday. You can't tell me that; no one can."

Michael slipped down in his chair and studied me. "Then we'll just have to pray that's what it is and that he starts to recover full movement soon. If that's the case, the wedding may be fine. Talk to him. See what he says."

I rolled my eyes. "Like the poor guy hasn't got enough going on in his head. I'm not going to make his day worse. I'll work it out."

"Cam—"

"I know. I know." I pushed to my feet and straightened my rumpled shirt and jeans. "But I'm going to give him some time first." I narrowed my eyes. "And if any one of you has missed *something*, you better run fast and far."

Leyton smiled wanly. "It won't come to that. This is your fiancé, Cam. You're one of us. Do you really think we wouldn't have pulled out all the stops?"

I didn't and shook my head. "No, but . . . no. Sorry. Now, if you'll excuse me, I've been instructed to eat something, although fuck knows how I'm gonna keep it down."

Michael made to follow, but I held up a hand. "I'm okay," I told him. "I need some space. Come see me later. And a heads-up for Josh —Reuben's father has been messing with Craig's head. He knows what's going on, and I doubt he'll keep it to himself."

Michael rolled his eyes and growled in his throat. "Fuck."

"Yeah, pretty much."

My phone buzzed just after midnight while I was dozing in the La-Z-Boy and Reuben slept. I hadn't woken him as I'd promised because . . . well, because there seemed no point worrying him any more at the moment.

I checked the text thinking it was my mother. We'd talked earlier and I'd told her she could contact me any time if Cory needed reassurance.

But it was Michael, giving me a heads-up. And he'd attached a link.

Shit.

Brian Taylor hadn't wasted any time.

I scrolled the news feeds both international and local and my fury boiled.

Is this the end of Reuben Taylor's rugby career?
Will Reuben Taylor ever play again?

Reuben Taylor, star All Blacks' fullback, struck down early in what would surely have proved a brilliant career.

All Blacks are silent over the fate of Reuben Taylor.

Then there were the more salacious ones.

Will the marriage of Reuben Taylor and Cameron Wano still take place in the face of this tragedy?

What will happen to Reuben Taylor's nephew?

Cameron Wano seen to leave the hospital in tears.

Cameron Wano says he can't face a life with Reuben in a chair.

What the fuck?

Father says the wedding is off.

Goddammit.

I shoved my phone in my pocket, then pulled it out again and fired off two texts. One to the All Blacks' media man to get him onto damage control and remind the world that Reuben hasn't been diagnosed definitively yet. The second text was to a number I'd avoided for two years.

Fuck it.

I typed a text and pressed Send before I could change my mind.

You're not a father, you're a sickness in every life you touch, including his. You won't break us up no matter what you do so shut your mouth before someone does it for you.

And if the media got hold of that, so be it. It seemed a perfectly rational response to his fuckery.

Reuben's chest rose and fell in quiet sleep, but I couldn't sit there any longer. If I didn't burn off my rage, I'd do something stupid like respond to some of the ridiculous online nonsense, and that wouldn't be a good thing.

I woke Reuben to tell him I was going downstairs and brushed off his concern about why I appeared so upset. The last thing he needed was to learn about his father's current arseholery before he had to. He quickly drifted back to sleep, and I took the nearest elevator to the ground floor intending to prowl the ER for some distraction. But the minute the doors rolled back, I realised my mistake.

Lights flashed and microphones were shoved in my face.

"Cam, what have you got to say about Brian Taylor's statement?"

"Cam, is Reuben paralysed?"

"Cam, is it true the wedding's off?"

"Cam, are you going to adopt another baby?"

My gaze jerked around at that one, the hesitation long enough for the group to cage me against the wall. My throat closed over, my pulse beating a tattoo against my ribs, and I held my palm up—the continual flashing of light blinding me until only coloured spots hung in my eyes.

"Cam, what will happen to Cory?'

"Cam—"

"All right, you lot, I warned you earlier." Josh pushed through the reporters to stand in front and began herding them back toward the main doors. "You're not supposed to be inside the building. Get out, now."

"But this is a public space," someone protested.

"Actually, it's not." I found my voice and pushed off the wall, chasing them down. "This is hospital property, and if you create a disturbance, security can remove you at will, or Josh here can arrest you. Take your pick." I made sure my glare hit every single one of them. A few smirked in reply, happy to know they'd rattled me, the jerks. Then they left, grumbling all the way.

"Sorry." Josh slipped alongside. "They got away from me. I take it you saw the headlines?"

"Bastard. Who does that to their own son? I'd cut off his balls if I thought he had any."

Josh snorted. "How is Reuben?"

"Sleeping. No change." I nodded to the reporters standing in a group outside the door. "The worst thing is, they're right."

"Who? The media?" Josh looked confused.

"Yeah, about the wedding, at least," I said.

Josh grabbed my arm. "Don't let them get to you."

I shrugged him off. "It's nothing to do with that lot. If there's even a hint Reuben won't make it to the ceremony, I need to postpone. If we don't do it before the contract details, then we forfeit the whole cost. And then there's the guests to consider. A couple of the Aussie team are flying here Wednesday, and we've got family coming in from down south and Samoa. The caterers have a no-change clause after Wednesday, and—"

"Hey, hey, hey." Josh's hands landed on my shoulders. "Slow down. You two have worked too hard for this. Could you maybe get another date?"

I rolled my eyes. "They're booked six months out."

Stella's baby and we won't be married.

I continued, "And even if things come right with Reuben, what are the chances he could cope with a wedding on Waiheke Island by next Saturday?"

And it wasn't Josh or Reuben who'd have to make all those damn calls. We couldn't afford to just sit back and cross our fingers. Someone had to make some decisions.

"Shit." Josh scrubbed his hands down his face. "What does Reuben think?"

My stomach clenched. "I . . . I haven't talked to him yet. He's got enough on his plate worrying about the fact he can't fucking move without adding the wedding into the mix." *Pinky swear*. I cleared my throat. "But I'll talk to him in the morning. Just keep those damn reporters out of my hair."

"Done. Now go back to your man and let me worry about them. Reuben needs you."

I shot him a killer look. "He's out like a light."

Josh smirked. "With you, I always find that helps."

Reuben

The one benefit of not being able to move from the chest down? It made pretending to be asleep piss easy.

I did doze on and off pretty much constantly due to the concussion, even with the cumbersome neck and thoracic braces that kept my spine stable, but not as much as Cam probably thought.

I wasn't avoiding him. Well, maybe just a bit. But finding myself inexplicably paralysed with no definitive promise of recovery had pretty much incinerated my thought processes and brought a whole lot of life into sharp focus. It was a strange sensation being able to feel things on my skin in places and yet not be able to move, and I briefly freaked out imagining being operated on while still feeling but not able to move.

Oh. My. God. Nope, not going there.

Meanwhile, Cam was busy doing Cam—protecting *me* while freaking the hell out on the inside. It was pretty bloody obvious by the haunted expression in his eye every time he looked at me and the way he'd clammed up about the injury, not wanting to talk about it.

To be honest, I was pretty much over that kid-glove stuff in a big way, and pretending to sleep stopped me from chewing his arse for keeping me in the dark, which I just fucking knew he was. Yes, Leyton and Will had talked to me, but I knew they'd have said a whole lot more to Cam, and he wasn't being forthcoming.

He was simply being Cam—taking it all on himself, as usual. And it was driving me batshit.

In our lives, he always grabbed the lion's share of the work, citing my travel and rugby commitments as reason—mostly without discussion, and half the time without me even knowing. He ran our complicated lives like clockwork, and yes, I loved that about him.

But it seemed more and more that I was scrambling for a foothold in that same life, feeling guilty for the load Cam carried compared to the small areas of responsibility he 'allocated' me. And we were about to add a baby to that. He couldn't treat our lives like his personal ER. I needed to show I could be that strong supportive person for *him* as well, if only he'd fucking let me.

I'd heard his phone go off and listened to his mutterings and soft curses at whatever it had been about. He was so pissed off, he was practically vibrating. But when he stroked his hand across my brow to tell me he was going downstairs, he never mentioned a thing about it, not even when I asked.

He'd brushed it off.

And now *I* was pissed.

Goddammit. I loved the man more than life itself, but he was the most stubborn motherfucker I knew. Cameron Wano was thrilling and frustrating in equal measure. Life with him was never dull, even though we could do with a little dull in our lives, to be honest.

I didn't need him to tell me what the options were with my injuries, but it would've been really nice to talk about it. I knew about stingers—I'd even had one in the past that lasted just seconds. And although transient quadriplegia was less common, it wasn't unknown in my world. I refused to believe it was anything more serious though. The odds were in my favour.

But as the hours went by and I still couldn't move, I'd started thinking. Even if I came through this, there was no way I'd be back on the field again before the next season. Funnily enough, the thought wasn't as terrible as it could've been.

Cam and I could get married and have an actual honeymoon,

even if we had to delay the honeymoon part just a little bit. But we'd also get a well-earned period of downtime together. Time to prepare for the baby. Time for me to really step up and be involved in the planning and organising for that. We'd absolutely made the right decision. If the paralysis stuck, then maybe we'd need to revisit this particular baby, but I refused to consider that just yet.

But there was no way in hell I wasn't marrying Cam next Saturday, no matter what state I was in, even if I had to marry him in my bloody bed. That certainty was the only thing keeping my brain from exploding. As long as Cam still wanted my sorry arse if things didn't go to plan with my recovery or if I didn't murder him first for not being open with me.

I pushed the thought away and focused on trying to move my fingers or even just my damn shoulder, but nothing sparked to life.

Dammit.

Exhaustion curled the edges of my mind and my eyelids fluttered closed of their own accord.

Cam

At 5.00, in the cool still of the morning, I was staring at Reuben from the La-Z-Boy next to his bed, lost in memories. A wet car park and a stolen kiss—the first time we'd met. He'd been so far in the closet that he'd thrown me off him and into a wall when a teammate had suddenly appeared. Our first coffee together when we'd agreed to try and be friends. Like that was ever going to last. The chemistry between us had been electric.

Then meeting Cory for the first time and having my heart stolen. The moment we gave up on the just-friends lark and shit got real. The hiding, the walking away, the coming back. Another hospital room just like this. On and on, we had so much history for such a short time together, so many damn hurdles we'd had to climb, including Cory's adoption and Reuben's arsehole father's interference and Craig's ongoing recovery, but we'd done it.

Reuben snuffled in his sleep and I watched for his hands to move, for some kind of indication we were going to be okay and that he was coming back from this, but nothing.

Nellie came and went. He brought me a coffee and a slice of something sweet I couldn't keep down for longer than five minutes.

Michael checked on me before heading to grab some shut-eye in one of the staff overnight rooms, and Josh texted to say all was quiet, finally.

I wanted Mathew here. I wanted Sandy.

I didn't want anybody.

I thought about Stella and the baby and wanted to throw up.

I thought about the wedding, and I couldn't fucking breathe.

It was too much.

At 6.00 I went to the bathroom, showered, changed into the clothes Jake had dropped off and ringed my eyes in battle-ready kohl. I gelled my hair, glossed my lips, and stared in the mirror.

What the hell was I doing?

I scrubbed it all off again and sat on the floor and cried.

By 7.00 I looked like I'd been ridden hard and put away wet, and not in a good way.

By 8.00 the doctors had been in, woken Reuben who remained groggy, done all their tests, murmured in a corner, and agreed nothing had changed.

By 8.30 Reuben was asleep again.

My skin felt tight like I was bursting out of it; suffocatingly tight. My heart had taken a permanent lease in my throat, and I had nail marks in my palms to go with the tooth marks on the inside of my cheeks.

I pulled my chair closer to Reuben, turned his hand over, and rested my face in his palm, imagining him touching me, imagining if he couldn't. He stirred and I rallied at the thought that he'd felt my touch, at least.

I ran my fingers through the light dusting of pale hair on his chest and imagined it rough on my back as he thrust into me. I brushed my cheek up his arm and drank in the sweat-stale scent of him, still good, still Reuben. And then I trailed my fingers over his face where I knew he was most sensitive.

He opened his eyes and I fell into those silvery pools, fell in love all over again.

"Hey gorgeous," he said, trying for a smile that didn't quite reach his eyes. "I love it when you touch me."

"Hey, beautiful."

He studied me with a soft expression. "You know we're gonna be okay, right?" He sounded so sure, and I wanted to ask why that was.

Maybe I was jaded from too many years of nursing. Too many times when I'd watched the chips fall the wrong way for people and I wanted to warn him not to count his chickens.

"Kiss me," he said.

And so I did, slow and gentle. He slipped his tongue between my lips and I relished the feel of his warm flesh filling my mouth as we briefly made out. My heart brimmed with hope again, drifting home, grounded from the exhausting and pointless cartwheels it had been spinning in my chest. Reuben was real. We were real. Our love was real. So yeah, maybe I could believe that we were gonna be okay as well.

He rubbed his nose against mine and held my gaze. "What did the doctors tell you last night? You were going to wake me."

"Oh." I schooled my expression. "Well, it was nothing more than what they told you, so I figured I'd let you sleep."

A flash of disappointment crossed his face.

"Basically we just have to wait and see if it comes back."

"*When* it comes back," he corrected.

I swallowed hard. "*When* it comes back."

"I'll be off for a while after this, for sure," Reuben said as I studied him. "That'll mean we'll have time to plan for the baby, together."

What the hell? I could barely put one foot in front of the other, let alone think about the baby. Other than believing we were crazy for exposing another family to our circus of a life, of course. "I, um, yeah. But maybe we should wait till we know about you first before we think about the baby."

More disappointment. "That's very pessimistic," he commented. "So, you don't want to talk about it?"

I ran from the scrutiny. "It's not that I don't *want* to. I just don't think there's any point until we know more."

Deep lines creased his forehead. "Have you changed your mind?"

I threw my hands in the air. "Reuben, what is this? You're lying in a hospital bed, unable to move from the neck down, and you want to talk about babies?" I needed him to stop.

His gaze turned wary, and a deep sigh fell from his lips. "Well, I guess that conversation's not happening. Is there anything you *do* want to talk about?"

I need you to get better. How the hell are we going to get married?

"I'm sorry." I buried my face against his arm. "Ignore me. I'm just scared."

"Then talk to me."

And I almost did. I almost blurted out how terrified I was when I saw him go down on the field. That I didn't know how I'd cope if he couldn't put his hands on my body again. That I had a million balls in the air and I didn't know how I was going to keep juggling them. That I needed him to tell me everything was going to be okay. That his dad was being an arse. That Cory was missing us. That I wanted to crawl in beside him and pretend that none of this was happening.

"What are you wearing?" His voice rolled through me like a warm curling tide, hitting me low in my balls, and I glanced up. The dark flecks in his grey eyes glittered.

I looked down at my clothes. "Um, Jake dropped off a few things."

"No." And then he smiled. "*What* are you wearing?" His gaze flicked down my front and I finally understood.

"Oh." I had to think about it. "Just briefs," I admitted. "Nothing special."

He scowled. "I thought so. Do you still have that go-to bag in your office for our surprise dates?"

I nodded, a smile tugging at my lips.

"Then change. You're . . . fading into the paintwork and you don't belong there." He smiled. "You *deserve* special, Cameron Wano, every day. And maybe especially today, I think you need it."

I smiled because he understood me so well and because he was right. I pressed my lips to his and then raced downstairs to change into the blue lace briefs I had stashed in that bag. I pulled them on and stood tall. And when I got back to his room, he made me show him.

"Much better," he growled and promptly fell asleep.

At 10.00, I pressed hard on Reuben's nail bed and watched for any sign he'd felt it. He . . . slept.

The All Blacks' media guy rang to read me the press release they had planned for noon and I approved it, only later realising that I still hadn't told Reuben about that little fiasco. It could wait.

At 10.15, Michael called in to say he and Josh were headed home for a break and a change of clothes and that Mark had taken over with the media.

At 10.20, Sandy and Ed popped in for a ten-minute visit. I turned down Sandy's offer to stay.

He frowned but accepted the brush off without comment. "What's happening with the wedding?" he asked instead. "Will you guys need to postpone?"

Jesus fuck. "Why the hell is everybody asking me that?" I snapped and instantly regretted it. "Shit, I'm sorry. I just . . . I just don't know, okay?"

He rested a hand on my arm, his eyes soft and warm, and I almost burst into tears, again. "Of course it's okay," he said. "It's a big decision and it's fucking complicated, I get that."

I shrugged. "And the rest."

"Yeah, well, maybe Reuben will be more awake later and you guys can work it out. You've got another day to let them know, right?"

Like that made a difference. It was a fuckton of stress either way. "We'll still lose a ton of money, but yeah."

He sighed. "Well, you know we're here if you need us. We'll help any way we can."

I kept from rolling my eyes by a whisker. "Thanks."

He frowned, then gave me a hug and a kiss on my forehead. "I love your stubborn arse, you do know that, right?"

I snorted. "Yeah, I think maybe I do."

At 10.40, Georgie and Craig arrived. I talked with Georgie for five minutes while Craig sat there staring at his brother and holding his hand. At least neither of them asked about the damn wedding and I could've kissed them for that alone. I left them to it and hid out in the sluice room for a bit. I was so tired of people.

At 11.15, the cleaner popped her head inside and I told her not to worry as I'd cleaned the countertops and was just finishing the sluice. She gave me a strange look, scoped out the sparkling stainless steel with an approving eye, and left.

At 11.25 I took my position back in the La-Z-Boy and tried not to scream with frustration. Reuben dozed on and off and I felt his stare at times, but he didn't talk.

I felt . . . relieved. And guilty.

At 11.35 Will appeared, did some sensation and movement tests, and had a quick read of Reuben's notes. "We wait," he said and left again.

I wanted to kill him.

At noon, I wandered down to the ward lounge to watch the short interview with Gary Knowles, the All Blacks' coach. He said Reuben was still having tests, that nothing had been confirmed, and that reports of paralysis were pure speculation. He ignored every question about the wedding, bless his heart.

He added that if the media wanted accurate updates, they'd do better not to take the word of a family member who was currently under a restraining order—something that was public knowledge since Brian Taylor had complained to the media himself on numerous occasions about being kept away from Cory. But the reminder put the cat among the pigeons and brought a smile to my face. It hadn't completely calmed the media frenzy, but it had taken the sting out of Brian Taylor's words.

Fuck him.

At 12.15, I fed Reuben a sandwich and a bowl of gluggy custard and curled up on the bed next to him. He went to sleep with me threading my fingers in and out of the hair on his chest. I sang softly as I worked, trying to stop the tremble in my body and the numbing dread in my head.

At 12.45, Reuben's day nurse tried to make me eat some soup and toast. I sent her packing. She didn't deserve it.

Ten minutes later Alison appeared from ER with the exact same lunch in her hands as Reuben's nurse. She ignored my bitching, slapped my hand, and watched until I'd eaten the whole lot. She kissed my cheek and left.

I smelled a conspiracy, but it was the first genuine smile I'd worn all day.

Not that it changed the facts.

Twenty-four hours and Reuben still had no movement.

Nothing had changed.

The wedding was in five days.

I couldn't just sit there.

I couldn't pretend things could simply go on as I'd . . . *we'd* planned.

Someone had to do something.

I had to do something.

Reuben had enough going on in that groggy head of his.

By 2.00 pm, I was making lists.

By 3.00 pm, I was making calls.

At 4.00 pm, I faceplanted on Reuben's bed next to his hand and let sleep take me.

CHAPTER TWELVE

Reuben

BODIES PRESSING DOWN IN A SCRUM; MY HAND WEDGED UNDER *someone's leg; pulling, twisting, but I can't move; numbness; nerves buzzing in my fingers; heat; bodies shifting; lying on the ground; a cool draft; lightness—*

"Reuben?" Cam's warm breath soft against my ear. "Reuben, are you okay?"

I peeled my eyelids open and blinked a few times to clear my vision. He wore a worried frown under adorably sleep-mussed hair with a red blotch on his right cheek where he'd been asleep on my burning hand.

My burning hand, whose finger was twitching.

I took a sharp breath and focused on that left hand. Definitely hot, tingling, and twitching. *Yes!*

"Reuben?" Cam repeated anxiously. "You were mumbling something. What's wrong?"

"Nothing," I answered. "The weight of your head put my hand to sleep, that's all. It's a bitch to get the fingers moving again." My mouth curved up in a huge grin.

"Your fingers . . . oh my god." He jumped back and stared at my hand. "You can move your fingers?"

I nodded, grinning like a loon. "Well, more like I can twitch them."

"Holy shit." Cam pumped twice on my call button, then cradled my face and kissed me fiercely. "Do it again."

I focused all my concentration and . . . my thumb twitched.

"Yes!" Cam's eyes flew wide, and he grabbed my hand and plastered kisses both sides of it. "Beautiful hand. Gorgeous, wonderful hand. Can you move anything else?" He reached for his phone.

I tried again, but nothing. "Just my thumb, and oh shit, look . . . my first finger too." I lifted it a centimetre off the sheet.

"Holy shit, he can move his fingers," Cam shouted into the phone. "Yes. Yes. Forget your damn dinner break. Get everyone up here." He threw the phone on the bed. "Leyton," he answered the question in my arched brow, then poked at my shoulder. "Try something else."

Both shoulders were a solid yes although barely a twitch, but my arms were still lumps of clay other than my hands where things perked up, my right better than my left. But I could also flex my toes, a smidge.

"Yes!" Cam roared. "How about sensation?" He used his pen to poke and lightly scratch at the spots on my body which had previously been dull to touch.

I nodded with a huge grin. "Better, sharper."

He threw the pen aside and pressed his lips to mine. I wanted nothing more than to wrap my arms around him, but had to be content with scratching the sheet. I wasn't about to complain.

"I love you so much." He peppered my face with kisses and then since no one had answered the bell, he ran for the door. "Nellie!" he shouted.

"Coming." The answer came from down the hall. "Hold your horses."

"He can move his fingers and toes."

"What?" Nellie was there in ten seconds flat, and I wiggled my fingers and toes as directed. He grinned broadly and headed off to call the team.

"Now get back here," I grumbled at Cam. "More kisses, please. A lot more. I need to test the sensation on my lips."

He grinned. "Is that right? As I recall, your lips weren't ever the problem."

"You can never be too careful about these things."

His mouth curved up in a slow, sexy smile and he did as he was told, for once.

By the time Leyton got to my room twenty minutes later, I had solid sensation to my elbows along with weak movement. An hour later I could lift my hands off my bed and shuffle most of the rest of my body. There were still a few patches of odd sensation, like random paint splashes on my skin, but whatever. It would take as long as it took, but I had no doubt I was on my way to a full recovery.

Cam stalked the room, ordering Leyton around like the doctor existed solely for his benefit. Underneath the impatience, he was obviously happy, but he also seemed . . . uneasy, floating sidelong glances my way when he thought I wasn't looking and frowning, a lot.

Leyton finally had enough of his helpful 'advice' and told him to sit down and zip it or he'd banish him from the entire ward for an hour.

Cam's jaw hit the floor and he stared at Leyton as if weighing the seriousness of the threat, but also with a certain amount of admiration.

Leyton had balls, for sure, and whatever Cam saw on the doctor's face, it clearly threatened follow through, because he slumped into his chair with an audible growl, glancing my way with a small smile that didn't quite reach his eyes.

"It'll keep," he warned, eyes flashing. "You have to come back into my ER at some point."

"I'm sure I'll survive." Leyton fired me an amused wink.

"I wouldn't be so sure about that," I whispered, and he laughed.

Three hours later, I'd been poked, prodded, and generally manhandled by Will and Leyton before being fed dinner and given a sponge bath by Cam. The latter had been an . . . interesting experience as Cam embarked on a mission to test my returning movement. All trace of his earlier unease was gone or well under wraps, I couldn't decide which.

My dick was still a little sluggish. Okay, a lot sluggish with zero sign of any kind of stiffening under Cam's careful and exacting ministrations. But the sensation was there, and he'd taken great pleasure in investigating every single one of my other *buttons* in some kind of personal itemised checklist he carried in his head. I didn't dare ask, but there'd been much humming and lots of small smiles, so I guessed he was satisfied with my progress.

The late hour meant our excited family and friends had to wait until the next day to visit. Michael was rostered in ER, so he'd been able to come up and celebrate with us in person, while everyone else had to make do with a video Cam took of me waving my hand just above the mattress. Cory and Cam's parents got a FaceTime appearance, and Cory showed off a brand-new truck he'd been allowed to choose from his favourite shop.

Cam's phone hadn't stopped buzzing since the news got out, and he'd finally shoved it on silent. The North Harbour, the Blues', *and* the All Blacks' coaches had all texted their personal congratulations and were planning a visit the next day followed by a coordinated press release.

No one was sure yet what exactly that release would say. My initial rapid recovery had slowed somewhat after the first ninety minutes, and although the ability to move had almost fully returned, there was definite residual weakness in some areas. Leyton wasn't unduly surprised and was confident that by morning I'd be almost back to normal, with maybe just a few areas that would need some strengthening work.

In the meantime, I was stuck with the stability brace until repeat imaging could be done in the morning. Until then they'd continue to treat me with supreme caution. No turning, no sitting, and only the quietest movements of my limbs that I could manage. Keep it low-key and careful.

Exactly what I was doing as I held Cam's hand in mine like a precious bird.

Any talk of what the incident might mean for my return to rugby, or even having a rugby career at all, was off-limits until the imaging and a later conversation. There was also still the concussion to consider, but since it was the first one of any significance in my career, I was hopeful. The transient quadriplegia was an entirely different matter, and I'd have to rely on expert advice about the impact of that on my career.

With only the nightlight to brighten the room, Cam was carefully snuggled against my side on the tiny hospital bed, his feet tangled with mine, his arm splayed across my chest. I badly wanted to feel his face buried in my neck, but the brace stood in the way and so we had to make do. Not that I was about to complain. Only a few hours before, I hadn't been sure I'd even be able to touch him ever again. I could wait to feel his face in my neck.

He'd gone very quiet, some of the earlier unease creeping back in. I wanted to ask him about it, but I sensed some of that same reluctance to talk that had been persistent since I'd been injured. I put it down to exhaustion, but I was done waiting on his timing.

"What would you say about me giving up?" I asked softly.

He jerked his head back to look at me, eyes huge. "Give up? You mean rugby?"

I nodded, thumbing circles on the back of those expressive hands.

He gaped. "First up, I'd ask if you've lost your damn mind. You love the game. If they say you shouldn't play again, then okay, we'll need to take that advice. But rugby is your life, Rube. You can't just walk away from it. Not if you don't have to."

"Can't I? And you and Cory are my life, *not* rugby. Rugby hasn't held that place since the day we met, although I was admittedly a bit slow on the uptake." He gave me a lopsided grin. "You, Cory, and the new baby that's coming our way—you're my life and my future, and I wouldn't risk that for anything."

He gave me a blank look. "Why on earth would you be risking it?"

I hesitated. Had I read his concern wrong? "I just wondered if maybe you were worried . . . about me going back on the field, after . . ."

He locked eyes with me. "If they clear you to play, then you should play, that's what I think." He pressed his cheek to my chest. "So you can quit worrying."

But it still felt like there was something he wasn't telling me. "Are you sure? This has been a big wake-up call about the risks of the sport and I'd completely understand if you harboured concerns."

He propped himself up on an elbow and looked hard at me. "Do *you* want to stop playing? Because that's an entirely different thing from whether *I* want you to."

Did I? I took a second to think rather than feed him some pat answer. It *had* been scary, waking up unable to move. I'd been fucking terrified.

I thought about the game, the crowd, the adrenaline, the camaraderie, the rush of the win, the stress, the pressure, the injuries. It wasn't an easy question to answer in the nuts and bolts of it, and so in the end, I went with my emotional gut response.

"No," I said firmly. "I don't *want* to stop. But there are a lot of things in life we might not *want* to stop doing but need to for any number of reasons. I'm not in this career on my own, Cam." I lifted my hand to let his silky black locks run through my fingers. "We both have to live with the good and the bad of it, and that includes the risk of life-changing injuries."

I held my hand out and he threaded our fingers together. "This life is about *us*, remember? And whether I play again or not isn't just my decision. *You* are my life. You and Cory. You're not just a part of it. And that means *we* decide this stuff, not me. What makes you happy, makes me happy. Because it's us."

His gaze slid away and I winced. Things still didn't feel right between us.

"I can cope just fine," he said, dropping his face to my chest. "And I can't be the reason you give up, Ruby. You'd hate me for it."

Heat flushed through my body and my pulse jumped in my throat. "Look at me," I said sharply.

His head shot up, his eyes wide.

"I don't want you to *cope*, Cam," I said testily. "Don't you get it? This is exactly the same as you saying that it's not too late to change my mind about the wedding, thinking you were holding my career back or making life harder for me. Well, I've got news for you, Cameron Wano, you don't have that kind of power. You might be the boss in the bedroom, but outside of it, we do this thing together or we don't do it at all."

He blanched but I wasn't done.

"I don't want you to be the stoic, fierce partner who handles everything my crazy career throws at us, not to mention all the family stuff, while I'm just the thoughtless fuck who just keeps shovelling pressure on."

His gaze shot to mine. "I never said that—"

"You don't have to. It's not what *you* think of me, it's what I think of myself. And I would never stop playing *just* for *you*. I'd stop for *us*. For what it would mean for us. All of us. Or I keep playing for *all* of us. That's what being together, what getting married means for me."

He stared at me, those huge tawny eyes battling some private war inside his head. I knew what I was asking was no small thing. Cam looked after people, protected them, went the extra mile, fought tooth and nail for those he loved, whether you were his staff or family or a patient or a kid at his drop-in centre. And I was asking two impossible things of him here. To make himself equally important. And to give up some of his incessant need to control shit.

I softened my tone and stroked his hair. "I guess what I'm saying is that I'm in this all the way, baby, whatever it takes. Us, together, you and me, Cory, and whatever other kids are in our future. So, are you with me? *Really* with me?"

It felt like some kind of turning point and my heart hammered in my chest.

He looked lost, almost fearful, and it was so unlike him my brain stuttered in my head trying to make sense of it. Even in the dim light, it was impossible to miss the way his face paled and he curled in on himself. Then he buried his face on my chest again and hid.

"I'm so fucking sorry," he muttered. "I didn't realise . . . I mean, I just thought . . . shit."

"Hey." I ran my hand down his lean back and watched him tense like a wary cat at my touch. "We're getting married Saturday, Cam, and it feels like I've waited my whole life for that. I know I have your heart; you show me every day and I'm so damn grateful. All I'm asking is that you move over a little in front and let me walk beside you. Let me take care of you as well. I might not do as good a job as you, but I want to try."

His jaw worked against my chest. "I'm not very good at that, am I?"

"We can practice."

He sighed and moved his hand toward mine while keeping his face buried. "Pinky swear."

The tremble in his voice caught me by surprise, and it took me a few seconds to get my clumsy fingers to behave but I finally got there. "Pinky swear."

This was the Cam no one saw except me and that most wouldn't believe existed—the endearing puzzle of a man I was head over heels in love with. A sassy, fierce, take-no-prisoners bossy boots and the soft-as-butter, vulnerable, open-hearted lover that lay just under the surface. Cam saw that side of himself as weakness. I knew it as the most precious part of who he was, and it killed me that he seemed to think he'd break apart if he let me or anyone else take care of *him*.

"And we don't need to decide anything about the rugby thing now," I reassured him. "I'm pretty sure I'm done for the season anyway. I just want you to think about it so we can have an honest talk. Would that be okay?"

He nodded without looking up. "Of course."

Of course? Hardly a resounding yes. But my energy was failing, and I didn't want to push. I kept hold of his finger and let my eyes close.

Sometime during the night, he slid off the bed and into the La-Z-Boy, but I doubted he slept. Every time I woke and glanced his way, he was staring out the window or scrolling through his phone, his jaw tense enough to crack teeth.

Something was wrong. Maybe I'd upset him more than I knew. Maybe he was having second thoughts about us, after all. Maybe the injury had stirred questions in him. Maybe he'd worried he couldn't live with me in a chair. It didn't sound like Cam, but how the fuck would I know when he wasn't damn well talking to me?

And when I finally woke at seven to a weak stripe of early morning light across my chest, he was gone.

The nurse came in with breakfast and found the note on my table.

Gone home to shower and see Cory. Ask Leyton to phone me about imaging results. I'm sorry. Love you. C.

It should've been reassuring, but fuck if it wasn't. He hadn't bothered to wake me when he left, and that alone scared the shit out of me.

What? He couldn't wait until after the doctors had come? That wasn't Cam. The note wasn't Cam. Nothing about the last twelve hours was Cam.

I relived our conversation from the previous night and cringed.

Jesus Christ, could I have been a more thoughtless arsehole? Already stressed with the wedding and the idea of a new baby, Cam had been hit with me being injured in a way that must've scared the shit out of him.

And what had I done the minute things improved? Gone and told him he needed to step back and chill out.

Fuck. Me.

I'd been a complete jerk.

I automatically reached for my phone only to remember I hadn't seen it since I'd been injured. A new nurse brought my breakfast and briefly looked for the phone when I asked but came up empty-handed. It was probably with Cam.

I managed to feed myself some toast before the doctors arrived to poke and prod. Leyton was clearly curious as to where Cam was, no doubt expecting the third degree once again, but I merely shrugged and said he'd gone home to shower. He frowned but didn't call me on it, finishing his examination with a bright smile instead. I had movement back in all my limbs, even if everything felt a bit like unset jelly, the right worse than the left.

When they were done, the others left, but Leyton pulled up a chair and smiled. "At this rate, if the imaging comes back clear again and you continue to improve, then I can see you home by the end of the weekend."

"I'm getting married on Saturday." I eyeballed him.

He frowned. "You might just have to—"

"I'm getting married on Saturday," I repeated. "If I have to do it in this room, I will. But I'd really like to think that I won't still be here if everything continues as it is. Would that be at all possible?"

Leyton sighed and sat back in his chair. "Let's get the imaging done and see how you are by Thursday. No promises."

"Yes." I did a tiny fist pump and Leyton laughed.

"No promises," he repeated sternly before he left, and I poked my tongue out at his back.

Then I was bundled off for another full round of imaging with the promise I'd be able to get rid of everything but a soft neck brace if the results were good. I wished with everything I had that Cam was coming with me and asked Leyton to call him and Michael and bring them up to date. He promised he would.

Two hours later I was back in the ward, but still no Cam, and no message for me either. *Goddammit.* I was past worried and quickly approaching thoroughly pissed off.

Was he trying to punish me? If so, he was doing a damn good job.

Leyton and Michael appeared in my room within minutes of my return, all smiles and thumbs up, so that was something. The awkward metal brace came off and a soft neck collar replaced it. I had to remain in bed—not that my legs were capable of holding me up anyway—but I was allowed to sit, thank God.

It felt like a prison sentence had been lifted.

Craig and Georgie came to visit, and it was incredible to hold my best friend in my arms—one of a million things I'd taken for granted. Even Craig came in for a hug, the tight lines around his mouth and dark circles under his eyes testament to a touching concern I hadn't expected. I held on to him longer than he probably wanted, but we'd survived our father, the two of us, and that was no small thing. We needed to find a better way forward.

He broke down immediately and apologised for telling Dad about my injury, looking confused when I said I had no idea what he was talking about.

Georgie blinked hard, a deep frown settling on her forehead. I made her show me the online commentaries and explain.

My blood boiled. Was this what Cam had been hiding? Protecting me yet again.

"Don't be mad at him," Georgie tried to soothe me. "You had a concussion, for fuck's sake, on top of everything else."

"I wasn't unconscious," I muttered. "He had plenty of opportunities to at least give me a heads-up, especially once I started to get movement back. I would've trusted him to handle it, but to not even tell me? And wasn't it you who said I needed to step up and call him on stuff?"

She rolled her eyes. "Jesus, Reuben, since when do you listen to me? And I didn't use those words, I don't think. Even if I did, I wouldn't have suggested you choose this particular moment to make a stand." Her brows knitted. "So, where is he now?"

I shrugged and tried not to show how hurt I was that I hadn't heard from him in nearly six hours. "I have no fucking idea. He at least knows about the imaging results; I asked Leyton to call him. Not that he's bothered to get back."

Craig punched me lightly on the arm. "You guys will be okay."

I glanced up and snorted. "And this is from your wealth of relationship experience, right, brother?"

He gave a low whistle. "Ouch. I might know shit in my own life, but I know you two are made for each other."

It was the closest he'd ever come to giving us his blessing, not that we needed it. Still, it felt good, and I'd been a dick, again. "Thanks. And I didn't mean it."

"Yeah, you did, you fucker," he answered with a grin.

They left when they saw my eyelids drooping, but it was only to pass Gary Knowles in the hallway, accompanied by the Blues' coach and the All Blacks' PR manager. Leyton arrived soon after, and the future of my rugby career was thrown on the table for everyone to hum and hah over.

I silently fumed. I'd wanted Cam to be here for this, and I was stung that he wasn't. What the hell was going on?

In the end there wasn't much to discuss. As expected, I was out for the rest of the season, and any return to rugby was dependent on my return to full strength and the recommendations of specialists down the track. A single episode of TQ was a potential contra-indication that would need a lot of consideration, and this early in my recovery, nothing was guaranteed.

The reality sank like a lead balloon in the room, but then conversation quickly returned to the positives and the fact that I was growing stronger by the hour. Together we crafted an optimistic but cautious press release.

We chatted for a few minutes about the offside tackle that had put me in here and the suspension of the prop involved. Gary handed me a personal letter of apology from the player, and I made a note to follow up with a call. Then they left to call their news conference to set all the rubbish rumours to rest, and I really hoped my dad would be watching. Arsehole.

A few friends and family popped their heads in for brief visits—word had clearly gotten out—although Michael and Sandy remained surprisingly absent. And still no Cam, although Nellie finally relayed a message to say he'd be back before dinner and that he was really happy I'd aced the imaging. He could've had them walk the damn phone to my room so I could talk to him myself, but nope.

How fucking thoughtful of him.

Nothing about any of this boded well.

I fumed and threw my pillow across the room. Well, more accurately, I dropped it off the side of the bed since I'd have lost an arm wrestle with a meercat.

There wasn't a lot I could work through until Cam decided to show his face again, but there was one thing I could do, and it was well past time.

So, when Nellie and Roberta came in to change my bed linen, I asked Nellie if I could borrow his phone and made the call.

"Who's this?"

I winced at the foul voice I hadn't heard close to my ear for a long, long time. "It's Reuben."

"What the fuck do you want?" my father asked, immediately wary.

"To tell you to keep your poisonous comments to yourself. I'm done with you fucking with my family and my career."

"Yeah, I heard that you'd walk again. Shame. I doubt *he* would've stayed with you if you couldn't fuck him."

Jesus Christ. Thirty seconds and I already needed a shower. "Shut your mouth."

"Or what?" Brian Taylor scoffed. "What the hell are you gonna do about it? It's a free country. I can say what the fuck I like. Have I upset your faggot *girl*friend? Is that why you rang? You better warn that fucker I don't threaten easy. Maybe when you're away sometime, I'll come around with a few of my mates and show him how real men fuck."

I sucked in a sharp breath.

"Or maybe I might just show that text of his to the police. I'm feeling so unsafe." He laughed in that ugly way that used to send me running as a kid knowing his belt would soon follow.

I wanted to punch him. "You touch Cam *or* Cory and I'll make sure you pay for it, understand, old man?"

"Yeah, right. Tell it to someone who gives a fuck. You might have Cory all tied up in a bow, safe and sound from his dear old granddad now, but that won't last. They'll drop that restraining order eventually and I'll be right there, waiting. You can't watch him all the time. Maybe he'd like to come on a holiday with his granddad? We could do with some bonding time. I hear he's doing well in that new fancy school of his. I think I might stop by. But as for that fuckhole of yours, Cam?" he chuckled in a low voice. "Well, I'm thinking that queer's fair game."

My heart thudded against my ribs. "You wouldn't dare."

"Oh, wouldn't I? Just watch me. Maybe he'll be a good enough fuck to turn me onto cock. Whaddya think? I might want to keep him."

I gasped. "Are you threatening to *rape* Cam? What the hell?"

He laughed. "Rape is such an ugly word. Call it therapy. He might even like it."

"Jesus Christ, that's a new depth, even for you. You touch him and—"

"And you'll what? You won't touch *me, son*. You're too fucking worried about tarnishing that golden boy All Black halo of yours. You step one foot out of line, and they'll dump your sorry arse. You might tick all their PR boxes now, boy, but you touch me, and my mates will cause such a stink in the media that the rugby bosses will be glad to see the back of you. You're just like all the rest of your fairy friends. No fucking balls. Nobody wants you in the locker room with them. You make any real man want to puke. They're all just waiting for an excuse to get rid of you."

And just like that, I was done with him. I had enough. "You have a *big* imagination, *Dad*," I drawled. "But you won't come near Cam for a few very important reasons, or you would've done it by now. You're nothing but a scumbag bully and no one who matters gives a shit about you or the bigoted crap you spout. The few people who agree with you are as sad as you are. You're all swimming in this tiny little goldfish bowl with a few of your mates, seeing your reflection in the glass and thinking that everyone's just like you. Well, they're not. So listen up."

"I don't have to—"

"Shut the fuck up," I shouted. "The first reason you won't come near my family is that Cam could whip your arse and your mates with a hand tied behind his back, and you bloody well know that. He's about as far from helpless as you could imagine. And how fucking embarrassing would that be, right?"

"As if—"

"Second, if you laid a finger on him, *or* Cory, you'll have half the Samoan population on your tail, and more than a few rugby players as well. Those are some big, big boys, and they don't forget easily. Family means everything to them. And you'd be shocked to learn just how many rugby players think Cam is the best thing for rugby since the name All Blacks was first coined. He's the new era in this sport, so you better get used to it, and you better be very, very careful what you say about him."

Brian Taylor grunted dismissively but said nothing.

Yeah, you absolute bastard.

"And third, you might not think much of the LGBTQ community, but let me tell you something, they could eviscerate your life in the media without stopping to take a breath."

"That's utter cr—"

"And finally, you total arsehole, I've just recorded this entire fucking conversation, and my next step is to hand it to Cam's killer lawyer sister to see just how far we can take these threats you've just made on Cam and Cory. Plus, I've got witnesses here who have heard every word you've said." I glanced at Nellie and Roberta standing with faces as pale as the fresh sheets on my bed, while Roberta held her phone alongside Nellie's.

I continued, "And if we can't get you in court the way we'd like to, and you say another thing against my family, I'll let the press have this recording and your words will be sprayed across the six o'clock news. Let's see how you like the press poking into every aspect of *your* life. I know damn well you've got more than a few nasty secrets hidden away. In fact, I can probably point them to a few myself, starting with taxes on the garage, *Daaaad.*"

"You little shit," he flustered.

I snorted. "I learned from the best. So be warned. The legal stuff is happening regardless. But if I read or hear another word from your filthy mouth in the media about us, I will do exactly what I said and give them the recording. Goodbye, *Dad.*"

I hung up and slammed Nellie's phone into his outstretched hand while I tried to fill my lungs past the mountain in my throat.

"Hey, it's okay." Nellie grabbed my shaking hands and rubbed some life into them. "Holy shit. I'd heard about your dad, but I had no idea. You were fucking awesome."

As the adrenaline settled, I blew a couple of deep breaths and raised my head. "Thanks for helping with that."

"An absolute privilege," Nellie said seriously with Roberta nodding furiously alongside. "Just let Roberta know where you want the recording sent to and she'll delete the original, right Roberta?"

More nodding. "What an arsehole." She blew a low whistle. "Now, how about a coffee?"

I snorted. "The great cure-all."

———

The confrontation with my father worked to release some of the steam I had backed up, but it didn't last, and by 2.00 pm when Cam still hadn't shown his face in my room, I was nothing short of wholesale furious with my fiancé—spitting tacks and pissing enough vinegar to keep the nurses out of my room and ready to rip the head off the next person who came through the door.

Which explains why I was completely unprepared to turn at the soft knock and find Cam, pale and uneasy, leaning on the door jamb as if he couldn't hold himself up and staring at me with desolate, red-rimmed eyes like his whole world had ended.

Fuck.

This couldn't be good.

My heart stuttered in my chest. "Cam?"

CHAPTER THIRTEEN

Cam

Earlier that day

I'D WALKED OUT WITHOUT EVEN WAKING HIM. LEFT A FUCKING note, of all things. A coward's way out.

But I hadn't been ready to face him, to tell him what I'd done in the wake of everything he'd said to me. He'd been right, more right than he knew, and I refused to add a lie on top of everything else.

Stunned pretty much summed up my feelings about our 'discussion'. Reuben didn't raise his voice, not to me, and man there'd been times he probably should've, but that wasn't his way. He gave me plenty of room in our relationship, seemingly content to let me go and watch the show. I'd tried not to abuse that trust, but clearly, I'd been running on default. Reuben was solid and quiet and just so fucking wonderful, and I'd taken that for granted. Not only had I taken it for granted, but I'd walked all over that agreeable nature without a backward glance.

My stomach soured at the thought. *Who the hell was I?*

Worse yet, he'd called me on it, and he didn't even know the full extent of what I'd done.

"We're getting married on Saturday, Cam . . ."

Except we weren't. I'd done exactly what he'd been talking about and postponed everything.

Without talking to him.

Thinking it was the right thing.

I mean I'd planned it all, right? He'd stepped back and let me do everything because that's what I'd wanted. And so what? That meant I could just go ahead and postpone it as well?

What was wrong with me?

Why didn't I wait?

Because I was cleaning house like I always did when shit got too much. Clean sluice rooms, clean the ER, clean our house, sweep old boyfriends under the rug, clean our lives, clean the slate.

Start again. Reboot. Take control.

Fucking, fuck, fuck.

How could I tell him that now? What would he think?

Would he think I'd given up on him?

Never.

I would never give up on him.

I'd given up on me.

Shit.

Reuben getting hurt, Stella and the baby, the wedding, the press, Reuben's fucking father. Nowhere to go.

Clean house.

Empty shit out.

Get the stressful things I *could* control off the list, whatever the cost.

Except maybe the cost would be Reuben this time.

And so I'd run home. I'd played with Cory. I'd showered and changed and had something to eat, all carefully avoiding my mother's pointed looks. And then when I was finally ready, I found her in the lounge waiting for me. My mother—the harbinger of caustic truth and a sure-fire remedy for my self-indulgent pity party.

"Do you think I'm controlling?" May as well jump right in.

She frowned. "Define controlling."

I rolled my eyes. "You know exactly what I mean."

She huffed and pulled me down next to her on the couch which signalled I was about to get one of her talks. *Awesome.*

"Cameron."

And there it was, that voice.

"What's all this about? You've been sulking around here like a kid who got caught with his hand in the lolly jar."

Eerily close to the truth.

I stared at my hands until she tipped my chin up with her finger. "Sweetheart, what's up?" She dropped her hand, looking concerned in the particular way mother's had no matter how old you were.

I blinked for a long second and then met her eyes. "I fucked up, badly." I barely recognised my own voice.

Her gaze narrowed, but the fact she didn't call me on my language only proved she knew it was serious. "Okay, tell me." She reached for my hand and tugged it to her lap.

I am not fucking crying.

"I don't even know why I did it. I um, shit, shit, shit. I cancelled the wedding, Mum. Well, I postponed it, I guess, although I can't get another date so . . ." I raised a hand to my forehead and sucked in a shaky breath.

"You postponed the wedding?" She said the words slow and carefully, as if she was checking she heard correctly.

"Yes, dammit. Yesterday."

"Okaaay. Was that suggested by the doctors? I mean it seems a reasonable thing to consider. What did Reuben think?"

I stared miserably at her. "I . . . shit, I, um, didn't ask him."

She said nothing. She didn't need to. My mother was rarely silent. I groaned and sank back into the couch cushions, pulling my hand free from hers so I could tear my hair out more efficiently.

"And what decided you to do that?" she asked carefully.

Excellent fucking question. I threw up my hands. "I thought . . . fuck, I don't know what I thought, but I did it. And now he's getting better, and he still thinks we're getting married, and he's so excited, and then we had this argument, or discussion, or something about me letting him walk beside me. Jesus, I can't even remember. Yesterday, it seemed so fucking clear. I thought it had to be done, that at least it would be one thing off my plate. But now he's okay, and he still thinks it's on, and I, oh fuck, Mum, I don't know how to tell him. He's going to hate me. It was exactly what he was talking about. We pinky swore and everything." I sighed and smacked myself on the head a couple of times for emphasis.

She blinked slowly which I figured was about the whole pinky-swear thing. I expected shock, frustration, maybe even anger, but all I saw was kindness and sympathy instead, which of course made things five billion times worse.

She was silent for a long time before she finally spoke. "Cameron Delany Wano—"

"Oh fuck," I groaned, and threw an arm over my face. "Why do I feel like you've been waiting my entire life to have this conversation?"

She snorted. "Not exactly waiting, maybe just expecting it at some point." She pulled my arm down gently. She was wearing a smile, and I felt twelve years old all over again. Cared for.

Safe.

The *same* safety I felt with Reuben on the few times I gave myself over to him in this way, raw and unsure. And, oh fuck, a thousand bells went off in my head with the realisation. Reuben had been so very right. He *was* there for me, always, I never questioned that. But it suddenly hit me that I hated the fact I needed him at all. And I hated confessing it even more, the admission rubbing like a hair shirt on my skin, scratchy and uncomfortable.

"You know you should be having this conversation with him, don't you?"

"I will," I promised. "But I need to get my head clear about it first."

She sighed and scooted in beside me. "Sweetheart," she began in that non-threatening voice she always used when any of us kids were being incredibly thick-headed. The same one that inevitably ended in me feeling like someone had scrubbed my emotional brain with a scouring pad.

She continued, "You were a kid who screamed 'different' from the minute you left my belly. And I don't just mean different in the fact of liking makeup and pretty things, or being gay, or being *fabulous*, because you know I love all of those parts of you, right?" She arched a brow, and I didn't even have to think.

I'd always known she loved me wholly and completely.

"Good," she continued. "You also have one of the biggest hearts I know, a sharp mind, merciless tongue, and a passion for protecting people. That's what makes you such a wonderful nurse, a gifted charge nurse, and a champion for those LGBTQ youth of yours. You'd fight for your staff and patients and kids until your last breath."

Warmth washed over me, which was kind of amazing considering how gloriously I'd fucked things up and the depth of the misery pool I was swimming in.

She drew a sharp breath. "All of those qualities *also* make you a great parent to Cory and partner to Reuben. They need that strength and fighting spirit. They need someone who can stand up to the media and all the crap that comes with Reuben's celebrity, and a person who'll fight for Cory to live his best life. You do all of that, admirably."

I rolled my eyes. "I sense a but."

She smiled softly. "*But* those qualities weren't just handed to you. You're fiercely protective, precisely *because* you know exactly how it feels to be ganged up on, to be threatened, to be ridiculed, even by that bastard of an ex of yours, Dom. And to make sure that never happens again, you take control whenever you can, and mostly that's worked for you. Giving up that control, however, has never been your strong suit, and if you try and take that into a relationship, you're asking for trouble. You don't like to show weakness, and you don't ask for help. You don't feel comfortable letting anyone else be your strength, and yet you want to be that for them. But that just means you hold all the power. You have to let Reuben share that."

I groaned. "He said exactly the same."

A smile tugged at her lips. "Smart man."

"You know, you might have led with this conversation a few years ago before I made an arse of myself."

She patted my hand. "You needed to learn this for yourself. And you of all people *needed* to make an arse of yourself. No better lesson." Her smile was wide.

"Not at the cost of Reuben," I muttered.

"Pfft." Her pat turned to a stinging slap and I jerked my hand away. "Give the man some credit," she admonished. "And since when do you give up so easily?"

She had a point. I straightened in my seat, took a calming breath, and she eyed me approvingly.

"That's better. You've spent your whole life putting up walls to keep a safe space around you, Cam. And even when those walls aren't so necessary anymore, they don't fall down of their own accord. You have to unbuild them. Do you trust Reuben?"

"Of course I do. No one more. That wasn't why I didn't talk with him. I couldn't imagine what he was going through and I didn't want to add to his worries. I guess I thought it might take the pressure off both of us."

She nodded. "Reuben's a good man, one of the best I know. He's got an excellent brain, good instincts, and he survived twenty-three years of having a total and dangerous dick for a father, while at the same time managing to protect his nephew. He's an incredibly strong man and I doubt he needs the protection you think he does. Plus, you need to consider if you were really protecting him or simply trying to stay in control and protect yourself. And it's not just Reuben. You didn't talk with *anyone*."

"Shit." My head fell against the back of the couch.

"Making decisions for someone you care about without asking isn't love, Cam. It's patronising, undermining, and even crippling. It says you don't have faith in them, in their capacity to prevail. Now, I don't for a moment believe you think that of Reuben at all. The question is, what are you going to do about it, and I can't answer that for you."

She kissed my cheek and left me a hollowed-out shell on the couch. *Mothers.*

I gathered the shreds of my dignity and headed back to the hospital, getting as far as the ER before being waylaid by Michael and Sandy who were holed up in my office in deep conversation. A conversation that came to an abrupt and telling end as soon as they laid eyes on me.

"Where the hell have you been?" Michael eyed me from behind my own desk, his expression one big pissed-off glare. "Reuben's been asking for you all morning. You missed his doctors' round *and* the imaging *and* the big rugby bosses think tank across his bed."

Shit.

"You would never do that without a good reason, but fucked if I can come up with a single one."

I slumped in the spare chair next to Sandy. "Hello to you too. And get out of my chair."

"No." He scowled. "You look like shit. Start talking."

Sandy took my hand. "What happened?"

Nothing. The word was right there on the tip of my tongue, itching to be voiced. It would be so fucking easy. Dodge. Smile. Snap. Sass and snark. It was all there for the taking.

Instead, I swallowed hard and told them.

Everything.

And when I was done, the office was bathed in silence, barring a soft hum of concern in Sandy's throat.

It didn't last for long.

"What the hell were you thinking?" Michael shook his head in disbelief. "You do realise he could be home by Friday, at least Leyton said that's what Reuben asked for so that he could still *get married,* even if he had to sit for it. And you cancelled without even talking to him?"

"Postponed," I argued weakly.

"Just . . . don't." He raised a hand. "If he were unconscious, I might understand, but—"

"I know, I know." I sagged in my chair. "You don't need to hammer it home."

"Don't we?"

"Oh, babe." Sandy's face was a single wretched frown. "I mean, it's not like we didn't know you were a control freak—"

"Gee, thanks." I scowled, reaching for a pen to fidget with before throwing it back on the desk. "And I don't know what I was thinking, all right? I just wanted the mess to go away. But you also don't know everything that's been happening—"

"Because you don't tell us." Michael pointed out while Sandy remained thankfully quiet, hiding the fact he already knew some of it.

I shot Michael a look. "I couldn't." Then I sighed. "We've been given the opportunity to adopt a baby, to be parents again."

Sandy made a good job of appearing surprised, while Michael just . . . smiled.

"But that's great news, isn't it?" he asked.

"It is," I agreed, feeling the swell of excitement that I'd tamped down for two days. "But it's also complicated. It's a young cousin of mine, and it would be a family adoption. They only asked us last week and we were supposed to give them an answer Sunday night."

"Oh, shit," he said.

"Yeah." I went on to explain all our concerns.

"But you decided to go ahead with it?" Michael studied me closely.

I nodded. "But then Reuben got hurt, and I started second-guessing everything. What happened if he didn't recover? Would

Stella and her parents still want us to be parents to Stella's baby if that happened? Could we even manage it? Would it be fair? How would Reuben cope? How could we bring the press down on their heads like that—I mean look at what happened Sunday night. Would that be fair on Stella?"

Michael's eyes widened and Sandy frowned. "Jesus Christ, don't tell me you turned them down as well," Sandy asked.

"No. No, I didn't." But it had been a close call, and that more than anything woke me up to the fact that something was messing with my thinking, something I needed to deal with.

"Thank fuck for that." Michael offered a deep sigh and a thoughtful expression. "But yeah, okay, I guess I can see how things might've gotten a little stressful. And it's not like I'm the poster boy for sticking around when things get tough."

"Ya think?" I gave him my best eye roll and tunnelled my fingers through my still-damp hair.

"But you could've talked to us," Sandy said flatly, raising a pointed brow my way while smoothing his green tartan skirt. "That's what friendship is about. Everyone hits the wall sometimes."

"It's like you don't even know me," I grumbled.

"Oh, believe me, we know you." His lips quirked. "And don't look so downcast. So you got your superhero cape a bit torn and dusty? Welcome to the real world, sugar. He'll understand."

I pursed my lips. "I'm not so sure."

"He will," Michael insisted. "But you have to tell him everything that was in that big beautiful, slightly screwed up brain of yours when you did it, not just the highlights."

A groan escaped my lips. "He's gonna hate me. Worse yet, he might decide he doesn't want to marry me after all."

"He loves you, honey. He's gonna understand . . . eventually." Sandy smirked and Michael bit back a laugh.

I narrowed my gaze at them both. "The two of you are enjoying this way too much."

"Do you blame us?" Michael flashed his dimples. "I thought I was the only one who fucked relationship shit up that badly. Not to mention, you chewed my arse ruthlessly when I hightailed it back to LA, and Josh and I weren't even together at the time. I'm feeling better by the minute."

I sank deeper in my chair and tried not to smile. That I had friends who knew me that well was still a novelty and more than a bit scary. It had taken a long while to realise that the no-man-is-an-island thing wasn't just a joke invented by sad individuals who needed a committee to make every decision in their life.

"I'm never gonna live this down, am I?"

"No," they answered as one.

"Just talk to him." Sandy grabbed my hand once again.

"I need a plan first."

Michael arched a brow. "And whose plan would that be, exactly?"

Shit. I slapped a hand to my forehead. "Mine. Okay, I get it. No need to be so smug."

"Oh, but there is very much a need." Michael batted his lashes. "Now, go on with you. Go and make a plan *together*."

And before I could register what was happening, I was hauled onto my feet into two sets of arms and hugged till my brains squeezed out my ears. Yet another of those horrifying changes in my life that I was frantically trying to adapt to. Being hugged. Having friends. People knowing my shit. Being—God help me—open.

When I was eventually released from the madness, my expression tried for stoic resignation but failed dismally when a traitorous smile crept over my lips instead.

Sandy poked at it with his finger and laughed. "Aw, baby, look at that. See, I knew you really liked us."

"Lies, all lies." I batted his hand away, then changed my mind and tugged him into my arms instead. "Thank you." I looked over his shoulder to Michael. "Both of you."

Michael gave a sly grin. "Just remember that next time I steal your parking spot outside ER."

I flipped him off. "If I *ever* find your car parked there, I'll be writing your phone number in the bathroom at Downtown G."

"Won't be the first time." He laughed. "And for what it's worth, any baby would be lucky to have you two as parents. Fuck the media, Cam. Fuck everything except the two of you and the family you're growing."

I made it all the way into the elevator before the tears I'd been holding back finally broke free, and I embarrassed myself in front of two orderlies and a staff nurse who rode the car with me. The orderlies gaped in open disbelief, while the nurse slipped me a Kleenex and squeezed my hand.

My reputation was in tatters and I couldn't find a single fuck to give.

I wanted every bit of that family picture Michael had painted.

I could only hope Reuben still agreed.

CHAPTER FOURTEEN

Cam

"Cam?" Reuben sat under a crumpled sheet and stared at me like he wasn't sure whether to kiss me or kill me, and all I could do was stare at those beautiful grey eyes and hope they still shone for me at the end.

Shame burned through me, my throat so thick with it I could scarcely breathe.

Reuben had always been an open book to me, his emotions not just worn on his sleeve but waved in great fucking flags above his head. And they were all there: fear, hurt, confusion, anger, and . . . disappointment.

The last no less than I merited.

"Hi," I answered, closing the door and sliding into the chair alongside his bed, my cheeks a hot beacon. "They tell me you're pushing to be home on Friday."

"Leyton isn't making any promises, but yeah, hopefully," he answered flatly, and I swallowed hard.

He was deservedly angry with me.

Still, he looked better than when I'd left, physically, at least. Beautiful as always, at least to my eyes. Blond waves washed and combed; someone had helped him with that—not me, of course, since I'd fucked off and left him. But those grey eyes were clouded, wary, and concerned—his expression so carefully schooled I wanted to slap him. I hated it. Hated to see that all too familiar guard back in his nature—the one he'd worn when he'd been buried in the closet.

But most of all I hated the fact that I was the reason for it.

I wanted to sink into those eyes, but I just couldn't, and so I kept my focus on the sheet in front of me and began the only place I could. "I'm so fucking sorry for disappearing on you," I said quietly. "I have no excuse except that I had some stuff to work out in my head."

"Cam?" Reuben tipped my chin up with his finger. "I need you to look at me, please. You're scaring me."

I was scaring *him*?

But I did as he said, and he wriggled onto his side to face me. He looked so . . . worried that I ran a finger across his soft collar and smiled. "Look at you. I bet that feels better."

"It does." He watched me with a quizzical look. "But I don't want to talk about me. Where have you been?"

I trailed my finger along his jaw and over his lips, marvelling at the plump softness and wanting nothing more than to sink my own against them, to forget about this conversation.

He grabbed my hand and tucked it against his chest. "Cam."

I sucked in a shaky breath and blew it out slowly. "I went home and saw Cory—he's good, by the way. I had a shower and something to eat, a chat with Mum, and then I came back."

He raised an accusing brow. "You left *ten* hours ago."

"I know. I stopped by the ER to talk with Michael and Sandy."

"Rather than be here?" Confusion filled his eyes. "I missed you," he said, and guilt wedged my heart a little further open. "I wanted you here for the rounds and the results and the visit from the coaches. It didn't feel right not having you by my side. We're supposed to be doing this together, isn't that what we talked about?

For Christ's sake, Cam, what's going on? And if you mention the word nothing, I will completely lose my shit, do you understand me?"

Shit. Showtime.

I nodded and pulled my clammy hand free of his. Then I shoved both of them under my thighs and forced myself to look at him. "Promise to hear me out. You can ask questions but just don't give up on me too soon."

"Yes, finally! Jesus, Cam, I'll promise anything if you'll just fucking talk to me."

"Okay, okay." I drew a sharp breath. "Well, remember what you said about not wanting me to simply be the partner who handles everything your career throws at us; the whole team idea thing; that you wanted me to let you walk alongside . . ." I hesitated. "That I had to stop protecting you."

His cheeks pinked. "Yeah. I've been thinking about that. I didn't mean it to come out quite as strongly as it did. That wasn't fair to you. And the timing sucked. After everything you've done—"

Oh god. I winced. "No. You were right. And the timing was actually pretty perfect."

His brow furrowed. "Then I don't understand."

I blinked slowly, then continued. "Remember you said we were getting married on Saturday and that you'd been waiting your whole life for that?"

The frown deepened. "Of course I remember that. What are you saying?"

"I'm saying that we're not."

His eyes widened. "Not what?"

I sent a silent prayer out into the universe. "We're not getting married on Saturday." I couldn't hold his gaze any longer.

"What do you mean we're not getting married?" he said, incredulous.

Fuck. Fuck. Fuck. "I cancelled, or postponed it, I guess, yesterday afternoon."

"You what? You . . . why the hell would you do that?" His gaze rolled up to the ceiling and his head fell back. "Oh, fuck."

"I'm sorry, Reu—"

"Shh." He held up a hand and continued to stare at the ceiling. "Just give me a minute, please."

I snapped my mouth shut and played with the hem of the hospital sheet, slowly unravelling a loose thread until I felt the burning weight of his eyes fall back on me. I steeled myself before I looked up, but it didn't help.

My gaze was met with hurt, grief, and utter confusion.

"Are you saying you don't want to marry me?" he asked in a coarse whisper. "That you don't love me? Is that why you kept telling me it wasn't too late to walk away, because that's what you wanted? Did you feel you couldn't tell me?"

Oh shit. "No! It's nothing like—"

"Was it because you thought I might not walk again?"

"No. Stop." I grabbed his hand and kissed the back of it. "I love you more than ever. And Cory, and everything about our life. I don't give a fuck whether you're walking or in a chair."

More confusion. "Then, why?"

"Because I'm an idiot. Because I fucked up, Reuben. I panicked. With you being injured, the baby, Cory, the wedding. I thought about all the people flying in, the deposits, the caterers, the press. All of it, and I just fucking panicked."

"And my father?"

I stared at him, then closed my eyes for a second. "Someone told you."

"The point is, why didn't *you* tell me?"

"Because you were—" I waved a hand over him. "You didn't need—"

"No, because *you* decided that I didn't need to know."

Shit. "Yes," I admitted glumly. "Because I decided. I was trying to—"

"Protect me."

"Yes." The air whooshed out of my lungs. "Turns out I suck at it."
His lips twitched.

"But as my mother has so painstakingly pointed out, that might've been just an excuse. I wasn't *coping*—Jesus, how hard is it to say those three words?" I grumbled. "And I guess I was trying to get some control back, in the wrong way, as it turns out."

Anger flared in his grey eyes. "Very definitely the wrong way. I might not have been in the best headspace to help, Cam, but I wasn't unconscious. And I deserved to fucking know and not just be side-lined. *My* father, *our* life, *our* baby, *our* wedding." He eyed me point-edly and I wanted to crawl under a rock.

"That particular point may have been made several times today, already," I muttered.

He fell quiet. I stole a glance and tried to pick up on his mood, but he was still guarded. Then he turned my hand and threaded our fingers together, and a tiny spark of hope flickered in my chest.

"We had time, Cam, for fuck's sake. All you had to do was talk to me. I've been thinking as well, believe it or not. Kind of hard not to with it only four days away. And it was pretty obvious the original plan might need tweaking—"

I snorted. "Right, tweaking."

He scowled at me.

"Sorry."

"But we could've worked something out."

"Like I said, I wasn't thinking clearly. I don't get overwhelmed, Rube, you know that. That's not me. Other people get overwhelmed. I sort them out. I line my eyes, dust off my fierce, and hand someone their arse on a plate. Just like in the ER."

"So, how's that working out for you?" He actually smiled and I almost fist-pumped the air.

I narrowed my eyes. "Not so great at the moment."

He snorted and shuffled a little closer. "Well, let me let you in on a little secret, Cameron Wano. Our lives together, you, me, and Cory and hopefully this new baby—"

Does that mean you're not dumping my sorry arse?

He grinned. "No, I'm not dumping your sorry arse."

Okay, so I'd said that aloud.

"Oh my god, you're blushing." He beamed. "Jesus, where's my phone so I can get that on record."

I may have growled. "I feel so fucking seen."

He laughed, which I took as another promising sign.

Then he continued, "Anyway, baby, our lives are *not* your ER. And neither are they a reflection of our bedroom—although let me be clear that I have no problem whatsoever with the dynamics that go down there." He slid me a knowing smile. "But Cory and I are *not* your nurses or *problems* to solve. And I am *not* some hapless guy who needs your protection, at least not all the time. I'm your *partner* and hopefully soon your husband."

"I want that more than anything," I said with what I hoped was enough force to convince him how very true it was.

He went still, letting the words float between us like the promise they were. Then slowly, like an incoming tide, he smiled, and that guard finally dropped. Light danced in his eyes and I had the distinct feeling of coming home.

"I love that you still want that as much as me," he said, eyes shining. "It means everything. But I want you to trust me too, trust that I can be there for you like you are for me. That you'll ask for help when you need it. You don't get to have the monopoly on being strong. And to be honest, it hurts to think that you don't see me that way."

"But I do see you that way," I stressed. "I know how strong you are. This is about my issues. Not about your strength."

"That doesn't stop it hurting."

I winced. "No it doesn't. And you don't deserve that."

"But it's also not all on you." He looked miserable.

What?

"I never made it clear I wanted something different. I just stood back and let you run our lives. If I'm honest, it made things easy for me, and that wasn't fair on you, either. Most of the time I enjoy sitting back and watching you set the world on fire. We both let this happen. I need to speak up more about what I want." A softness filled his eyes. "In fact, I think I should practice that right now. Get up here with me. I really, really need to hold you."

He shuffled back to make room so I could lie on my side, pressed up against him. A nurse popped her head into the room with a blood pressure pump. I glared and she left.

I leaned in to brush my nose across his. "*You* are my strength," I said, meaning every single word. "The fact my knucklehead brain has ignored this too often doesn't change the truth of it. And the almighty fuck up that's happened because I couldn't get my head out of my arse only proves just how much stronger you actually are than me. I'm so fucking sorry."

I chanced brushing my lips across his, and his hands came up to cradle my face, staring into my eyes.

"But be patient with me," I pleaded. "I might disappoint you, again. I'm not sure I know how to be anything different."

"Not true," he said with a stern look. "You have never ever disappointed me. Puzzled me, sure. But *never* disappointed. And I don't want you to be *different*. I love your fierce. I love that take-charge attitude you have. I love every single part of you, Cam, and I love this life we're building. I just want us to hold hands and make the big decisions side by side. I'll step up if you step over. Pinky swear?"

He held up a hand and I wrapped my pinky around his.

"Pinky swear." Fucking sappy, foolish heart doing flip-flops in my chest. I wrapped both his hands in mine and reached up to press our lips together. "I love you so fucking much, baby." I nuzzled my nose against his. "But that doesn't solve the problem of me screwing up this wedding. I'd like to say I could just go back to everyone, eat crow, and tell them to go ahead, but there's no way you'll be ready for a ferry trip to Waiheke Island for a long arse day, not by Saturday, even if your miracle happens and you get discharged in time. And I don't know how to fix that."

"It will happen, no miracle needed." He tapped my nose with his finger. "Then how about *we* fix it. And I don't care about the big wedding, I never did. You, Cory, and our family and friends will be perfect."

I frowned. "That's still quite a few people, and it's too late to get—"

"Shh." He put a finger to my lips, but it was the intensity of his expression that silenced me. "I believe it's my turn to ask, this time around," he said, the flecks in his grey eyes darkening to almost pitch. "Cameron Wano, will you marry me on Saturday, if we can? Will you be a father to Cory and any new babies that come along? Will you love me and help me and protect me when I need it?" He brushed his thumb across my wet cheek.

I turned and pressed a kiss to his rough palm. "Goddammit, you made me cry, again. I will." I sucked in a ridiculous sob. "If *you* agree to love, help, and protect me, *especially* when I *don't* think I need it."

He smiled. "I will. Now—"

"Hang on." I rummaged in my pocket, and then took his left hand and slid the ring I'd bought him back where it belonged. "I've been keeping this safe since you were admitted."

He stared at it then sighed. "That feels so much better. And now, Cameron Wano, you may kiss your fiancé." He waggled his eyebrows. "A wandering hand or two would also be appreciated, just so you know. I've got reflexes to check."

"Is that right?" I slid a hand under the sheet and wrapped it around his soft cock. It jumped in my hand and he shivered. "Mmm, the light switches appear to be working," I murmured against his lips, sweeping my tongue through for a lingering taste deep inside.

He groaned and his hips lifted, his cock beginning to plump.

"It appears the dimmer is working too." I gave a gentle stroke and bit down on the curve of his shoulder. "An excellent sign."

"Oh, excuse me. Sorry." The same nurse stood in the doorway, wearing a smirk.

I slid off the bed and whipped my hand from under the sheet as Reuben choked back a laugh.

"I can always come back later." She made no move to leave.

"It's fine, Roberta." Reuben waved her in, looking guilty as sin. "Cam was just testing my . . . reflexes."

"Oh." She wandered to the bed and wrapped a blood pressure cuff around Reuben's arm. "That must be some new-fangled technique from the ER that us lowly ward nurses have yet to be shown. You'll have to give me the salient points." She threw me a shit-eating grin and I noted the name on her badge. She'd fit in well in the ER.

I tapped the side of my nose. "Very top secret. But for the record, his reflexes are excellent."

She snorted. "I'll make sure to note that down *and* to pass on the details at shift changeover."

I narrowed my gaze. Oh yeah, definitely ER material. "You do that. I have a rep to maintain and that should do the trick nicely. And if you think you might like a change in work environment, come see me for a transfer."

Her eyes blew wide. "Really?"

"Really. Now hurry up. Reuben has a whole list of reflexes that need my particular attention."

She laughed and finished her work quickly, but Reuben grabbed her hand before she left. "Do you still have your phone?"

She nodded, pulling it out of her pocket.

"Let Cam hear."

I frowned but Reuben just patted my hand. "You'll see."

And as I listened to the conversation between Reuben and his father, my eyes blew wide. "Holy shit, Rube. This is fucking gold." I didn't give a shit about the threats the jerk made about me; it couldn't have been better for getting him tied up over a barrel. It was absolutely perfect.

"Send it to Cam's phone and mine, if Cam has it?" Reuben looked my way and I nodded. He relaxed. "Good. But don't delete it until we talk to Cam's sister. Thanks, Roberta."

She smiled and closed the door behind her when she left.

I crawled back onto Reuben's bed. "Damn, Rube, that was fucking brilliant."

I waggled my brows. "Not bad for someone you thought needed protection, huh?"

My cheeks grew warm. "I'm so sorry."

"It's okay . . . now." His mouth quirked. "And to be honest, I should've done that or something like it a long time ago, and that's on me. To some extent the old bastard was right. I *was* being careful about the PR. I didn't want to ruffle any feathers, but it meant leaving you and Cory way too exposed. You should've been my first priority, and I'm so sorry for that. But this is the new me, right. Stepping up when I should."

He slipped an arm across my waist, his fingers dipping beneath the waistband of my jeans and searching for my crease. "So, about this wedding on Saturday . . ."

I hastily undid the buttons of my fly and his touch burned lines across my thirsty skin.

"I was thinking we're both going to be pretty busy over the next few days with hospital appointments and rounds and stuff, and I want you part of all that." He gave me a pointed look.

"Don't worry, I'll be here," I promised.

"Good." He withdrew his hand and offered it to me. I sucked his fingers into my mouth and slicked them up. He returned them to my crease and my eyelids fluttered closed. "Plus, I want us to talk to Stella and her parents and see if they're still happy to go ahead, if you agree?"

My heart kicked up a notch and my eyes flew open again. "Yes, absolutely. Jesus, Reuben—" I lifted my head to check the door, but we were fine. "If this is you stepping up for what you want, I am so fucking on board. We should've had that conversation a long time ago."

He grinned, holding my gaze. "I want."

I sent him a lewd smile and lifted my leg over his hip so he could reach my hole. He slid a fingertip inside and fucked me slowly, the moan that fell from my mouth as filthy as the dark look in his eyes.

"You're a damn tease," I growled, pushing back to get him deeper.

"Yeah, that's about all I'm going to manage, sorry." He blushed and withdrew his hand, and I grabbed it to suckle that finger in my mouth. His irises flared as he watched before I let it go.

"Rain check." I winked. "Now, back to the wedding."

"Right, the wedding." He looked a little dazed. "How about we outsource the whole thing." He regarded me with an amused expression.

Surely, he didn't mean— "Outsource?" My mouth dropped open. "You mean let someone else—"

"Yes, exactly. Let someone else do it for us."

My hand flew to my chest. "Holy crap, Reuben. Have you lost your fucking mind? I'm gonna need a fuckton of sedatives to cope with just the idea of that."

"I figured it could be a good test run?" He eyed me pointedly.

Bastard.

"A birthday party is a test run, baby," I said. "Choosing new curtains for a spare room is a test run. Changing the colour for summer annuals is a test run. Switching up Friday take out is a test run. But planning an alternative wedding in four days is *not*, in anyone's books, a test run."

"Oh, I have great faith in you." He bopped me on the nose. "But if you want to wait, that's fine."

"No, I don't want to wait. I want to marry you this Saturday." I'd fucked things up and I was going to bloody well unfuck them.

"Would it help if I said I wasn't thinking of just handing it to *anyone?*" He ran a finger around my lips, and I sucked it inside for a nibble. "We have a very capable group of friends who love us dearly, know most of the plans already, and pulled off a great bachelor party. Some of those things we had in place for the wedding that you *postponed—*"

I winced.

"—can probably be salvaged. That photographer you liked is a friend, right?"

I nodded.

"And Canelli caterers can deliver some of the stuff they were going to cater onsite. Their website says they do that on arrangement. It wouldn't have to be a total redo."

"How did you know that? About Canelli's?"

He smiled like I was a small child. "I might've let you loose on the planning, sweetheart, because I wanted you to have what you wanted, but I read every single thing you filed on our desk at home, looked at every email related to the wedding that came our way, and read every brochure you left lying on the coffee table. I might not have had the time to do it myself, baby, but I was with you every step of the way. And I was so damn proud of you."

Something warm broke over my heart and I got up on my elbow and peppered his face with kisses. "I was a fucking idiot, wasn't I?"

He grinned. "Is that a rhetorical question?"

I slid a hand down his chest and under the sheet to squeeze his dick.

The grin froze in place.

"Now, you just keep nice and still," I warned him, enjoying a thorough grope. "Not everything is gonna change, you know."

"Fuck, I hope not," he said in a strangled voice, not moving a muscle.

I kept up the slow stroke as his eyelids fluttered closed. "Sensation intact?"

"Yeah," he croaked. "I might not crest the hill, but the view on the way up is mighty inspiring."

I smiled and closed my mouth over his for a languid kiss, no hurry to get anywhere, just happy in his arms. His safe arms.

"After your frolic up the hill—" I trailed a line of kisses along his cheek to his ear. "—I think we should call Sandy and Georgie."

He opened his eyes and I fell into their soft grey warmth. "Yeah, baby, after that we call Sandy and Georgie."

CHAPTER FIFTEEN

Reuben

"For Pete's sake, Reuben, will you stand still for two seconds so I can get this damn thing straight?" Georgie fiddled with the pink tie while simultaneously blowing a stray lock of hair off her nose.

"It's not going to *stay* straight with the bloody soft collar I have to wear, is it?" I grumbled. "You'll hardly even see it."

She fixed me with a glare. "You will see it, but more importantly, so will Cam. That's why I'm going to staple the back of the knot to the collar."

I checked to see if she was joking, but apparently not.

She shrugged. "It'll keep the rest hanging right. And don't think for a minute that this is overkill," she muttered, tugging again and cursing under her breath. "Cam will have my tits in a vice if I send you in there with a single thread out of place, and you know it."

I bit back a smile and lifted my chin because, hell yeah, he would.

Cam's detailed instructions to our *planning team* had been to keep the wedding ceremony brief and relaxed so that I could actually enjoy it and not be looking for a bed halfway through. To that end, Sandy had dialled back the ceremony from its original 4.00 pm timing to noon.

For the same reason, the reception was being held under a marquee in Cam's parents' oversized backyard. Cory would be comfortable, all the dogs could be in attendance, and I could crash in a bedroom if I needed some downtime.

Exhaustion remained my biggest hurdle. I was whacked most nights from doing absolutely nothing. But with the wisdom of hindsight, I wasn't sure if handing the reorganisation of this rebooted wedding over to somebody other than Cam had been a smart move or not.

Firstly: Yes, there was no way Cam would've had time to do it himself. We'd both attended more medical conversations around my injury, recovery planning, and rugby future than I thought was humanely possible before they finally discharged me on Friday. It was a discharge Cam had a lot to do with, judging by the alarmed expression on Leyton's face after he'd been taken for a 'walk' so Cam could discuss exactly why Leyton was still holding out, not to mention Cam's smug smile when Leyton agreed I could leave.

Admittedly, there was no real need for me to stay other than an overabundance of caution on Leyton's part. I'd been working with the physio every available moment she could spare, determined to get out on time, and I was doing great. Not to mention, it wasn't like Cam was going to let a single hair on my head be harmed. Six days from my injury and I suspected he was now one of the pre-eminent experts on TQ injuries in the whole of New Zealand, and he certainly wasn't past regaling Leyton with his knowledge on the subject at every opportunity. An invite to the wedding so Leyton could personally eyeball me was enough to seal the deal.

I'd recovered all my sensation and movement, although there was still weakness on my right side in comparison to my left, especially in the legs. It continued to improve, but I'd need a fair bit of strength training before we knew just how much. No one was prepared to offer an opinion on whether I'd recover to pre-injury levels, and the thought didn't bother me as much as it probably should have. I was just so fucking grateful for what I had.

I was stuck with a soft collar for the immediate future, although I could remove it at night or lying down, something which had vastly improved the experience of my designated Cam cuddle time. My cock was fighting fit and looking to make up for lost opportunities, but Leyton had been very clear in the sexy-times lecture initiated by Cam, who was nothing if not thorough in his questioning, and the very straight Leyton had turned a deep and intriguing shade of crimson you didn't see very often.

In summary, there was to be no penetrative sex for a little while in order to protect my spine, and I was to stay passive and on my back as much as possible. We had to be creative, and Cam had to do all the hard work. Those were our instructions.

Leyton clearly had no clue what he'd set in motion, because Cam had veritably radiated wickedness at his words, the practical application of which had necessitated a hastily made Do Not Disturb sign for my hospital room to protect innocent eyes from his creative tomfoolery.

Second: Yes, Cam had done his level best not to freak out completely or worry about every little thing our friends were doing without his say so. I was immensely proud of him. But there had also been some miserable fails along the way—like finding him locked in the staff toilet with his cell phone, stalking Georgie's social media, and calling the photographer and caterer *just to check*. I'd hidden his phone for the afternoon.

Then there was the time I caught him eavesdropping on Sandy's hushed conversation with Michael in the hallway outside my room. I'd dobbed him in and Michael had shut Cam in the cleaning closet with one of the nurses on guard until he and Sandy had finished.

Third: Yes, our friends had been good about keeping Cam in the loop and getting his feedback about the really important stuff—all except Michael who was currently riding high on my personal hit list for his merciless teasing. Teasing, which inevitably resulted in an agitated, irritable fiancé and an endless barrage of questions and doomsday scenarios fired my way for hours at a time—something akin to death by a million needle pricks.

Take, for example, Michael's text requesting Cam's decision on whether he preferred steak and cheese, or chicken curry pie for the rejigged main course option. Add that to a million others like it, and by the time I was ready for discharge, Cam looked like a pissy alley cat strung out on catnip and cruising for a fight.

So yes, I fully understood Georgie's concern.

Happy with the tie, at last, she smoothed my crisp white linen shirt and patted my chest. Cam had wanted me in a classic black tux from the start, simple and elegant. And although the choice of pink for the tie fuelled my imagination, I had no idea what he was wearing, something I was almost more excited for than the wedding itself.

"There," she said. "If he doesn't give it at least a nine point five out of ten, I'll kill him myself."

"You'll have to get in line," I quipped. "There's a whole queue of people crowdfunding his demise after this week."

She laughed. "I have to admit it's been fun watching him squirm and trying to pretend like not running everything isn't driving him completely batshit. I'd give him a solid nine out of ten for effort, even though the actualisation of the intent barely made a four and could've done with a little more finesse. Still, it can't have been easy for him."

I snorted and brushed her cheek with my thumb. She looked stunning. Elfin features, a cheeky smile, and a heart big enough to swim in. "Yeah, Cam doesn't do subtle or restrained. It's like putting a time-release muzzle on a great white. You can still see all the teeth and there's that look in their eye that says the clock is ticking."

"Right? You do realise that when Michael told him I wanted to change my dress from floor length to mid-calf because of the change in venue for both the wedding *and* the reception, Cam blew up my phone with *suggestions*. I had to turn it off because I'd been two hours in the dressing room sending him photos, and the sales assistant was beginning to lose her shit. And also because we . . . disagreed on the final choice."

"Hah. Well, I love what you're wearing, and he will too." I held her hand and she shyly did a twirl, the white taffeta cocktail dress with its line of tiny black buttons down the back billowed over a black tulle underskirt that screamed 1950s in the best possible way. She looked gorgeous.

"Oh yes, I'm positive Cam will love it." She pulled a face. "Because it's the one *he* chose, dammit. He was right, even though I didn't want him to be." Her mouth turned up in a sly grin. "But I told him I'd bought the other one."

I laughed. "Oh my god, you're positively evil."

"Yeah, well, he deserved it." Her eyes danced with mischief. "He drove me up the damn wall." She walked over to the bed and grabbed the soft collar for my neck.

"Bloody thing," I grumbled.

"Suck it up," she admonished. "You wouldn't be allowed to get married without it so don't be a baby."

I tipped her chin up to look in those smiling eyes and chuckled. "You know, I've always loved this patient, tender side you have. It's one of your many gifts."

"This is true." She poked me in the stomach with her finger and I almost doubled over. "And don't you forget it." She stood back. "Yes. You'll do nicely."

"Knock, knock, knock." Mac pushed the bedroom door open and gave me an approving once over. His gaze lingered on my face and his mouth quirked up. "Well, don't you just look positively fucking edible."

I snorted. "You better keep those comments out of the AB dressing room if you're looking to stay in the closet. Besides, I'm not quite sure the world is ready for a flirty All Black prop who's built like a tank and could bench press the Queen Mary. They had enough trouble with my slender model."

He laughed and brushed a tiny piece of lint off my trousers

before grabbing my jacket from the bed. "Here." He held it out and I slipped my arms inside.

"Holy crap, is this really happening?"

"You better believe it, sunshine." He brushed my shoulders. "Just keep thinking who's waiting for you at the other end. You're a lucky man."

I grabbed his arm. "I am. And thank you for doing this for me."

He stared, the corners of his huge green eyes crinkling with affectionate warmth. "You are most welcome." He stood back to take a longer look, his finger to his lips, and then nodded. "Fabulous job, Georgie."

She blushed. "Thanks. I had great material to work with."

"Wow, you look amazing."

I spun at Craig's voice, surprised to see his eyes shining with what looked like tears. "You scrub up pretty damn good yourself."

I ran my gaze over both of them in their matching black tuxes, white shirts, black ties, and pink rose boutonnieres. The stitching on Tom's tux barely contained the mountain of rippling muscle beneath, whereas Craig's slender frame stood out in stark comparison. Apples and oranges, and yet they somehow fit.

"Is Belinda coming to the reception?" I asked Craig. His newish girlfriend was a whole staircase up on any of his previous ones—smart, sensible, and with an actual job, which was always a good start. Plus, she was excellent with Cory.

He nodded as a small face appeared around his right hip. Cory—dressed in the cutest little black tuxedo with a pink flower pinned to his lapel and pink shoes. Cam said Cory had been adamant about buying the shoes to match, and he looked so damn adorable I teared up on the spot, which sent Georgie running for the Kleenex to blot my face before I smudged my eyeliner.

I'd wanted to surprise Cam and I'd been practising on the downlow for months with colours and techniques.

"Pappy!" Cory walked into my arms, carefully avoiding Mac who had yet to be accepted in Cory's inner circle. "Dad made me Vegemite toast. He makes it better than you."

I glanced at Craig to find a smug smile in place. I returned him a wide grin. "Well, maybe he can show me how to do it right, then."

"Happy to," Craig answered, and we stared at each other for a long moment.

We'd been trying to do the family thing better. He hadn't been in contact with our father since the hospital debacle, and he'd promised not to pass on the change in wedding plans or send any photos. I could only trust he kept that promise, but so far, so good.

I didn't know how we'd managed it, but the press were apparently still in the dark with some even spotted heading over to Waiheke Island, just in case. But that wouldn't last. They knew we hadn't cancelled altogether, and I had no doubt word would get out as soon as we all started moving. We knew eyes were on us.

Which was why we'd kept the news of the baby completely under wraps. Only Georgie, Michael, and Sandy knew. When Stella and her parents had agreed to come to the hospital to meet with us, they'd been over the moon to hear we still wanted to adopt Stella's baby as long as she was still interested in us being the adoptive parents. Michael had explained about my injury in order to allay any concerns they might've had, and we'd agreed to approach the issue of the media as a team and deal with it the same way.

Stella's second ultrasound was due in a few weeks and we were beyond excited that she wanted us to be there. The immediate goals were to get the formal processes under way, including Cam laying groundwork for the extended leave he'd need from his job, and then try to keep a lid on things for as long as possible.

However, as Cam and I knew from painful experience, that didn't always work out, and there would need to be a strategy for when shit inevitably hit the fan, planned or otherwise, most likely otherwise. The secret was driving us crazy, but it was the right thing to do, and we could only pray it held. We needed the wedding under our belt at the very least before that particular can of worms was leaked to the press.

"Okay, you lot." Ed stuck his head through the open doorway. "Let's get this show on the road?" He jangled the limo keys in his hand. A friend in the business had agreed to let Ed drive to keep a better lid on the wedding. And we'd accepted Ed's offer of his and Mark's house to get ready in for the same reason. Plus, Tink was one of Cory's favourite 'people' and an integral part of the wedding party.

"There's someone special waiting for you." Ed smiled softly. "And he's not the most patient of men."

Holy shitballs. A kaleidoscope of butterflies took flight in my stomach, warmth flooded my body, and my heartbeat cranked up a couple of notches or seventy. I'd been waiting on this moment for a long, long time.

And now it was here.

Georgie once again dabbed at the tears gathering on my lashes. "Don't you dare make me fuck up my makeup," she sniffled, her own eyes alight and shining.

My gaze slid from her to Ed, to Mac, and finally to Craig and Cory and the lumbering bulk of Tink pressed against Cory's side.

My heart filled to bursting and a huge smile broke over my face. "Okay, let's do this."

CHAPTER SIXTEEN

Cam

"OH MY GOD, HE'S GONNA HATE IT." I GLARED AT MY reflection in the mirror. Is it too late to change the colour? Reuben's always liked my green eyeliner the best."

"You're wearing pink, you dipshit," Jasmine snapped. "You are not putting green eyeliner with pink tulle, for fuck's sake."

I stared down at my outfit. "Oh right." I was losing my fucking mind.

"Now stand still so I can get your grubby finger marks off my foundation, again."

"Sorry."

She stared at me. "Who are you and what have you done with my insufferable brother? You *never* say sorry and your fabulous is a bit thin and tatty around the edges. Pull yourself together or Reuben will wonder if they swapped you out for a more agreeable model."

"Sorry." I winced. "Fuck. Point taken. I need something to irritate me back into queen-mode."

"And how's the blushing bride?" Michael pushed his way through the curtains and froze, his mouth falling open.

"And there it is." I winked at Jasmine. "I think I'll be just fine, now."

She laughed and started packing my makeup.

"Damn, baby." Michael walked a circle around my fidgety self before taking both of my hands in his. "You look fucking beautiful."

He held my gaze, but I wasn't going to cry. *I wasn't.* "Stop it," I hissed, following with a loud sniff. "Dammit to hell and back, pass me another bloody Kleenex. If you make me smudge this makeup, Michael Oliver, I'll bury every X-ray request of yours to the bottom of the pile for the next fifty years, and you'll have our favourite X-ray tech, Lucinda, up your arse with crampons on a daily basis."

"And he's back." Jasmine grinned and kissed me on the cheek. "Right, my job here is done. Fifteen minutes till showtime, folks." She grabbed my hand. "See you down there, little brother."

I held her beautiful, crazy, smart, and calculating eyes and whispered, "Thank you, Jazz."

She sniffed back a tear and left, passing Sandy, Jake, and Mathew on their way in. They looked amazing in their black tuxes, light pink shirts, and black ties. Jake still had a bit of a beaten puppy look about him after his breakup with Trent, but he was rallying hard.

Mathew whistled long and low. "Holy smokes, bro. Look at you. Is that a . . . harness?" He reached out a hand and I slapped it away.

"It is. And I don't need you pawing at it. What do you think?" I did a little twirl.

"You look beautiful." Sandy wiped at his eyes.

"Jake?" I turned to my cousin who was still staring with his mouth wide open.

"I, ah, sorry." Jake cleared his throat. "I just, man, I don't have any words. You always look great, Cam, but you've just blown it out of the park. Reuben's going to lose his fucking mind."

I turned back to the mirror and smoothed a hand down the waistcoat. "That's the general idea."

"Seven minutes till we start walking," Michael reminded us.

"Okay, gather around," I said, holding out my hands and flicking my fingers.

"Oh, fuck me, no." Jake's eyes bugged. "If you're going to do a group hug, then I might have to vomit. This new, touchy-feely Cam version 2.0 is freaking me the hell out."

"Get over here, sexy." I grinned at him. "I give you full permission to punch me in the balls if I start chanting."

"I won't need your permission." Jake sidled over and tentatively slipped his hand into mine. "It will be my personal contribution to world peace."

I chuckled, then leaned in close. "Are you okay?"

He shrugged. "Trent texted this morning. Nothing important, and I'm not gonna let it fuck up today. I'll tell you another time."

Bugger.

Michael squeezed my hand. "Okay, so what's the deal?"

I looked around at some of the best men I knew and put Jake's boyfriend problems to the back burner. "Right, well you might want to take notes because you've as much chance of hearing this again as the Hurricanes have of winning the Super Rugby this year."

They glanced at each other and chuckled.

I waited until I had their attention once again and then made sure to catch each and every eye. "There's a lot of people I need to thank for making today happen, but no one more than you guys. I screwed up badly this week—a sentence I guarantee you are unlikely to hear from me ever again. And if you breathe a word of it to anyone, I will fuck you up, understand?"

There was an almost choreographed nod of solemnity that I didn't believe for a second.

I narrowed my gaze. "I know it may come as a surprise, but I don't ask for help very often—"

"At all," Jake added cheerfully.

"*Anywaaaaaay.*" I pinned him with a glare. "You rescued me, rescued *us.*" I might have flushed. "I don't know the details of who did what, which I'm inclined to think was a deliberate ploy so that I couldn't run anyone down after—"

Everyone laughed thinking I was joking, and I was . . . mostly.

"—but I know you all pitched in, and Reuben and I are so damn grateful for what you've done. Thank you for being there for us, for making sure today happened. I love every one of you, even Michael." I flashed him a grin and swallowed hard. "Okay, that's it."

"Aw, bro." Mathew went to hug me, but I sprang out of his reach.

"Have you lost your tiny little mind? You'll crimp my tulle."

"Two minutes till curtain call," Sandy warned.

I gathered the tulle to stop it dragging on the floor and then grabbed the Kleenex Sandy held out for me.

"Shove a couple in your waistband," he said.

I did as he suggested, then held my hand out for more. "Just bring the damn box," I grumbled.

He grinned and shoved the box under his arm.

Michael stepped close. "Give me that; you're creasing it." He took the tulle skirts from my hand and fell in behind me.

I spun and took a second to register the sight of my blustery friend holding my wedding train as if it was the most natural thing in the world and wondered how my life had found its way to a place where this kind of thing happened.

"Come on, he's waiting for you." Jake elbowed me gently.

And I knew that for the eternal truth that it was. Reuben would always wait for me without question, whenever I needed him to, as I would for him.

My mind skipped back three years to the memory of that wet parking lot and the gorgeous blond-haired beauty who left the rugby after-match inside to find some quiet. Instead, he found me. And I remembered briefly wondering at the time, what lucky person would get to claim his heart, never dreaming it would also be me.

I took a deep breath and blew it out slowly. "Come on, girls, I've got a damn All Black to marry."

Sandy pinched my cheeks, which earned him a furious scowl,

and then led the rest of us through the curtains of trauma six, our yet-to-be-commissioned brand-spanking-new treatment room. The hall was eerily empty, which got me wondering for a second, that was until we got to the nurses station where I was brought up short.

Holy fucking shit.

An honour guard of practically every one of my nurses, on- and off-duty, and most of the medical and ancillary staff as well was lined up on either side of the corridor all the way to the elevators. They clapped and woo-hooed, wolf-whistled, and dabbed at their eyes, all of them holding walking canes and crutches above their heads in some kind of makeshift arch.

I lost my shit on the spot, a broken cry of appreciation falling from my lips as I blubbered shamelessly into my fist. Sandy stepped to my side and shoved another bunch of Kleenex into my hand, though I figured it would be nowhere enough.

The day had barely started, and I'd cried three times already before I'd even laid eyes on Reuben. We'd be lucky if we didn't have to swim out of the chapel.

Sandy retouched my makeup and smiled fondly. "You deserve this," he said. "You both do."

I nodded like a bobblehead, then faced the lines of people and gave a deep bow. "Thank you all. You're the best people I know, and I can't tell you how much this means to me."

Silence fell in the corridor for a long, emotionally charged moment before Hayden Wilson, our head of radiology, broke into song: a beautiful Maori waiata that I recognised from our inaugural meeting of the Auckland Med queer focus group. He'd come along that day as an ally, his deep baritone sending shivers up my spine. I took a deep breath, gathered my fabulous around my heart and spine, and started walking. I thanked people as I passed, but when I came to Hayden, I stopped for just a second to let his voice soak in, and then I leaned in and kissed his cheek before moving on toward the corridor that led to the chapel.

When I'd heard Sandy's idea for us to be married in the Auckland Med chapel, I gave him credit for the inspired choice. The chapel was close to the ER, easy to isolate, wouldn't be high on the media's list of possible venues, and allowed for the hiccup of Reuben not being discharged in time. And lastly, because it was on the hospital grounds, it gave Mark and Josh a lot of control for backup security.

But more than any of those excellent reasons, I loved that my staff could be part of it and maybe see a tiny piece of this softer part of me that Reuben seemed so damn keen to show the world.

The very thought made me want to stab a fork in my eyes, but what did I know?

The short walk to the chapel from the ER was via a back corridor used mostly by staff. But our little party caused quite a stir nonetheless, especially since most of the ER staff not tied up with a patient or providing coverage tagged along in a motley crew of supporters. Hayden also followed, his beautiful waiata echoing through the hospital.

I felt the heat of stares as I passed, heard the faint rumble of clapping and shouts of congratulations, but nothing shook my focus from the man I knew was waiting for me.

I am not going to cry.

I am not going to cry.

I am not going to fucking cry.

And I was doing just fine until we turned the corner to the chapel, and there he was, Reuben, standing outside the chapel doors. Six foot three of hard-muscled, big-hearted gorgeousness, with long blond waves kissing his shoulders and those devastating silver-grey eyes, and all mine.

We locked gazes and the world fell away.

He mouthed I love you and I mouthed the words back, my heart jumping in my throat.

We wanted to walk in together, side by side, but I'd completely underestimated what I'd feel when I laid eyes on him. And when his face lit up in the biggest smile, those devastating dimples popping all over the damn place, my knees went to jelly and he sucked every drop of oxygen from my lungs as he always did.

Cory stood with a hand around Reuben's hips, the small bag with the rings dangling from the other and Tink glued to his side. *How in the hell had Tink got the hospital's okay to be there?*

"I might've told them Tink was his service dog," Sandy whispered with a waggle of his eyebrows.

Okay, so I'd obviously asked that question aloud and my tongue was on its own mission separate from my brain. That didn't bode well for the rest of the day, but what the hell. As long as I said yes at the right time, we were golden.

I leaned close to Mathew. "For fuck sake, kick me if I don't say yes when I'm supposed to."

He snorted. "You got it."

"You need to start moving if you intend to actually marry the guy," Michael whispered from behind.

"What? Oh, right." I straightened my shoulders, pulled up my sass, and planted my boots on solid ground.

The others took their place at my back and I met Reuben's warm smile. He held out his hand, and time stopped for just a second as everything inside me calmed like a deep lake on a windless day.

I took a breath and drank in the sight of him, composed, focussed . . . and so damn happy. His gaze travelled the length of me with undisguised appreciation, taking his time, letting me know how much he liked what he saw, and my heart filled. And when we locked eyes again, his smile grew, like nothing else mattered in the world except this minute and this joining. That what we were about to do had some greater meaning in the universe, and maybe it did, in our universe at least.

My handsome, huge-hearted, gentle love. This beautiful man who drew a softness from me I didn't know I had; who loved me in every way it was possible to love another person; who held my heart safe in his hands; and who somehow wanted *me*, every sharp-edged, lace-lined part of me, and who couldn't seem to get enough.

I wanted to remember every second of this forever.

Somehow, I kept moving, one foot in front of the other, my heart afire.

Heading for Reuben.

Heading home.

I returned my love's smile, cocked a hip, much to his amusement, and then sashayed over to take his hand before leaning in to whisper, "You looking for a cigarette?" Repeating the very first words I'd ever spoken to him.

He beamed and ran his nose across my cheek to brush mine. Goosebumps ran over my skin.

"You were the most beautiful man I'd ever seen. You still are." His gaze ran the length of me. "And you look absolutely stunning. I am so fucking proud of you."

"You too, baby." I couldn't drag my eyes from his face, astonished at the shadow of charcoal that framed his eyes.

"You like?" He sounded nervous.

"I love." I cupped his cheek. "It makes the light grey of your eyes pop even more. I never knew you wanted to try—"

"I wanted to surprise you." He lifted my hand to his lips and kissed the back. "I needed help to get it straight because my hands were shaking so damn much."

"Not too straight, I hope." I winked, then frowned and straightened the tie under his neck brace.

For some reason, he laughed.

"And are you wearing that item of clothing we bought?" I arched a brow.

His gaze turned molten. "I am."

I pictured the tiny pink jockstrap I'd bought him and was thankful the tulle was a forgiving piece of clothing.

"And can *I* assume that whatever you've got under that skirt matches that sexy-as-fuck leather harness?" He tried to lift the tulle and I slapped his hand, much to the amusement of everyone gathered around.

"Now, that would be telling. But I have one word for you —chains."

His pupils blew wide.

Michael cleared his throat alongside. "Gentlemen, can we maybe move this show along before I have to find you two a room?"

"Shall we?" I turned to face the chapel doors, keeping my gaze locked on Reuben.

He slid alongside, threaded my arm through his, and kissed my forehead. "I can't wait."

We turned to check on Cory and he offered a small smile. He had the rings safe in a bag in one hand, whilst the other held tight to Tink's collar. Sandy was walking alongside for support, and to take Tink, while Geo waited at the front to escort Cory to his seat once his job as ring bearer was done.

I winked at Cory who looked nervous but quiet, his favourite train shoved in his pocket just in case.

"You look very handsome," Reuben whispered, and Cory's lips quirked up at the compliment.

We turned back around and nodded to Ed to open the doors. He did, and the sound of Haley Reinhart singing 'Can't Help Falling in Love' swept out into the corridor. I looked to Sandy and whispered, "Thank you." It had been my first choice for walking in.

But when I heard Reuben's gasp, I quickly turned back around and gaped at yet another honour guard waiting on us, this one a line of Reuben's rugby friends and players, all standing with a smile and an outstretched arm, welcoming us to walk between them, all the way to our celebrant waiting at the front.

Behind the guard, the chapel swelled with all our friends and family, standing and grinning, some wiping their eyes.

Reuben blew out a long breath and patted my hand. "You ready?"

I covered his hand with my own. "I've been ready for you forever."

He nodded. "Yeah, we've got this."

I smiled. "Because it's us."

He closed his eyes and breathed into the moment before opening them again. "Yeah, baby, because it's us."

EPILOGUE

Four weeks later

Reuben

It was D-Day, the day of Stella's second ultrasound which they'd kindly delayed to give me a little more time to recover. In a couple of hours, we were going to see our baby for the first time, and I couldn't fucking wait.

Cam threw our bedroom curtain aside, his wedding ring catching the light.

It brought a smile to my face every time I saw it, reminding me of that first glimpse of him outside the chapel on our wedding day. It still took my breath away—the way he'd sashayed toward me on that cloud of pale pink tulle, wearing that familiar cocky grin—every step parting the slit in his skirt for a peek at those white million-buttoned and sexy-as-shit high-heeled ankle boots and that black garter. And above the skirt, another million-buttoned pale silk waistcoat with a thin black harness visible underneath, and all atop acres of olive skin that I knew like the back of my hand.

So fabulous, so sensual, so masculine, so . . . Cam.

I palmed myself, hard at the thought again. Because when I got to peel all those layers off later that day, I'd found a black lace jockstrap covering a soft pink silicone cock cage, the key to which was handed to me on a silver chain. But since the moratorium on anal sex hadn't lifted until a few days ago, we'd had to wait for the full enchilada experience until then.

And we hadn't really stopped.

Hence the mountain of crushed tulle in our bed, the garter on Cam's thigh, and the cock cage twirling on his finger.

Damn.

And hanging that tulle on the clothesline every day was getting to be embarrassing.

"What time is it?" I grumbled.

"Seven." His black negligée draped softly over that beautiful spiral tattoo on his arse cheek, almost within reach.

I thought about grabbing it for all of two seconds, but the sizzle in my eyeballs had me pulling the covers over my head instead. "Go away. It's too early."

We'd talked late into the night and made out lazily until eventually he'd fucked me slow and deep into the early hours. But even then, we'd been too nervous to sleep, tossing and turning in each other's arms until I eventually drifted off sometime after four.

I lay under the covers and waited with a smile on my face and counted the seconds as they passed, knowing Cam hated being ignored.

Five, six, seven—

He landed on me with a growl.

Touchdown.

"I want you again," he muttered, biting my shoulder through the duvet.

My cock immediately answered that siren call as it always did.

"You can run, but you cannot hide." He dragged the covers to my feet and rolled me onto my back as the cool morning air licked at my skin. Then he ran a heated gaze the length of my goosebumped body before straddling my hips and pinning my arms above my head.

"Door?" I looked around his lithe body.

"Still locked," he answered with a sly grin, then cocked his head. "I could fuck you till you begged me to let you come. I bet you're still hot and wet from earlier." He leaned to the side and slid a finger into my well-used hole. "Mmm. So good." He licked a stripe up my throat as he finger fucked me, and I groaned. "Whaddya think?"

I sent him a pointed look. "I think your mother's coming at eight, and we have Cory to get ready."

"Damn." He pouted. "Always the sensible one."

"We're gonna have lots of time in the next week," I reminded him.

After the ultrasound we were headed to Queenstown, a combined honeymoon present from all our friends—a week's stay in an upmarket, super secluded B&B in Drift Bay, right on the shores of Lake Wakatipu. Called Lake Dream Suites, the newish place had received tons of glowing reviews and was apparently run by a property developer whose husband owned Southern Lights Coffee Company, my favourite roastery.

I couldn't wait.

Cam's mother was taking Cory, and we had a whole week all to ourselves. No rugby, hopefully no media, and no interruptions. A chance to catch our breath before the madness of Christmas, the new year, and a growing family took shape.

I brushed a few mussed locks of black hair from his forehead. "Has anyone heard from Jake?"

He stilled. "Other than two texts to his parents to say he was fine and not to worry, no. Fucker. I'll give him *fine* the next time I see him. He'll be so *bloody* fine he won't be able to walk for a week with his balls wrapped around his neck and plaited down his back?"

I snorted. "Maybe he's looking for closure."

Cam grunted. "He'll get his foolish heart trampled again is what he'll get. Anyway, enough of my idiot cousin. I know we said we wouldn't talk about your rugby career until we got to Queenstown—" He got up on one elbow and looked down at me. "—but I don't want to wait. I've been thinking about it, a lot."

My stomach clenched, but whichever way he went, we'd be okay. My recovery was going well. There was a little residual weakness on my right side, which strength training was already improving, and the soft collar had been ditched a few days ago. I was sidelined until the next season and would need a full clearance from the TQ and concussion specialists. I was hopeful but I wasn't taking bets, and if it all fell through, I had Cam and our family to fill any gap rugby might leave in my life.

Cam cleared his throat. "Don't look so nervous." He smiled. "Nothing has changed for me since the first time you asked. If they clear you, I want you to play. If there's a genuine question about your safety, then that's different. But you love rugby, Rube, and yes, I know you love us more, but if you're cleared, it would only be fear holding us back, and we promised we wouldn't do that again. So my vote is, you play."

My hand cupped his jaw. "And you're sure?"

He frowned. "Of course I'm bloody sure. We promised, full disclosure from now on, right?"

"Right." I rubbed my thumb over his cheek. "Full disclosure."

He grimaced. "No hiding how I feel about things. Not about the media, or you being away, or Cory, or the new baby. We talk about it all. I don't try and protect you, and you let me know what you want, as well." He eyeballed me. "It sits about as comfortable as a drag queen's tuck, but I'll do it. You too."

"Me too." I grinned.

"Good. So stop with the checking."

I saluted and pulled him down so I could kiss him, thoroughly.

"Mmm." He smacked his lips and waggled his eyebrows. "I vote we take this to the shower before Cory wakes up. I want you to come so far down the back of my throat that it blows out my arse. You game, Mr All Black?"

I cradled his face. "How is that even a question? Ten bucks says you blow before I do."

"Pfft." He eyed me sideways. "It's like you don't even know me. I'm putting fifteen on you."

I shoved him off my chest. "You're on."

Cam

Reuben took my hands in his to stop them from shaking and kissed my cheek. "Breathe, baby."

Easier said than done as I stood transfixed to the slightly blurry, black and white form floating on the monitor.

Hell, my brain had checked out the minute Stella lifted her shirt to reveal that beautiful gently rounded belly.

A baby.

Our baby.

And Oh. My. God.

What the hell were we thinking?

What if I was no good with babies?

I mean, I was okay with Cory, but a teeny tiny baby?

Reuben would be great. Of course he would.

He was a fantastic dad.

But me?

I was a sharp-tongued killer queen with zero experience caring for small bundles of fragile flesh.

What if I dropped them?

What if I ruined their tiny little life?

What if they grew up and hated my gay-fem arse?

What if all their friends laughed at them because their pop wore makeup?

What if—

"Stop it." Reuben leaned close. "I can hear your brain stalling from here. You'll be fine. We've got this. You're gonna be a great dad, just like you are to Cory."

I sent a scowl his way. *How did he do that?*

He bopped my nose.

"I wish we could've brought him," I whispered.

He kissed my forehead. "I know, but we can show him the imaging pictures later and maybe bring him to the next if Stella has one. Right now, it's too soon."

He was right, of course. We'd started reading Cory books about new babies and siblings and families, laying the groundwork. He'd met Stella, and we'd begun to talk about the baby in her particular tummy. He'd taken a look, run a gentle finger over the bump, and then gone back to his truck. So far, so good.

We planned to include him in choosing a colour for the room and picking out soft toys, and we'd start using the baby's name after today. But it was going to take time for him to absorb and adjust to the idea; that was the advice we'd had from other parents with children on the spectrum. Which meant there was no way he was ready for the reality of a scan this soon.

Mary-Anne, the ultrasound tech, slid the transducer lower on Stella's belly.

Stella gasped. "Oh my god, is that a leg?"

"Where?" I squinted at the monitor.

"Indeed it is." Mary-Anne chuckled.

"Oh, shit there!" I squeaked, crushing Reuben's hand in mine as my heart jumped in my throat. "Look! Look! A leg!"

"I can see, baby, I can see." Reuben whispered in my ear. "They usually come in pairs so keep a lookout."

I elbowed him sharply.

"Let's see what else we can find." Mary-Anne slid the transducer a little more to the side and Stella's free hand shot our way, fingers wiggling for connection.

Reuben uncoupled my hand and placed it in Stella's slender one. I glanced back with a frown as he nudged me forward. "Go on, baby," he said softly. "I'm right behind you." He wrapped both arms around my waist and laid his chin on my shoulder.

Colleen held tight to Stella's other hand, while Stella's father stood with a hand on his wife's shoulder and a wad of Kleenex at the ready.

"Aaaand there's the other leg." Mary-Anne pointed to the screen. "With the requisite five toes on each foot to match the five fingers apiece on each hand, right there." She angled the transducer to show the second hand. "And with the head on the side like that, you can see the left eye, a cute-as-a-button nose, and there's a thumb in that beautiful mouth."

We all leaned forward, oohed and aahed, and then laughed in chorus.

"Just like their mother." Colleen reached up to kiss her daughter on the cheek. "Sucked her thumb until she was three."

"Mum!"

Colleen laughed.

I wanted to hoot and fist pump the air, but I was having enough trouble simply getting the breath to move in and out of my chest, past my heart wedged in my throat, as I watched that tiny little fist shoved up against the sweetest lips there ever were. How was this miracle possible? How fucking amazing. How . . . everything.

I turned my head and kissed Reuben's damp cheek, my own eyes swimming with tears. "Holy crap, Ruby. A baby. A whole baby."

Stella turned her gaze to mine and beamed. "Your baby, boys. Yours."

"Oh my god, how are you so calm?" I kissed her hand as Reuben's arms tightened around my waist and I caught another wet sniff on my shoulder. "I'm losing my damn mind here. Look at you, girl. You did all that." I pointed to the screen. "You are so freaking amazing. I'm in awe of you."

"This is true." She laughed and squeezed my hand, and I

might've melted just a little bit more for her. We'd become close with
the whole family in the four weeks since the wedding, but something
special had sparked between Stella and me. With our age differences,
I really hadn't known her that well, other than as a cousin I occasionally met at family get togethers.

But far from the quiet, almost timid girl I thought her to be, the
Stella we'd come to know more recently, was a sassy, smart, kind
young woman, and she fitted into our lives like she'd always belonged
there. Maybe it was because I was going to be taking the primary on-
the-spot parent role that would've otherwise been hers, but whatever
the reason, Stella and I had a fierce bond, and I knew in my gut that
this was going to work.

Reuben popped his head around my shoulder, kissed my wet
cheeks, and wiped them with a Kleenex.

I caught another of Colleen's laughs and turned to find her
smiling at us.

"I'm screwed, aren't I?" I said, shaking my head. "I'm gonna cry
for the next thirty years, right?"

She snorted. "And the rest."

"Good lord. Michael's gonna have a field day."

"Um, have you seen him with Sasha?" Reuben reminded me.
"He doesn't have a leg to stand on, babe."

That was true and the thought sparked an evil warmth in my
belly. "Thank you. If he even looks like giving me shit, I'll remind
him how much he freaked out at Sasha's first movie 'date' and then
proceeded to spy on them from five rows back for the first twenty
minutes of the movie. Josh couldn't stop laughing for a week. Yeah,
I've definitely got some wriggle room."

"And he's back." Reuben's hand covered Stella's and mine, and
Stella gave him a broad smile before turning back to the monitor.

"Okay, family." Mary-Anne sat back and looked around the
room. "Do we want to know about the bits and bobs between the
legs?"

"You saw?"

Mary-Anne smiled. "Yes, Charge Nurse Cameron, I saw. The baby has been quite active, and I've had a couple of good views. The first I wasn't so sure about, but the second was nice and clear."

Everyone looked to Stella.

"Your call, sweetheart," I said, but she shook her head firmly.

"No, this is your baby. You guys get to decide."

My gaze darted from Stella to her parents, who simply nodded. "What she said."

I spun in Reuben's arms to find an intent look in his eyes. We hadn't considered it might be solely our decision. I tucked a stray lock of his blond hair behind his ears and cradled his face. "Baby?"

He kissed me softly and shook his head. "I'm up for the surprise if you are. And we talked about not making assumptions, right?" He looked to Stella.

She nodded firmly. "No assumptions."

I stared at Reuben for a minute, lost in the miracle of this incredible man I'd married. Then I turned to Mary-Anne. "You heard the man. We're gonna wait."

She smiled and put the transducer aside. "Gotta say, I love a surprise."

Reuben slipped from behind to alongside me. "However," he addressed Stella and her parents. "We have actually decided on a name."

"Yes!" Stella clapped her hands. "I was hoping you would."

I took a deep breath and smiled at Reuben. "Bearing in mind the no assumption thing, their name is Kennedy."

"Oh," Stella gasped. "I love it." She pulled her parents in for a hug. "Kennedy. Kennedy."

"It's a wonderful name." Colleen winked over Stella's shoulder. "They're going to be surrounded by so much love."

I went up on my toes and wrapped my arms around Reuben's neck. "They will. Because it's us."

He kissed me softly. "Because it's us."

THE END

Thank you for taking the time to read

YOU ARE CORDIALLY INVITED
An Auckland Med Wedding

I love these guys so hard, and if you enjoyed Cam and Reuben's journey to their wedding, please consider taking the time to do a review in Amazon or your favourite review spot. Reviews are a huge help for spreading the word. Thank you so much.

But wait.... there might be more...

You may have noticed a couple of unfinished story lines in the book. Somewhere down the track we might just find out what happened to Jake, and will Mac ever meet his match? Stay tuned.

ALSO BY JAY HOGAN

Have you read Jay's Painted Bay Series?

OFF BALANCE

Painted Bay 1

When JUDAH MADDEN flees his tiny suffocating home town in New Zealand for the dream of international ballet stardom, he never intends coming back. Not to Painted Bay. Not to his family's struggling mussel farm. Not to his jerk of a brother. Not with his entire life plan in shreds. And certainly not into the tempting arms of MORGAN WIPENE, the older, ruggedly handsome fisheries officer who seems determined to screw with Judah's intention to wallow in peace.

But dreams are fickle things. Shatter them and it's hard to pick up the pieces. Hard to believe. Hard to start again.

And the hardest thing of all? Finding the courage to trust in love and build a new dream where you least expected to find it.

Readers rave about Off Balance

by Jay Hogan

"This story gutted me in places and had the tears flowing but in other spots I laughed so hard that tears also came."

—Xtreme Delusions ButtonsMom 5 stars

"Judah and Morgan have superb chemistry and their flirting dialogue and interactions are the hottest and sassiest I've ever read! So much fun and sizzle – it had me grinning from ear to ear! The passion and angst in this story bring the storyline into technicolour with plenty to keep the reader engaged."

—Kimmers Erotic Book Banter 5 stars

"I urge you to pick up this complex piece of perfection. Happy Reading!"

—Bayou Book Junkie 5 stars

MORE BY JAY HOGAN

AUCKLAND MED SERIES

First Impressions

Crossing the Touchline

Up Close and Personal

Against the Grain

You Are Cordially Invited

SOUTHERN LIGHTS SERIES

Powder and Pavlova

Tamarillo Tart

Flat Whites and Chocolate Fish

Pinot and Pineapple Lumps

STYLE SERIES

Flare
(coming 2022)

PAINTED BAY SERIES

Off Balance
(Romance Writers New Zealand 2021 Romance Book of the Year
Award)

On Board

In Step
(Coming 2022)

STANDALONE

Unguarded

(Written as part of Sarina Bowen's
True North— Vino & Veritas Series and published by Heart Eyes
Press)

Digging Deep
(2020 Lambda Literary Finalist)

ABOUT THE AUTHOR

JAY IS A 2020 LAMBDA LITERARY AWARD FINALIST AND THE WINNER OF ROMANCE WRITERS NEW ZEALAND 2021 ROMANCE BOOK OF THE YEAR AWARD FOR HER BOOK, OFF BALANCE.

She is a New Zealand author writing in MM romance and romantic suspense primarily set in New Zealand. She writes character driven romances with lots of humour, a good dose of reality and a splash of angst. She's travelled extensively, lived in many countries, and in a past life she was a critical care nurse and counsellor. Jay is owned by a huge Maine Coon cat and a gorgeous Cocker Spaniel.

Join Jay's reader's group Hogan's Hangout for updates, promotions, her current writing projects and special releases.

Sign up to her newsletter HERE.

Or visit her website HERE.

Milton Keynes UK
Ingram Content Group UK Ltd.
UKHW021323241123
433202UK00018B/271